F.U.L.T.O.N. COUNTY 404

Yesterday We Became Millionaires...

Today We Are the Most Feared in the City...

Tomorrow We Will Be the Most Hunted Men in America...

God Forgive Us All.

* * *

*F*rom the works of author K. F. Arnold comes a decadent tale of greed and redemption set in the Capitol City of the South. Based on true events, F.U.L.T.O.N. COUNTY 404 chronicles the deadly modern-day war being raged between Mexican and African-American Cartels over control of Atlanta's multi-million dollar narcotics trade, and the ongoing Federal manhunt for some of the *C*ountry's most dangerous outlaws.

The gripping tale is an awe-inspiring look into a seething underworld where professional athletes, politicians, and entertainers all come to play in a high stakes arena of pleasure and sin. From City Hall to the highest ranks of the Atlanta Police Department and the U.S. Justice Department, no one escapes this deadly web of sex, politics, and murder.

404

F.U.L.T.O.N. COUNTY
404

K. F. ARNOLD

REVELATION7

Atlanta   London

R7 Publishing
An Imprint of Cooper Global Group

This saga is a tragic work of fiction. Infamous Names, Celebrity characters, Seedy places, and Criminal incidents are products of the Author's rather distorted imagination, and not to be construed as real. Any resemblance to actual events, city locales, political organizations, prominent politicians or persons living or dead, or soon to be deceased, is entirely and uncontrollably coincidental.
A hurt dog will holla every time.

First R7 E-Book publishing: July 2006
First R7 Publishing Paperback printing: January 2007
First CGG / R7 Publishing Paperback printing: September 2007

www.myspace.com/fultoncounty404

Printed in Atlanta, GA

R7 Publishing ©, Fulton County 404 ©, and the M.A.N. from Atlanta™ brand are trademarks of Revelation7.

Author Interviews & Press Contact:
Rseven7@lycos.com

UK and EU Contact:
CGGPress@aol.co.uk

MAXXWORLD MANAGEMENT

PART I

*"And it came to pass in those days, when Moses was grown,
he went out unto his brethren, and looked on their burdens..."*

11 Exodus ii

1

PUNCHING THE CLOCK

There are seven ways to die in Atlanta. The casual thought stabbed him as he stepped out to the balcony. *Seven...at least.*

From his penthouse perch, Michael Drake glared at the intermittent webs of lightning that pierced the night sky. Heavenly electric fire burned wafting bands of black clouds that hovered over a teeming city as he climbed to the top of the railing, and wobbled dangerously over the edge. *One more step.*

His free fall would end a dizzying twenty stories below where cars crawled along West Peachtree Street, dotting the faded concrete, and faint streetlights beamed over ant-sized pedestrians rushing for cover as the first splatter of water drops fell. The staccato rumble of thunder rattled his ears, snapping his lofty trance. Bloodshot eyes whipped toward the pale half-moon hanging ominously overhead.

God's pissed off tonight. Maybe his tears can wash away my sins...melt the dirt off this whole stinkin' city.
Then again he figured, as he unrepentantly swiped holy beads of soothing rain from his boiling forehead....
Probably not.

Cool rain fell in thick crystal sheets, its moist scent carried on a howling breeze that refreshed the stale midnight air. Michael inhaled the welcomed gust, and sighed a deep breath of tension that mixed with the raw stench of brandy escaping from his rumbling stomach.

Buzzed from the alcohol coursing through his blood, he strapped a diamond-faced Rolex to his wrist, and painfully slid on a three-karat pinkie ring, its platinum band snugly tightening on his swollen left hand. The expensive garments, bold and elegant, felt more like a costume than ever--just useless, overpriced accessories for a clown suit he was forced to wear in a multi-million dollar circus.

Every move's center-ring in the big top.

Sparkling buildings rose into the Atlanta skyline. Angled and beveled rooftops, outlined by shimmering lights, jutted into the foggy horizon like glowing mountain peaks. It always amazed him how human ingenuity and craftsmanship could create such magnificent structures. They were towering man-made temples of glass and steel built in the worship of big business, free enterprise, and All-American capitalism.

A skyscraper's enormous heights whisked ambitious souls far away, shielding them from the filth that circled in the real world below. For the price of a college degree, any smart man, or tough woman for that matter, could just educate and elevate themselves to a higher nest in a small, three-walled cubicle or a swank, spacious corner office locked away from mediocrity, crime, and poverty.

A leather briefcase, a grey suit, and a necktie, a power skirt, wingtips or heels, and a leather briefcase full of condemning evidence.

That's all it took to safely wrap you up in the comfortable blanket of the American dream. *Ain't that some bullshit.* Michael smirked at the idiocy of it all. *Nobody's safe. Nobody.* Four years swimming in the sewer of Atlanta's underworld had proven that much to him.

If karma was a kind friend, and reincarnation a possibility, maybe in the next life, dirty Uncle Sam would let him trade in his hard-earned Ivy League degree for one of those suit-and-tie jobs.

Yeah, I could damn sure handle that.

He would be resurrected as the almighty CEO of a Fortune 500 company with stock-options, a supermodel trophy wife, and live out his dying days at a lakeside mansion in some far off country--or retire in solitary peace to a villa on a tropical island so remote you couldn't find it even if you had a map. *Paradise.*

Amused, he smiled at the thought, then...*Poof!*
Like soft dreams melt in the heat of reality, he realized that
to be reborn he'd first have to be buried. *Six feet deep.*

The brief smirk, and the subtle peace that came with it, vanished into thin air. Mike shook his head at the morbid irony, and checked his watch. The second hand flowed too fast.

Time waits for no man.

Closing his eyes, he spread his wings, and stepped off the edge....

2

*G*reenwalt's Auto Body was a small, two-bay garage hidden just off a busy stretch of Bankhead Highway. By day it was a nondescript local business--tires changed and rotated, spark plugs gapped and replaced, oil changes, lube jobs. There was nothing out of the ordinary, nothing to convey an otherwise reputable front. But night time had fallen and all that was by day was eerily put to rest.

Bathed in dull shadows, four men moved about one service bay, each focusing on his job, methodically preparing his weapons: 9mm Glock handguns chambered, Mossberg pump action shotguns racked with heavy load buckshot, modified Soviet SKS rifles harnessed, and thirty-round banana-clips jammed into hungry A-K 47's.

Calmly, they dawned Kevlar bulletproof vests, covered them with black jackets embroidered *Fulton County Sheriff,* and laced up dirty, steel-toe combat boots. Velcro straps tightened black batter's gloves over deadly fingers, and black cotton ski masks rolled down over the crowns of their heads.

American justice in all its costumed glory.

A black, unmarked police issue cruiser sat in the next bay, its doors spread wide, and an open trunk compartment lay bare. With city government license plates, and a chrome searchlight mounted from the driver's door, the car was only as legitimate as it needed to be. The four sheriffs tossed empty duffle bags into the trunk, and secured the guns up front. The car doors swiftly slammed shut in delayed calamity, hiding the occupants behind darkly tinted windows.

A growling motor barked to life. Halogen headlights ignited. The garage door jerked, sliding upward on rusty metal guides, drawn by a clinking metal chain. A bright flash of lightning pierced the air, glaring over the rain soaked streets. It was a perfect night for their mission. A stirring fog and heavy rain would cloak them from the prying eyes of potential witnesses. *And dead men don't testify.*

"Time to put in work," the driver grinned with a gold and diamond plated smile as he locked into gear, and punched the gas.

With a banshee's shriek, peeling tires propelled the car into the street, and it streaked away, its taillights disappearing in the dreary haze of a rainy night in Georgia.

3

Michael Drake lumbered back into his condo, and slid the glass balcony door shut, locking it. The *click* of the door latch trapped him, as another dark tide of emptiness washed over his body. He gulped, holding his breath, going under. *Stay alive.*

He was sinking, drowning in a spacious, loft-style living room sparsely lit by a fire red, art-deco lamp standing guard in the corner next to some leafy, orange Caribbean plant he didn't particularly like. It smelled funny. *More props on center stage.*

From that single source of light, the dense shadows fell on the rest of the room, dark and desolate, exactly as he wanted. Light had begun to annoy him lately, as if the brightness would shine on him, exposing the traitor he really was, or worse, the monster that this fragile, shallow lifestyle was turning him into. He stared listlessly at the scenery, *sinking* deeper underwater, fighting not to breath. Starved lungs filled with the lifelessness of the possessions and controlled props that littered his stage.

All that's missing is a studio audience.

There was that burgundy Italian leather furniture, this sixty-inch flatscreen HDTV, those imported Tuscan vases, and hand-crafted Persian rugs. He was hopelessly trapped inside twenty-foot walls bleeding red, Ralph Lauren paint, and a gaudy mix of contemporary paintings.

Man, this really ain't me.

All the high-end digital gadgets: laptops, PDA's, digital cameras, laser printers, and chirping Nextel phones were more scenery in another episode of reality TV.

Lights, camera, action!

Mike Drake rubbed a powerful set of hands over his face, grinding clinched fists into his sleepy eyes, trying to force himself into character. *Sink or swim.* It was too close to the final curtain call to be this out of it, too dangerous a stage not to be on point.

At least seven ways to die, he recollected again, counting on his fingers....

Gunfight, car wreck, stabbing, cirrhosis of the liver, drowning in the Chattahoochee river, overdosing on dope, or maybe...if ya lucky...ya get to die of a broken heart.

"Irene? Marlene? Where are you ladies?" he unconsciously sang out loud, as if he'd actually expected an answer. "C'mon, girls! Rise and shine! I know you're tired."
He slowly spun around, searching the room. "So am I."

This was unlike him, to be forgetful, to be so disoriented. In the last year, he'd began to drink a little more, *a lot more* each day, soaking his liver, constantly clearing the cobwebs from his mind, dulling the razor sharp emotions just enough to help him get this treacherous job done.

"There ya go baby dolls," he whispered. His *ladies* were sleeping comfortably on the marble mantelpiece over the fireplace.

"Time to wake up, ladies." He gently cradled them in his hands. "Daddy's gotta get on the grind." Michael solemnly kissed each of his twin Sig Sauer .357's and secured the chambered pistols in his waistline, draping the tail of his black silk shirt over the fitted gun grips. *Irene* and *Marlene*, as he'd affectionately endeared them, were named after his two favorite aunts, *God rest their souls.*

* * *

Winter 1986. "C'mon here child, I swear!" Li'l Mike Drake was dragged away, kicking and screaming, to live with his bible-thumpin' aunties. This was right after his enterprising, superfly father, *slick as he thought he was*, got caught ordering a fast take-out order for twenty-one kilos of Peruvian flake during a rather dubious DEA investigation. In fact, Big Poppa Drake hadn't even been the main target of the drug sting, but *slick as he really wasn't*, he was reeled into the net nevertheless, and the hefty charges of conspiracy to distribute cocaine buried his world beneath a ton of *white bricks. Literally.*

Ol' Self-righteous Poppa, a solid crook of honor, *too real for his own damn good*, gave up no names in a brutal four-day marathon of intense interrogations. During the heated plea-bargaining process Slick Poppa even took on the pending jail time for his horny teenage mistress so she would gracefully be spared the pains of federal prison. The reward for his selfless heroism and adherence to the almighty concrete code of silence was a federal sentence of fifteen years to the door.

Mike Drake shivered, still haunted by that frigid November morning when his father hugged him, offering hollow words, *"Keep ya head in the game, son. The strong survive, the weak surrender!"* Then he left to enjoy his first class reservations at the Atlanta Federal Penitentiary.

Thanks for a shitty life, Ol' Man. I sure hope hell is warm and cozy. It was the same chilly day his father's loving sisters came to drag little Mike away to redemption.

"Praise the Lord!" Feisty, God-fearing, take-no-shit southern women in their own right, Aunt Irene and Aunt Marlene had always taught young Michael to carry one bible and two guns. After all, "Even David had to kill Goliath with a rock," they often repeated until the seed of war was deeply planted in the boy's fertile mind. *Amen, brother...Amen!*

* * *

Standing at the bar, Michael gulped down a warm glass of Remy XO that he had somehow forgotten to finish. With the final taste, he burped and escaped the depressing tide, bursting through the surface, gulping for air. He grinned, sated by the warm cognac spiraling toward his cold heart. *Ahhh, the spice of life.*

Straightening his shirt, he caught a glimpse of himself in the brass-framed, three-panel mirror mounted behind the wet bar. The dark-skinned, stone-faced triplets reflected in each glass pane stared back at him with piercing brown eyes. He was sure that none of the ghosts were the *real* him, even though all three followed when he moved, and they mouthed back in a slow, southern baritone when he grunted, "What the hell you lookin' at?"

As he grabbed his car keys, and stuffed nine-thousand dollars in crisp hundred-dollar bills into his pocket, he quickly calculated his odds of survival....

I ain't going nowhere near the Chattahoochee River tonight...sweet Irene and Marlene, locked-and-loaded, gonna raise hell on any knife-toting maniacs...shit, it's damn near impossible to overdose on fine brandy...and she'll be lying naked in my bed long before the sun comes up.

"That leaves me just about three ways to end face-up in the morgue." At three-to-one odds, he liked his chances. Either way, it was time to go to work.

Showtime.

4

FEDERAL

United States District Attorney David Namath stretched his tired arms above his head, and pressed his palms against the double-paned glass window towering in front of him. The layered glass was cool to his touch, and a welcome reprieve from the sweaty hands he'd worked up over a nineteen-hour workday.

The conference room window high above the Sam Nunn Federal Building afforded a monarch's view of the town Namath was charged with overseeing, and for the first time in years, he stopped to appreciate the scenery under a stormy night's light show.

Peering over the water-soaked city, he felt more powerful than ever. In less than a month, he and his overworked staff would be finalizing its bribery and conspiracy case against former Atlanta Mayor Russell Campbell. The popular Mayor had lied, perjured, and obstructed his way through this case for five years, and now Namath would finally get his chance to bring this circus to an end. This conviction alone would be enough to catapult his political career to new heights, but heaven had sent David Namath an even greater gift.

Throughout the course of the Campbell investigation, it had been obvious that the high levels of corruption were not a sudden aberration. Damning evidence had proven that there were obvious patterns of criminal activity dating back to city administrations well before Mayor Campbell's scandal broke headlines. Luckily for those politicians, their administrations hadn't been Namath's responsibility, and had summarily escaped the judicial wrath that was about to fall upon the more recent inhabitants of City Hall.

Namath's office had uncovered a nest of illegal activity inside the Atlanta Police Department and City Hall including bribery, extortion, racketeering, and theft by County Officials and acting City Council. Greater still, there was a chance, if all the cards fell in place, that Namath and his legal troops could bring down the standing Mayor of Atlanta.

For five years *Operation Enigma* had been covertly spinning a net over the Atlanta drug-trafficking trade. As the operation expanded, the interlocking web of investigations began to reveal damaging criminal accusations against some of Atlanta's most prominent citizens, and high-clientele corporate and entertainment guests. Millions of dollars of illegal drug funds had been laundered and was now entrenched in the Atlanta economy, and in the process, the city had become a lawless playground. U.S. Attorney Namath now had the option of choosing who he would go after next, and at this level, the biggest fish always demanded the most attention.

Behind Namath, a dark oak conference table stood covered with case files, dossiers, surveillance photos, affidavits, witness and confidential informant lists, along with transcripts from thousands of hours of recordings from authorized and illegal wire-taps--all the key ingredients Namath would need to cook up the biggest drug trafficking case in his stellar legal career. Everything he'd ever wanted was in his grasp, and Atlanta was the city that was going to hand it all to him.

His ascension in American politics would follow a natural and time-tested progression. As the U.S. Attorney for the Northern District of Georgia, he was overseeing one of the most active crime zones in the Western World.

Over the last two years, Namath had seen his share of television time with one press conference, or post-trial interview after another. Washington, D.C. would see what he had accomplished here in the South. He'd made all the right moves, and courted the proper political allies. *Just like Rudy Guiliani had done in New York--bring down major crime figures, politicians, celebrities. Dispense justice evenly but publicly. Clean up the city. Then move into politics.*

The current White House Administration under President George W. Bush was in a political tailspin over the ineffectual war in Iraq, and utterly distracted with domestic squabbles over illegal immigration, and embryonic stem cell research. The present U.S. Attorney General Roberto Gonzalez was reeling from an embarrassing scandal over his controversial firing of numerous U.S. Attorneys. In two years, a Presidential election would foster in an entirely new administration--one that could not ignore Namath' presence.

Mayor. Senator. Congressman. U.S. Attorney General. President. Namath smiled, gratified by the brightness of his future.

"You know what I love about this city?" Namath subconsciously blurted out.

"Excuse me?" Special Agent in Charge Angela Cooper mumbled without turning to him. She had been sitting quietly for the last ten minutes, staring at the large diagram hovering at the front of the conference room.

"Do you know what I like about Atlanta?" he restated. "It's too big for its own good sometimes. I suppose that makes our job easier. When people cross the line, they're so far out of their comfort zone. By the time we get a case, the criminals have already exceeded their capacity to outsmart us."

"I'm glad it pleases you so much to shoot humans in a barrel," she said distractedly. Agent Angela Cooper was a twenty-two year veteran of the Federal Bureau of Investigations, and acting Special Agent in Charge of the Atlanta Field Division. She was a petite black woman, in her mid-forties, brilliant, with a commanding presence. Born and raised in Atlanta, she was a proud Spelman graduate, and later earned her Ph.D. in Electrical Engineering from Georgia Tech. Patient and calculating, she was a refined woman of few eccentricities.

She wore little jewelry, and showed even less emotion. Her controlled persona was that of a dignified, Southern Baptist preacher's wife--a mild mannered exterior that masked the vicious adversary she was when facing the complexities of her job. She was every bit as ruthless and cunning as the men and women she hunted.

Under Agent Cooper's reign, the Atlanta Field Division had infiltrated some of the most prolific narcotics organizations in history, but the scourge of the South was not limited to smugglers. Her division had successfully investigated scores of child pornographers, pedophiles, murderers, internet spammers and scammers, and even crossed paths with a multi-state serial killer. A Lenox Square Mall security camera had recorded the *Greensboro Strangler* enjoying lunch in the food court with a teenage girl hours before she became his eighth known victim. Agent Cooper kept a copy of the ominous video in her bedroom DVD player. The men she dreamed about capturing were the type of people mere mortals ran from in nightmares.

"I forget you're a native," Namath said. "You're the last of a dying breed."

"That I am," she muttered.

"I didn't mean to sound so obtuse," he apologized.

"I'm not here to persecute the masses. We have a real purpose. Now if you and I both get what I want in the process, well, that's just an extra perk."

Operation Enigma. The bold, block letters headlined the fifteen-by-fifteen foot organizational chart standing at the front of the room. The board was plastered with color photos of key suspects, names, dates, and locations. The tentacles of the massive criminal enterprise spiraled outward like a wiry octopus. The display told an epic tale that began in the nutrient rich fields of Peru, where the coca was grown, harvested, and processed. The chart outlined the supply chain from Cali, Colombia to Mexico, across the U.S. border to Corpus Christi and Houston hubs, all the way to Atlanta.

"This is our time, Agent Cooper. We reel in Jorge Vargas, track his channels back to Mexico, and we write our own tickets," Namath calculated with pride.

"Forgive me if I don't share the same lofty White House wet dreams you have." Namath smirked at her snide remark. "But it will be worth everything we've poured into this to see him fall," she finished. "Vargas is a monster among men."

Agent Cooper brushed the strands of hair cascading across her forehead. She was a seasoned investigator with a bigger agenda than Namath's or so she believed. But right now her lurking concern was not Vargas, or the majority of the dozen or so faces staring back at her from the operation billboard.

The politics and the sound of Namath's voice soon faded into the background. Her eyes trailed over the color photos of a somber, stern-faced *Jorge Moreno-Vargas* who was positioned above two well-groomed heads mounted on massive, brawny necks—cartel soldiers *Manuel Avila* and *Hector Avila*. And there was the beautiful, tanned *Adrianna Guevara*.

To the far right, the organizational chart extended to its furthest branch where it completed its reach into the heart of America's southeastern states. It was the final photo that held the most worry for her. Agent Cooper batted her dreary eyes and left her thoughts trained on the man who controlled the entire Atlanta hub for the Vargas cartel.

It was a picture of Michael Drake.

5

FLESH & BONES

The florescent lights lining the marquis of *Magic City* glowed like a lighthouse beacon calling the city's elite, black businessmen to the shores of its carnal playground. A steady stream of luxury, four-wheeled land yachts cruised into the parking lot turning it into a fantasy dealership with an inventory of European coupes, Italian getaway cars, SUV's, roadsters, and metal-flake painted, old-school Chevys mounted on monstrous twenty-four inch polished chrome.

Nearby, a one-man, soul-powered cooking hut billowed smoke from its ventilation pipe as its busy chef prepared salted pork barbecue ribs, sausages, and steak sandwiches for the drunken, hungry crowd that would spill from the club. All the while, this opulent, carnival-like atmosphere cast a mocking glow over the hapless lives scurrying along its fringes.

A block away, clans of homeless men taunted passersby with stolen goods offered at wholesale prices, or short of inventory they simply whispered foul-breathed pleas for cash donations. But when the potential customers or donors refused a purchase, or respectfully declined to give a free heartfelt handout, they were barraged by a wicked storm of foul-mouthed reprimands--country curses and damnations spat from hungry bellies. Dirty fingers waved in hatred for not feeding the needy. *Lord loves a cheerful giver.*

Across the street from the strip club, a stream of wrinkled passengers escaped from dusty Greyhound buses that lumbered into the bus terminal like aged dinosaurs. Wrinkled, downtrodden Atlanta natives returned home from some unknown expedition with tattered luggage. Sweet Jamaican mothers cradled crying newborns. Wide-eyed Pakistani students joked in their Urdu tongue, while tender young Midwest daughters dreamed of igniting their singing careers in the new Motown of the south. Cash starved Dominican sons trafficked with rolling tote bags stuffed with the finest crops of marijuana and cocaine--spiritual medicine for their new homeland. The troop of ragged souls herded into the terminal like third world refugees, dreaming, praying, willing to starve and die just to get a fresh start in Atlanta.

Good luck my friends.

2:00 AM. And the steady, torrential downpour that engulfed the town had finally broken. Thin clouds of steam floated from the hot concrete as stifling humidity clung in the air. And amazingly all of the city's sins were still in tact.

It'd take a wrath o' God flood to wash this grime away. Michael Drake locked into reverse, backing his steel gray Lamborghini Mercialago into an empty parking space near the front door of *Magic City.* As he climbed from the cockpit, he smiled, amused that his flashy ride brought little fanfare in a parking lot full of new Bentleys, Porsches, and gas-guzzling Hummers. *Business is good in the city.*

It was a wicked Monday night in a restless town with nothing much to do on a Monday, and Atlanta's most infamous strip joint was the only place to be. The moderately sized building was a far cry from the mountainous skyscrapers that Michael admired. And no toilet paper college degree or fancy suit-and-tie ensemble would guarantee you a corner office around here. Still, the money was just as green as any corporate paycheck and it was all tax free. *Screw the IRS.*

In Atlanta's underground economy, commerce and exchange, wholesale to retail, was not negotiated in skyscrapers, office suites, or the boardroom, but rather in the seedy confines of its *titty bars.* They were the playgrounds for the rich and famous who would never grace the glossy covers of *Fortune, Business Week, Forbes,* or *Fast Company* magazines.

These street ordained bars were sovereign country clubs for the underground entrepreneur. *Safe-havens for certified hustlers. A nursery for growing legends. Kindergarten 101 for baby ballers.* The streets knew it. The law knew it. And everyone allowed it just the same. *God Bless America.*

"Big Mitch! What's really happenin'?" Michael casually greeted a burly, muscle-bound bouncer guarding the front door.

"Another day, another damn dollar," the bored bouncer matter-of-factly returned. "The economy's slow, ya know?"

"Dig that." Michael slipped the guard a folded fifty dollar bill for his troubles and side-stepped the metal detector surrounding the door frame--an unspoken courtesy afforded to a dying breed of concrete cowboys who would only relinquish their guns when they were pried from their cold dead fingers. Metal detectors were for the small timers who didn't have the balls to keep their steel handy.

Michael's muscular frame melted into floating shadows as he stepped into the controlled darkness. Pounding music reverberated from loudspeakers, the bass numbing his ears. The powerful scents of cheap cigars and overpriced *hydro* weed mixed heartily with the wave of designer body sprays camouflaging lusty funk, sweaty nipples, and wet pussy. The pungent symphony of odors flared at his nostrils awakening his senses. The sights and sounds of this late night circus were too familiar, too alluring. And he was becoming all too comfortable, too loved in this shady environment.

Dollar bills wafted through the air like falling leaves, fluttering to the floor, landing at the feet of naked bodies grinding on stage. As Michael moved through the crowded room, diamond-studded men nodded in respect, and friendly gold-digging dancers gave notice with a gracious wink or a flicker of a soft tongue lashed across glossy, painted lips.

Good evening, ladies. Caramel-toned vixens, voluptuous redbones, dark chocolate hued queens... *What's your fantasy?*

Michael inhaled the attention, wallowing in the shallow fame, his chest filling with the addictive vapor of ego. It was an illusion draped inside a lie. He was a master magician. And his name was ringing in the city. *I'm on top.*

Michael collapsed in a seat at the bustling bar where an overworked waitress promptly brought him a short glass of his favorite brandy stock. She smiled gratefully as he kissed her cheek and slid a folded fifty-dollar bill into her shirt pocket.

"Thanks, Mike," she moaned and coyly stroked his face. *It's heartwarming to know that a man can get all the love and respect he can afford.*

Taking a sip from his glass, Michael swiveled in his chair, carefully scanning the room, assessing the playful array of urban cartoon characters, impostors, posers, and pretenders mixed in with undercover vice cops, bounty hunters, and DEA, FBI, and ATF agents.

Bunch o' Goddamn fools. The cadre of hustlers, killers, and thieves laughed and joked, intermingling with the very men who would, in due time, destroy their burgeoning criminal enterprises...*Brick by stinkin' brick.*

In the crowded VIP section, Michael noticed a table of rambunctious, sharply dressed lesbians, fondling, licking, pleasuring themselves with a horde of appreciative dancers.

Bulldyker money is still green as green gets.
Whatever floats ya boat, li'l momma.

In just two free-living decades, Atlanta had become the new San Francisco of the south and the sexual revolution was in full swing. More often than you think, girls played with girls. This was a simple fact of life. *A sign of modern times.* And the sooner you realized it the sooner you could make it pay.

Deep in the shadows, a howling pack of fifty comrades with thick wads of cash in hand, wore black t-shirts emblazoned with *"BMF For Life"* logos. Four over-sized bodyguards stoically stood watch with loaded guns mounted at their side.

Over the past year, the Detroit-based Black Mafia Family had made its presence well known throughout the city.

With reckless disregard for secrecy, they flexed their muscle in outrageous spending sprees at local malls, raced caravans of new Ferraris through the Buckhead party district for fun, and inadvertently managed to grace the front page of the *Atlanta Journal & Constitution* with a cowboy-style shootout with one of music mogul Sean "Puffy" Combs' former bodyguards. Outmanned and outgunned, the bodyguard died in a hail of bullets that night, arguing over a woman who had chosen to run with the new money in town. *Poor bastard.*

Then there was that giant "The World is BMF's" billboard looming prominently over Interstate-85, touting their radiant, smiling pictures as they announced their record companies forced entry into Atlanta's high profile music scene. And who could forget the great urban tale of BMF hiring a helicopter to fly across the city while they dropped big face hundred-dollar bills over downtown's Fourth Ward? They were fast becoming legends in their own minds, in their own time. But Atlanta has its own way of dealing with concrete legends, in its own time. And the clock is always ticking. *Always.*

"Mike, my baby." The soft words soothingly brushed his ears. The warm touch of her hands graced his neck, and his heart stuttered. Adrianna was stunning--a statuesque import, born of Peruvian parents who had fled South America to start a new life in Atlanta. She was five-foot-eight, and mocha-skinned with a beautiful mane of sandy brown hair that trailed fluidly to the small of her back; a hypnotic set of light hazel eyes sat beneath cat-like eyelashes. A hot pink two-piece bikini hung to the contours of her supple breasts and thick hips. The skimpy outfit glowed beneath the glare of fluorescent strobe lights swirling overhead.

As she leaned in to kiss him, Michael's trained eyes cast quick judgment. Her dilated pupils were glazed and distant. Her eyelids batted too softly. Her casual motions were cosmic, too free flowing, as if she was under a snake charmer's trance.

"Look at ya! Whole world's at ya feet and you're still poppin' that man-made poison into ya system," he grunted with the loving disdain of a father scolding his baby daughter. "That makes you a lab rat, ya know?"

"C'mon now, baby," she purred, "don't be mad at me, alright. I just had one." She coyly waved a single finger, tracing her manicured nail across his lips. "It helps me stay loose. And hell, I don't see you backin' away from the bar." She thumped the half-empty glass in his hand.

"That's your problem now. You're way too loose!" Michael lashed out. "Loosey Lou!"

"Listen, smart ass! My father, he was the only living saint I ever knew. And he died a long time ago!" she snapped.

"Poor ol' man...he's turnin' over in his grave knowin' his baby girl's in here sellin' her butt-naked soul!" he stabbed back with full force, hoping that it hurt her. *This was tough love, whatever that meant.* Her gorgeous faced softened, and the flame ignited in her eyes. His dart had hit its mark, but she was tougher than she looked. "I'd hate your arrogant guts if I didn't love you so much, Mike!" she bellowed, poking him in the chest.

"You don't love me woman, you love my money."
He playfully grabbed her wrists, and drew her into his arms, kissing her neck, inhaling her flowery scent. Her soft hair flailed across his face as she giggled and pushed him away.

"I hustle for my own money, baby boy," she admonished, waving a tiny fist full of crumpled bills. "And you still ain't my daddy!" She wagged her long tongue at him, spun, and sauntered way, throwing extra swagger into each high-heeled step, teasing him with the G-string view of her jiggling ass.

"I'm twice the man ya daddy ever was!" Michael smirked lustfully and gulped his drink down. *Ya sexy ass.*

He hated that she was addicted to those damn pills, and loved how horny they made her even more. This was their game. *Love and abuse.* No apologies, no excuses. Speak or forever hold your peace. There were grumpy, old married couples that weren't this happily dysfunctional.

"Damn, I'm playin' with fire," he warned himself. and spun back to the bar. "Bartender! See this empty glass? Don't let it happen again," he joked. Suddenly, a hand patted him on the back.

"Mike Drake! Just the man I needed to see!" a tall, thin man greeted with forced bravado. In no hurry to bump into any old friends or new enemies, Michael reluctantly glanced over his shoulder. The two greeted each other casually, pounding fists. Trust and mistrust sealed in a single gesture.

"Fat Todd, what can I do for ya?" Michael asked nonchalantly. *Took six months to bait this fish. Can't let him off the hook now.*

"My pipeline's dry. I need to talk to you 'bout gettin' some work." Fat Todd leaned in closer, acting out his part like a spy on some top secret mission. "My folks just got jammed up in South Carolina. Now I got no *connect.* Can you believe that? I'm starving out here!"

"Like I need to inherent your problems," Michael frowned on the insult. *Attack his honor. Make him prove his worth. Quickest way to make a man wanna do business with you.*

"You offend me, Mike. C'mon, this is me ya talkin' to. That's never been the way I operate and you know it. That Lamborghini I sold ya...you had any problems?"

"Can't say that I have," Michael admitted.

"There it is. From L.A. to New Orleans. South Carolina all the way to downtown Atlanta, my name's clean. I make my own moves, take care of my own problems. I'd never turn the heat on another man just to save my own ass. That's a major code violation."

"One that could easily get you killed," Michael inserted. Fat Todd nodded in agreement and smiled wickedly. *Murder is a revolving door.*

"It's just that my *connect* got greedy and got caught up in some other mess he didn't have no business gettin' into. Credit card fraud. Identity theft. That kinda low level nonsense," Fat Todd pleaded his case, deflecting the attack on his reputation. "Now I'm all alone out here in the wilderness."

"You can always do business with the heavyweights over there." Mike nodded toward the BMF clan who was now drenched in a storm of money and naked women. "The bad boys from Motor City are giving it away by the ton. All you gotta do is ask."

Fat Todd saluted the reveling BMF crew and shook his head. "They're sittin' on top of the world right now. You know how many out-a-town crews been through Atlanta flexin' their muscle in the open like that? Too many to name, and all of 'em end up the same way. When I'm old and gray I wanna be able to look back at my past from my front porch, not a dirty prison window."

Spoken like a true hustler. Todd was shopping for better prices. Michael raised his glass to his lips, seeming to measure what he'd been told. "How much weight can you handle?"

"Depends on your ticket." Fat Todd flashed a cheshire-cat grin. "For the right price I'll scoop up fifty *birds.*"

"I'll go sixteen-flat a *brick,*" Michael offered. "But ya know, that ticket, that's just for you. I'm tryin' to work my way into City Hall." *That's it, pull back easy, reel the prize fish in nice and slow.*

Fat Todd rubbed his chin, calculating the price tag on sixteen-grand times fifty kilos. *Eight-hundred-thousand easy. Chump change.* Todd smiled, approving of the best deal he could get anywhere in town, and not get robbed or indicted in the process. "Run it," he said.

"I'll give you a call Wednesday night, around seven. Make sure you got the cash on deck or we never do business again," Michael warned with a smile.

"Bet!" Fat Todd beamed joyously and walked off with a grand stride.

Michael took another slow sip as he watched the lanky, long-armed man leave. Standing just over six feet tall, and weighing in at a svelte one-hundred-sixty pounds, soaking wet on a full stomach, Todd Graham was anything but fat. But he was damn sure lucky. By some stroke of fate, the guy had ended up married to the Mayor's daughter--a chessboard move which essentially gave him free access to a world of social and political privilege far beyond this one. But around here the cash was too quick, too nice, too easy, and he never gave up his true hustle.

His poor, sweet, dear mother-in-law. The first black woman to ever hold the top office in the capitol city of the south had absolutely no idea. If she did, she sure as hell couldn't admit it. *Wait'll they hear 'bout this shit down at City Hall.* The lights dimmed.

"If you ain't sippin' or tippin', ya broke ass niggas can get to dippin'!" the DJ threatened over his mike. "All real-deal, trillsville. Straight up, no flex! Due up next, it's super-booty on duty! Comin' straight at ya on center stage, live and in the nasty flesh, give it up for the sexy, Miss Diamond! OWWWW! Open up ya wallets players, and don't forget to pay ya pussy bill!"

The music cued and the soft spotlight tracked Adrianna as she took center stage amongst a drunken parade of howls, cheers, and applause. Like a dream in motion, she was a certified crowd favorite.

Michael watched her soft eyes meet his, connecting the small distance between them. Beneath the driving music, he could hear what she wanted, and she definitely knew exactly what he needed.

This shit still ain't me, he tried to convince himself.

Suddenly, that damned nagging, pitch-black sadness washed over him again. To see her like this was so erotic, so nice...*So painful.* Here was this angel, cast from heaven, falling to earth. *Now she's dying in a joint like this.*

This woman could have graced the cover of any fashion magazine, walked any runway from Paris to Milan. She was real beauty, her toned body full and fluid.

None of that anorexic, pale-face couture shit favored by them French fags, and New York City queers.

Green paper flew to the stag as Adrianna slowly undressed, seducing lustful hearts and empty souls. The lights flared, finally exposing her bare beauty, suppressing her fears, muting her dreams. The fee for her demise was paid. Piles of cash blanketed the stage, crumpling beneath her gentle steps.

As she kneeled, twisted, contorted, and grinded on stage, her sensual performance hypnotized the horny audience. She was making love to a crowded room, but Mike knew every sinful emotion, every slutty position was really all for him. These suckers would never get to touch her the way he could.

Yeah...there are seven ways to die in Atlanta.
And this one's worth my last fuckin' breath.

6

The pine table and four wooden chairs quickly slid out of the way, and the faded rug rolled back, revealing the panel door hidden beneath. The squeaky padlock popped off with the twist of a key. Alejandro and Cesar, two sweaty Mexican teens haphazardly piled air-sealed bundles of cocaine into the secret compartment hidden in the kitchen floor. There were ten kilos to a sealed bundle, ninety bundles in all--a ton of pure *snow* to blanket the city.

"Think about it, Cesar. By the time me and you are twenty-one, we'll be millionaires!" Alejandro beamed with a rich accent. "One day, when Uncle's old, he'll pass *la familia* on to us! We'll be the hottest crew around. Hot cars and nice suits for breakfast. Fuckin' supermodels for dinner!"

"I want a helicopter too!" Cesar dreamed, "like Uncle Jorge's or a big, big one like the Marines got with two propellers....Vrrrrrr!" Cesar imitated, whirling his index fingers like chopper blades.

"We'll get two. One for the day, and one to go out in at night," Alejandro decided, "I'll be the Don and you...you'll be my right hand *hermano.*"

"How come you're in charge? Me, I'm the smart one," Cesar complained. "I'm even better lookin'."

"Why else? 'Cause I'm your older brother, and my hairy *cajones* are bigger than yours!" Alejandro laughed, grabbing his crotch. "Now hurry up. If we get done early, I wanna go fuck those black chicks again." Alejandro humped the air and tapped his watch.

"Ayyy! They strippin' at the *Blue Flame* tonight?" Cesar asked excitedly. "I love to get pissy drunk and watch 'em shake those big asses." Cesar danced around the table, clumsily imitating the stripper's gyrating moves. "Boom! Bam! Boom!"

"Sluts are there every night, just like the money," Alejandro answered. "Gettin' naked, it's a way of life for these country girls. They're born this way. I was gonna pick 'em up after they get off work. But we can get there early and hang out a while...if you hurry your slow ass up! *Vaminos!* " Alejandro slapped his baby brother across the back of the head.

"Ayyy, I'm moving!" Cesar grunted. They quickened their pace, finished in the kitchen, and replaced the furniture.

Moving into the garage, the two playful brothers joked as they neatly lined up forty plastic lawn bags stuffed with compressed pounds of Mexican weed, fifty pounds to a bag--a ton of fresh herb to season the city.

"Alejandro! Cesar! Stop playing around so we can get to the airport on time!" a voice boomed from the back of the house.

"Whatever you say, *El Gordo!* " Cesar joked, puffing his cheeks, mocking the fat man's meaningless order.

"Chingate!" Alejandro chimed in...*Go fuck yourself.*

"I hear that. That's no-no funny!" El Gordo shouted back. "*Idiotas!*"

In the master bedroom, a plump, balding Mexican man stuffed in a sweat-stained silk shirt lumbered with heavy breaths, stacking piles of bills--filthy ones, fives, tens, dirty twenties, coca-laced fifties and fresh, big-faced hundreds. As bands of currency flipped through a state-of-the-art Giesecke & Devrient money counter, its digital screen blinked numbers that fluttered like red demons.

Beep! The counter signaled and stopped.
"Ahh, lousy fakes...waste of my time!" El Gordo huffed and removed the counterfeit bill from the machine ladle. He raised the bogus bill to the light, examining the minor inconsistencies in ink and print. *Not a bad fake, eh amigo?* Convinced, he burned the bogus bill with his cigarette lighter and started the money counter again. With nimble fingers, El Gordo snapped

thick rubber bands around the stacks of counted loot and stuffed them into cardboard boxes, readying them for the long journey back to Mexico City.

For another twenty minutes they all went quietly about their business, the house buzzing like a beehive--immigrant worker bees storing sweet green honey for the cold winter. Distracted by their work, and hypnotized by their greed, they were peacefully unaware of the black police cruiser creeping to a slow stop in front of their house.

Four silhouetted bodies pounced from the stealthy car, and raced across the front yard, flowing amidst the shadows. The first armed sheriff scrambled to the porch, covering the front door, while the other three darted along the dimly lit sides of the house. The cloaked trio finally crept up to a back door leading directly into the kitchen.

A small sectioned window in the door reflected human images; Alejandro and Cesar walked back into the kitchen and sat at the table, popping open two ice cold brews. "All you bought was Coronas? What's that German beer we..."

Suddenly, a flash grenade crashed through the window, bouncing off the kitchen sink, flaring with a searing, blinding light! Two smoke grenades instantly followed, spewing a cloud of choking vapor!

"La policia!" Alejandro and Cesar simultaneously sprung to their feet, stumbling clumsily, gagging for air, reaching for their waists, fumbling for their guns, dizzily trying to fight off the swirling vertigo. Deep inside the smoky blindness, they heard the back door crash open.

Multiple voices barked, *"Sheriffs' Department! Get on the ground! Get the fuck down! Sheriffs' Department!"*

Clamoring in white darkness, gun barrels aimed at the heart of the cloud of fumes! "Reach for the sky muthafuckas. Ya know what it is!" There were jagged screams! Guns targeted! Panic ignited, fueled by the deafening crackle of automatic machine gunfire!

Impulsive youngsters, their hearts driving, Alejandro and Cesar backed up, arms flailing, triggers squeezed!

"Ay, mierda...I'm shot! *Fuck thiiissss...!*"

Spanish screams echoed before painfully drowning into gasps of gargled blood.

In the back room, El Gordo dove behind the bed, cowering next to the boxes of cash. An eerie silence fell over the house. The trembling El Gordo squeezed his eyelids together, trying to wake from this nightmare. His heart pounded till it ached, and blood vessels throbbed behind his reddened ears.

The door slowly creaked open. A thin veil of grey smoke trailed in small swirls across the threshold.

"You got one chance to live fat boy! If ya in there, step out easy. Real easy! This ain't no game, and I ain't fuckin' 'round!" a deep, jagged country voice warned from behind the door frame.

"Vete pa'l carajo!" El Gordo grumbled...*Go to hell!*

"I don't speak none o' that bullshit!" the unseen sheriff returned coldly. "But I'll kill yo' ass in any language you want, amigo!"

El Gordo whimpered, tears rolling down his fat face. Horrified, he rubbed his trembling fingers over a pendant at the end of his gold necklace, and mumbled a solemn prayer to Saint Francis of Assisi--the Catholic patron saint of solitary death--in desperate hopes of an earthly pardon.

EL Gordo saw the barrel of the pistol first. A man in the ski mask step around the corner next, his Mossberg shotgun still aimed for the kill.

"It's just you in here?" the masked sheriff asked.

"Si..." El Gordo quivered, and stood to his feet, his hands raised high. "No mas, senor. Por favor no me mates!" he begged for his life. *No translation needed.*

The gunman's head tilted to the side, and through the knit mask, a wicked smile formed. *No mercy.* His gloved finger tensed, the hairpin trigger *clicked...BLAM!*

A thunderous shotgun *blast ripped* through El Gordo's chest, pummeling him backwards. He landed on his back, gasping, spitting blood, convulsing in shock, still whispering his last rites. His teary eyes stared at the roof, seeming to penetrate it, burning a clear path to heaven. On the road to the pearly gates, he could see a lofty vision of Saint Francis bound in a blanket of light, but there would be no holy pardon tonight; his rapidly pounding *heartbeats* slowed to a final *thump....*

The black police cruiser backed up to the house as the garage door quickly opened. One by one, the boxes of cash were hastily dumped into large duffel bags and tossed into the open trunk. The bundled kilos were lifted and stored next.

"That's all o' the powder, but we ain't got no room for all this weed!"

A second masked sheriff reached inside a plastic bag, grasping a clump of weed, examining the dark, seedy crop.

"It ain't nothin' but some bullshit Tex-Mex regular no way. Just take what we can!"

RRRIIIIINNG! The jingled tune of a cell phone played in the distance.

"Who we got callin' us in the middle of our work day?" a masked sheriff joked as he made his way back into the house, searching for the source of the call. In the kitchen, he rolled Alejandro's body over and pulled the chirping phone from a bloody shirt pocket. The digital screen read: DRAKE.

"I'll just be damned! We got big time Mike Drake on the hotline!" the sheriff yelled out to his crew.

"Answer it!" a voice barked back. "Tell 'em he gone have to find some mo' Mexicans!"

The sheriff turned off the cell phone and thoughtlessly dropped it on Alejandro's motionless body.

"Wait yo' turn, Drake. We comin' to see ya."

Out in the garage, the masked sheriffs managed to get twelve giant plastic bags jammed into the trunk, and six more in the back seat, leaving barely enough room to sit. Filled to capacity, they dove inside the car, doors slammed, and they slowly rolled away.

It was a good take for half a night's work. Before long, the powder would be cut, whipped, and flipped into *Saint Cash*, the patron saint of dope boys and strongarm thieves. There would be no police reports filed, at least not until the bodies stiffened and began to smell, and the flies started to feast.

No sirens. No ambulances. No backup needed.
No court dates. No judge and jury. No jail time.

American justice in all her glory.

7

"Dammit, Alejandro! Pick up the phone. I ain't got all night!" he yelled into the cell phone as it rang, but still no answer.

4:20 AM. And this impromptu stop was out of their way. *Them's the rules. Never stray from your path. Get the money. Get the girl. Get home alive.* All they were supposed to do was stop by the stash house to drop off the seven-hundred-thousand in cash that was sleeping soundly in a hidden compartment in his trunk, and then call it a night. *But that woulda been too much like right.*

Alejandro and Cesar are waitin' on me to get there so they can make their pre-dawn trip to the airport with the loot. He gripped his cell phone. *And here I am, my ship way off course, floatin' out in dangerous open waters, waiting on her.*

Adrianna had begged him to make one quick stop.

"*It was a quick side-play,*" she had whined until he caved. "*A chance to make some extra dough later on.*"

Michael impatiently watched from his car, the rain spilling over his windshield, blurring his view as Adrianna entered the *Krispy Kreme* doughnut shop on Ponce De Leon Avenue.

* * *

Just over a hundred yards away, a Ford Tempo with Florida license plates sat parked on the main strip. A blonde, female driver carefully aimed her Nikon camera, its 35mm shutter clicking in rapid succession. Special Agent Jessica Lewis patiently panned the telephoto lens, keeping it trained on

Adrianna as she shook the water from her coat, and confidently strolled through the doughnut shop.

"That's it sweetheart, take us right to the top," Agent Lewis triggered her camera again.

The passenger door opened and a rain-soaked male counterpart climbed into the car, balancing a tray mounted with two steaming cups of coffee. "I miss anything?" Agent Dan Yates asked.

She clicked another barrage of photo frames. "We're just getting under way."

"Damn shame she's about to wreck this kid's NFL career," Agent Yates regretted and blew the smoldering steam from his coffee.

"I never liked football anyway," she admitted.

"Hold it. We've got a marked police car rolling into the parking lot," he noticed.

Agent Lewis trained her camera on the police car.

"How's our girl holding up?" he asked, bolting upright. "Keep your cool, kid. Stay on course."

Agent Lewis pivoted, aiming the camera back at the doughnut shop. The lens framed two men already seated inside as one waved to Adrianna.

"She's good." Lewis reported from behind the camera. "I don't think she even knows the cop is there."

* * *

*T*his here's a bad idea. Michael could barely see the two men who greeted Adrianna with hugs. They all huddled together at a table next to the window.

For the next twenty minutes, they talked with bold, exaggerated hand gestures, like they had a grip on life, like they would live forever. *Dealing. Negotiating.* This was an unauthorized move outside the chessboard, and Mike knew he would have to keep an extra careful eye-out just for her sake. *Nobody lives forever...and money can't save you.*

Through the torrent of falling water, he watched her weave her timeless spell. The one woman that constantly haunted his dreams was beautiful, smart, and reckless.

And all money ain't good money.

From the corner of his eye, Michael tracked a police car as it pulled into the parking lot and stopped. The interior light of the squad car lit up, the cop inside seeming to check his dashboard computer before he reached for a clipboard.

Probably just stoppin' to fill out a patrol report. Pretending to be on duty during a rain soaked night in a city that would have to patrol itself. Cops hate to get wet for no good reason.

Thunder clapped and lightning burned over the parking lot in a white spark of brilliance. Michael wiped the fog from the windshield, but there was too much rain to make out the officer's face. Stubbornly, he squinted through the beads of water until his head ached under the strain. His Nextel phone chirped. It was *him* calling.

"Jorge! What's the word, amigo?" Mike cordially spoke into the receiver.

"All's well in this world of treachery, my friend," Jorge grumbled. "Where are you? Is my angel Adrianna somewhere around?"

Dangerous question. It was way past closing time for Adrianna's line of work and Jorge knew it. Mike paused, forming his answer.

"I saw her earlier tonight over at *Magic City*, but I had to go hit a lick. This whole damn city's bleedin' money."

"Oh, yes!" Jorge continued with conjured surprise. "I wasn't aware of the time. I'm an hour ahead of you."

Sure you forgot, ya dirty bastard.

"I'll be back early in the morning around eleven. Pick us up at hangar C-14 this time. I've got a brand new toy to show you," Jorge confided. "Be sure to bring my beloved Adrianna. Tell her I miss her, or love her...something...whatever a woman likes to hear."

"Sure thing, Jorge. She'll be glad to hear it," Mike finished sarcastically and killed the call.

"*His beloved Adrianna,*" Michael restated in a

meditative whisper. He really didn't like the way Jorge had said it. It was condescending. Maybe, Jorge knew more than he was letting on. Maybe, it was a slither of Mike's own jealousy poking its head from beneath the surface. Annoyed, Michael tapped the steering wheel, contemplating his third alternative; he was just being paranoid. *Paranoid my ass.*

In the past four years, paranoia had become his best friend next to his twin guns and a warm bottle of brandy. In this line of work, paranoia was an essential and dependable life preserver. When utilized properly, and readily available, it could save a drowning man's life just in the knick of time. *Problem is, it's impossible to throw a life preserver to yourself once you go overboard.* And he sure as hell couldn't count on the cutthroats he did business with everyday to offer a lifeline. *It's every man for himself out here on the Georgia plains.*

He soon looked up to see Adrianna scurrying across the parking lot, her heels splashing in small puddles of collected water. She dove inside and slammed the door.

"Hey, woman, watch yourself now! You're drippin' water all over my ostrich skin seats!" he complained.

"You li'l boys with your Tonka toys. I promise, after we pull this lick off, I'll buy you a brand new one," she whispered softly with the glow of greed skirting in her hazel eyes.

Adrianna giggled and wiped strands of wet hair from her face. Tossing her head back, she gripped the bundle of locks with both hands, pulling them behind her, fanning the hair across her back. He sat dazed by her beauty, watching the contours of her neck as a tiny river of water trickled down to her shoulders.

"After we pull what off?" he asked, breaking the spell she'd unknowingly cast over him.

"Just a li'l move I got going down." She kissed his lips and reached for the dashboard, blindly punching buttons.

"Ahh, c'mon, Mike! Doesn't this Italian piece o' shit have any heat? I'm freezing!" She helplessly poked away at the controls while he watched. She could feel his eyes pressing on her. "I'm cold...I'm wet...I'm high...I'm horny! Are you gonna heat me up or what?" she begged, seductively sucking her tongue.

Michael cranked the car and adjusted the temperature dial. Warm air rushed into the cabin, tossing strands of her damp hair. *I'll heat ya sexy ass up, alright. Wait 'til I get you home.*

"So who are these cats you just met?" Mike pointed at the men still sitting in the doughnut shop.

"One of them's some kind o' basketball player, I think. The other one's this guy I used to go to high school with. Angel, he's alright. He knows how to get to the money."

"The other guy, who does he play for?"

"How should I know? Somebody in the NBA I guess. L.A. Clippers? Or no, is it Minnesota? Anyway, he just needs a small favor that's all." She was holding back on him. He could smell the fumes of deceit.

"Regardless of who he does or doesn't play for, he can't fix any games for you, or shave any points," she continued, trying to deflect his line of questioning.

"Who said anything about puttin' on a fix? I'm an honest, degenerate gambler."

"I really am worried about you," she warned. "This gambling's gettin' to be a serious thing for you. You always had a really addictive nature anyway."

"You oughta getcha own talk show. You could be the stripper therapist," he teased.

"Doubt my feminine intuition all you want, but you still need help."

"A small wager here and there ain't never hurt nobody. And what the hell kind of favor do these cats need?" he persisted.

"The kind of white favors that only my friends like you can supply," she answered in frustration. "Now stop askin' so many questions and let's go. I swear I gotta get some smarter men in my life." Adrianna placed her shivering hands over the air vent, absorbing the heat. He palmed her hands, sharing his warmth.

"Does Jorge know about this side hustle or do I have to be the one to tell him?" Mike threatened.

Adrianna snatched her chilled fingers from his grasp, and snapped, "Tell him. But he'll be way more pissed at *you* for helping me do this behind his back."

"You can't blackmail into a deal."

"I just did. So leave Jorge out of this, and I'll make sure you get your cut of the check."

She knew Mike better than he knew himself. He could never ignore that dangerous fact. She was counting on greed to reel him in, and the fear of death to keep him on her side. *Damn, I love this woman.*

"Jorge just called. Says he'll be back tomorrow."

"Did he ask about me?" she asked excitedly. Mike cringed at her exuberant reaction to another man, then checked himself. *Jealousy is real.*

"Of course the mad Mexican asked for his prized pussycat. Wanted to know if his li'l mamacita was with me."

"What'd you tell him, slick?"

"Told 'em you couldn't talk with ya head in my lap. She'll call you back, Jorge...after she swallows." Mike gulped loudly and exploded in laughter.

"You're a real funny guy!" She jabbed his arm with a solid punch. "We'll see how funny you are when I never let you touch me again, playboy." Mike's laughter stopped abruptly. It was cool to play rough, but not that rough.

"Heeyyy, woman! Mike tossed his hands up in surrender. "I gotta throw a flag on that penalty. A man and his balls got needs." Adrianna opened her lips, readying for a verbal assault on his manhood, when Officer Alexander drove past.

"How long was Alexander sittin' there?" she asked.

"The cop? He pulled up right after you went in," Mike answered. "Why, you workin' with him?"

"He's a long way from Zone One Precinct," she mumbled. "That can't be a good thing."

"Who is he to you?" Mike asked jealously.

"Just the devil with a badge and a blue uniform," she murmured with a glimmer of dread.

Mike twisted the ignition, and the Italian car growled to life. That's when he felt her hands loosen his belt, and yank on his zipper.

"Drive fast," she moaned.

Mike locked into first gear, and jetted up Ponce DeLeon Avenue, streaking past the black Ford Tempo just as Adrianna's head disappeared in his lap.

8

4:48 A.M. The strip along Bankhead Highway was eerily dark and few cars roamed at this early hour. The black sheriff's cruiser crept southward, cloaked in a relentless spray of rain, as it approached the Zone One Police Precinct. The growling car's weighty load pressed the suspension down low over its spinning wheels.

"Slow down right quick," Danny Diablo called from the back seat. The driver eased off the gas and lowered the radio. Danny racked his gun, and climbed from the back window, straddled cowboy-style, firing over the car roof, blasting 9mm shots at the police precinct! Four hollow-tip bullets pierced the concrete walls while two more punctured and splintered the glass façade.

"Diablos, mutha fuckas! Haahaaa! Kill or be killed!" Danny Diablo vowed loudly, as he slid back inside the car, howling with his brothers like drunken pirates.

9

PLEASURE BEFORE PAIN

5:02 A.M. The condo door flung open. Adrianna was hanging in his arms, their tongues curled together, her legs wrapped tightly around his waist, as he carried her across the threshold, and kicked the door closed. Michael clumsily pulled the twin Sig Sauer .357's from his waistband, kissed them, and set them on the bar.

"Goodnight, Irene...goodnight, Marlene," he wished them and plunged his face into Adrianna's breasts. She threw her head back and purred

"One of these days," she gasped between erotic moans, "one day...*ohhh!*..you're gonna tell me why you named those guns Irene...*ewww!*..and Marlene."

"One day, baby," he promised, as he slid his hand beneath her red Chanel dress, and ripped her panties from her hips, "but not right now."

Damp clothing peeled from moist skin, littering the floor in a haphazard trail to the dark bedroom. Ripping the silk covers back, he dropped her naked body on the bed.

"C'mon, fuck me, daddy. Fuck me like I like it!" she squealed in anticipation. She always liked it rough. He preferred it any way he could get it. Wasting no time, Mike climbed into bed, spreading her legs, as he quickly slid his tongue over her hardened nipples. *Foreplay was for fags.*

Michael pressed against her clit and rammed inside her. She moaned and dug her nails in his back, their heartbeats pounding in harmony--writhing, touching, tasting each other. *Forbidden fruit is always the sweetest.*

An hour later, the edge of dawn broke through the night, bathing the room in a pale blue haze. Michael lay staring at Adrianna as she slept, memorizing the curves of her cheeks, wondering what it was, or who it was that she dreamed about. The beige silk sheets rose and fell slowly as she breathed.

The alarm clock *buzzed.* Mike punched it to sleep for interrupting his time and space. Adrianna's sleepy eyes slowly pried opened.

"I hate you," she sighed.

"Not as much as I hate you." He brushed a wave of hair from her face, tucking it behind her ear. She batted her eyes and he hoped that she knew what he was really feeling. And if she didn't feel the same about him, it didn't matter.

We've stolen one night.

Yawning, Adrianna stretched and climbed from his bed. Mike lay with his arms smugly folded behind his head, watching her naked, sculptured frame disappear into the bathroom. He reveled in the heightened sense of sexual gratification a man gets from making love to someone else's prize. Everything about their relationship was wrong in every sense of the word. *That makes it perfect.*

In the bathroom, Adrianna leaned over the sink, staring at her drained face in the mirror. Her heart sunk, and she fought hard to remember everything that was right about her world. *Fast cars, rich men, designer clothes, diamonds, cash, premium grade drugs, plenty of rough sex, too many friends I can't trust...bad men pay for my love...kill to have me!*
I can't breathe.

She winced, her face cowling in sadness. Refusing to cry, she slammed her eyelids, squeezing them until her temples hurt. A trickle of blood fell from her nose, landing in tiny droplets in the stainless steel sink.

A faint whimper escaped from the bathroom. Mike rose in bed. "That emptiness you're feelin' right now," he began softly "that's not just a nasty side effect of the X-pills wearin' off. The higher we fly, the harder it hurts when we come crashin' down. That's reality settin' back in. But that ain't what's really hurtin' me and you."

"You and that goddamn Doctor Phil got the answer to all our problems, don'tcha?" she fired back furiously as uncontrollable tears streamed from her reddened eyes. Her jittery fingers spun the hot water nozzle, sending a spray of water into the sink. The sight of her blood swirling in the draining water fed her nausea.

"Nah, I ain't got all the answers, but I got the one answer you and me both need!" he yelled above the running water. "Just like the Holy man, I can save your soul!"

The water stopped running.

"You can stay loyal like a dog to Jorge if you want. Do your thing. But I can give you something, Jorge can't."

"What's that?" her weary voiced wafted from the bathroom.

"A way out of all of this."

"You have any idea what that's going to cost us?" she sighed. "The life you know here is over. You could never come back to Atlanta."

"Pennies compared to what we gain."

"Who ever said anything about gettin' out anyway. We like living the way we do. We run free. Do what we want when we want. People would die to live our lives," she tried to convince herself.

"People die *from living* like this too,' he joked.

"What makes you think Jorge would ever let us just run away together," she wondered. "You do dream big."

"Let me? I ain't gotta ask his permission for shit," Mike frowned.

"Doesn't matter with Jorge," she explained. "What's his is his, and you're in business with him, so what's yours is still his. He's just letting you borrow his product and his power."

"Ah, man!" he groaned, and collapsed backwards against a pile of pillows.

"What is it?"

"I was so busy trying to get you naked that I forget to drop off a load of cash last night," he remembered. But

Alejandro and Cesar had never answered the phone anyway.

"Drop it off where?"

"To the jackass brothers...Alejandro and Cesar!"

"Don't talk about them like that. They're cute boys. Even if their uncle is a ruthless, sadistic snake. It's not like Jorge's gonna miss the money."

"When it comes up missing, I'll tell 'em you took it," he threatened.

"How much is it anyway, so I'll know when he comes askin' ?" she edged.

"Enough," he stated bluntly. *She hates money secrets.*

"It's too early in the morning to be yappin' about money I can touch!" Adrianna barked, and pulled herself together. "You're turning into a greedy pig just like Jorge!"

She's mad now.

"Oink, oink, baby!" he jabbed back, pushing her buttons. "It's never too early to get to the money, Miss Lady. Remember that next time you want a six-thousand dollar purse...or an overpriced pair of them high-fashion, *Sex in the City* pumps from some Euro-fag designer whose name I can't even pronounce."

"You're a homophobic racist," she scolded.

"Hell you say. I'm a heterosexual prophet and sex king!" he laughed. "No God-fearing man should willingly take it in the ass. Ain't natural."

Michael reached for the remote, and fired up the giant plasma television mounted on the wall facing his bed. The TV was already locked on Channel 2 Action News, his favorite source for eye-in-the-sky reporting, and commentary on local mayhem. *This is reality TV.* Watching it was part of his sacred morning ritual. The first thing he did every day, no matter what.

"Turn to channel five, I wanna see if that playboy weatherman is drunk off his ass again," she said just to pick at his morning obsession.

"Don't test my addiction to channel two news, woman," he warned and turned up the volume. The smiling fresh-faced reporters ran through the slow-moving morning traffic, a rather dismal weather forecast for the rest of the week, and an early morning police standoff with a deranged man in southwest Atlanta. Somebody even had the audacity to fire several shots into the Zone One Police Precinct on Bankhead. Mike erupted in laughter. *Young cats got balls these days.*

"Only reason you're so loyal to that stupid channel is 'cause of some deep-seeded, sexual fantasy you Atlanta creeps got about Monica Kaufman. She's the first news lady you li'l country black boys saw on TV that looked like your mamma, and y'all been pussy whipped ever since."

"Your theory is sick...and disturbing," he attacked.

"But horribly true." Mike dialed his cell phone.

Between the flow of news stories, the weatherman made casual warnings about some category-five storm brewing off the Gulf of Mexico. *Katrina* was the hurricane's name. Apparently, New Orleans and parts of Mississippi were bracing for her watery onslaught.

"Plant Man, this is Drake. Huh?" Mike relayed into his cell phone. "Of course I know what time it is. I wanna slap four-hundred-thousand on the Spurs...game two." Mike paused. "Cavaliers don't do shit. Bet it. Gimme another two-hundred-thousand on the *Over*...at one-ninety-five-and-a-half."

He paused for the confirmation.

"That's what I ordered. And make sure you leave this six-hundred-grand in winnings on my account at the Wynn Hotel Las Vegas!" he predicted and hung up. "Free money."

"You got to know when to hold 'em...know when to fold 'em!" Adrianna sang out *The Gambler*, in her best Kenny Roger's voice.

"Only good bet is a sure bet," he defended. "Plant Man's got his hooks in this shady NBA referee that owes some big time gambling debts. The fix is in, baby!"

"You have a problem," she said. "Get help."

There was a 'Special News Report' about an outbreak of teenage prostitution in the city. Young girls were the easiest prey for the new age of pimpin' in the south. Next, after the commercial break, the commentator promised to give us a few tips on how to avoid the high price of natural gas this winter.

"Get up and get dressed," Adrianna demanded as she stepped from the bathroom, plugging brilliant diamond earrings into her lobes. Her soft makeup was restored to its pristine, pre-sex state. Michael climbed from the bed, and caressed her face. Their lips met in a slow, warm embrace.

"Only this much beauty could hide so much pain," he whispered, peering into a sad pool of hazel eyes.

"Vargas is waiting. You know how he gets when I show up late."

"You remember you belong to me," Mike said sternly, making no attempt to mask his hatred for the man that he was hunting. "I don't move when he barks. I move when the money shakes."

"When Jorge finds out about us...he's going to torture me fast and kill you real slow," she warned, as she slid back into her red Chanel dress.

"Not if I get rid of him first."

"What good is lying to ourselves, Mike? We need Jorge more than he needs us. And you...you're up to your neck, sinking in Mexican quicksand." Adrianna stepped into her heels. "He'll never let you leave him alive."

In due time li'l momma, he thought. *In due time.*

10

THE MEXICAN CONNECT

A warm dawn calmly broke over Dekalb-Peachtree Airport, a small private airstrip just fifteen miles north of Atlanta. The emerging sun cast a mystical orange tint above the gray strips of runway littering the tarmac. On the horizon, a giant steel bird ascended from the heavens, touched its wheels down, and slowed to a crawl, as its turbine engines ebbed to a steady whine.

The polished black Gulfstream G550 rolled off the runway, and disappeared inside an aluminum domed hangar where a bulletproof, white Chevy Suburban with pitch-black tinted windows waited. The truck doors swung open. Adrianna and Michael climbed out of the SUV, staring in awe at the shiny new airplane.

"One thing's for sure," Mike admitted, "the man travels first class all the way."

"And you want me to give *this* life up?" Adrianna rolled her eyes at Mike, dawned her Versace shades, and strutted away. "Not a snowball's chance in hell."

The bay door of the jet lowered and two massive bodyguards stepped off first. The dark haired soldiers were Latino monsters Hector and Manuel Avila. Towering at an even six-foot-four, the identical twin brothers were a combined five-hundred pounds of Mexican muscle with an unquenchable appetite for tequila, a lust for loose, busty women of all ethnic persuasions, and a passion for random violence any way, any time, any place they could get to it.

Their animated boss Jorge Moreno-Vargas poked his head from the aircraft door next, and smiled grandly at the sight of Adrianna posing in a red mini-skirt and stiletto heels. It was an expensive outfit he'd purchased for her last birthday.

"What do you think of my new plane, Mike?" Jorge's arms flew up in joyous pride. "Forty-six million dollars U.S. I bought the most expensive model they had. It's even got a Jacuzzi in it!"

Michael scratched his head in bewilderment.

"With gas prices these days, you got any idea what it's gonna cost you to keep this sucker fueled up?" Mike asked jokingly.

"Ahhh, damn Georgie Bush, junior! Republican, frat-boy pussy!" Jorge exploded. "I'm not going to stop living my lifestyle of the rich and famous because your redneck President is too dumb to stay out of Iraq."

"You gotta point, Jorge," Mike nodded.

"Damn right I do. Adrianna, come!" Adrianna raced into Jorge's outstretched arms, her joyous squeals echoing in the large hangar.

"*Mija*, you are the most beautiful creature God has given the world," Jorge moaned into her ear. Adrianna blushed and kissed Jorge on the lips, lingering slowly, giving him time to taste her.

"Welcome home, Papi! You miss me?" she purred as she groped his crotch. Michael gritted his teeth, and uncomfortably shifted his weight from one foot to the other. Just seeing Adrianna touch him was becoming unbearable.

Jorge Moreno-Vargas was a short, powerfully built man in his mid-thirties. He was regal in his persona--a king among peasants. But the stress of power and murder had begun to slowly age him and strands of gray highlighted a coat of curly black hair. He was born down and dirty, a poor bastard son pushed from a whore's womb in Sinaloa, Mexico. A self-educated man, Vargas was a car thief before entering the trafficking business with the help of his uncle, the legendary smuggler Juan Guerra.

At the age of twenty, Jorge Vargas illegally crossed the border with his mother and sister to start a new life in Corpus Christi, Texas. But in the last ten years, it was here in Atlanta that he had sliced off his biggest piece of the American pie.

"Mi amigo!" Jorge cheered as he embraced Mike in a bear hug, hoisting him from his feet like a small child. Mike simply smiled, suppressing the bubbling disdain he held for the man gripping him. Jorge dropped Mike back down and wrapped an arm over his shoulder as they walked toward the Chevy Suburban.

"I didn't know you could get a jet painted polished black," Mike noted.

"Are you kiddin' me? For forty-six million in cash, they would've painted me polished black!" Jorge jeered. "Then, I'd be your Mexican soul-brother!"

"Everything go as planned?" Michael asked.

"Doesn't it always?" Jorge sneered. "Lousy DEA couldn't stop us even if they really wanted to. And why would they want to?" Jorge chuckled heartily, liquor vapors blowing from his proud chest. "We're the good guys. Me, you, the twins! If it weren't for us, they would have no jobs!" Jorge laughed until he turned red. Manuel and Hector joined in the banter; not that they thought it was funny, but it's always polite to laugh at the jokes of a man who pays you well.

Maybe, I ain't the bad guy. Fighting drug traffic was just as lucrative as dealing in it. That was the irony in this masquerade. Legalization was a pipe dream for the doped-out users who felt that they were in control of their own lives and their junkie habits.

The FBI, CIA, ICE, the DEA, all the conservative, Republican alphabet-boys, they wanted and needed somebody to hunt just as much as men like Jorge Moreno-Vargas needed somebody to outsmart. *This shit is chess not checkers.*

* * *

Ten minutes later, the white Chevy Suburban was racing north on Georgia Highway 400 amidst a growing stream of early morning commuters. The busy, three-lane strip was congested with cars filled with nine-to-fivers--real people, living normal lives in a world that seemed a million miles away.

Jorge sat in the back seat, slowly caressing Adrianna's bare thighs, his probing fingers tracing at the edge of her dress hem.   Seated next to them, Mike glared from the tinted window, trying his damnedest to ignore the scene. *I'm gonna cut his hands off.*

"What's the payload lookin' like this go 'round?" Mike asked, deflecting the venomous thoughts pooling in his skull.

"Nine-thousand kilos," Jorge stated in a whim. "Our friends in Cali have shown us all the love our hearts can handle."

"You mean all that I can handle," Mike corrected. He and Jorge chuckled at the divine truth. It was a simple process. The Colombian suppliers paid the Mexican delivery boys entirely in cocaine--no cash needed. All Jorge had to do was transport five-thousand bricks to the Colombians' associates in Dallas. The remaining tons he could keep. This modern day payment method kept the paper trail to a relative minimum. But unloading at least half of Jorge's end of the shipment on Atlanta was Michael's prime responsibility.

The Mexican might be *the connect,* but it was a black man that had to unload it. The cutthroat streets of Atlanta wouldn't let a Mexican, or any other outsider, hold on to that much dope for too long. *This ain't Mexico, amigo. And 'round here, Mexicans don't run shit.*

It was also for the sheer sake of peace, and a good night's sleep that Jorge preferred to receive his *mercancia* from the relatively gentile and business-like remnants of the Cali cartel. The ever vigilant Bogota and Medellin cartels were a little more temperamental, and wholeheartedly less forgiving these days.

"I need you to handle...let's see...three-thousand kilos. The rest I give to Hector and Manuel for their workers up in

Memphis and Birmingham," said Jorge, like he was passing out Christmas gifts to naughty, not nice, little boys and girls.

"Think you hombres can handle that, or do ya need my help in Tennessee and Raleigh too?" Michael asked the twins.

"We don't really need you here in Atlanta," Manuel sneered. "Jorge here thinks you're good for public relations. You're the right *color*. Me, I think you're *dead weight*." The three of them exchanged worthless smiles, and there wasn't a grain of love lost.

"Be nice to each other, boys. We're brothers in business. Like the United Nations of trafficking!" Jorge laughed and buried his face in Adrianna's bulging breasts.

"Stop that, Jorge! That tickles!" she chuckled and squirmed as Jorge snorted and came up for air.

"How long do you think it'll take to finish your end?" Jorge inquired greedily, his dark eyes seething at the thought of another multi-million dollar payoff. Jorge was always happiest talking about the money.

Mike shrugged, "I don't know. Maybe five, six weeks. Probably longer."

Jorge frowned. "A month? Why so long this time?"
"Two-plus tons of work that's why. That ain't kiddy weight, Jorge. Then we got too many crews stockin' the city. We got them BMF cats fronting everybody they meet a brick, then these Dominican cats are coming down from New York settin' up shop," Mike complained, feigning a worried scowl.

"You know what the problem is with you Georgia boys? You're too accommodating," Jorge said. "You let people just walk into your town and have their way with you for the right price. This town's like a nasty street whore waiting for her next *john*."

"That's her plan, Jorge. Atlanta...she invites you in with welcome arms, gains your trust. She keeps you relaxed. But she's an unfaithful slut. She don't love nobody but herself. While you're workin' and partying yourself into a coma, she robs you blind. Sooner or later, she'll suck the life right outta ya. It ain't nothing but a set-up," Mike explained.

"Well, if y'all hate this place so much, why don't we just pack up and get outta town?" Adrianna chimed in, tired of the useless chatter. "We can all be miserable in the French Riviera."

"Leave?" Jorge said in disbelief. "And abandon all this wonderful money? This place is a gold mine."

"We've put in a lot of work over the last three years," Mike continued. "The streets are singing my name and that ain't good, ya know?"

"Better your name than mine!" Jorge squawked in hysterical laughter. Michael never cracked a smile.

"It's only a joke. I'm kidding!" Jorge mockingly apologized.

"Sooner or later, it all goes bad, Jorge. When we least expect it, one of these young cats gets banged up, and the next thing you know he's trying to introduce me and you both to Uncle Sam."

"Ah, you're just paranoid!" Jorge accused as he waved his stubby hand. "The money will keep us free."

"Just 'cause we don't see 'em don't mean they ain't watchin' us," Mike warned. "Them Feds, they hate to lose. So they let you work good for years. The whole time you're comin' up, thinking you're on top of the world, they're in the shadows spreading their net, drawing ya whole clique in for the kill."

Jorge pondered the lesson for half a second. "To hell with the Federales. To hell with Georgie Bush. And damn the border patrol," Jorge joked as he poured himself a drink from the wet bar. Simple reason should have warned him that Michael was right and that maybe they should slow down. But greed distorts reasoning, melts common sense, and blinds smart men.

"Or maybe you're tired of our arrangement. Maybe you want to up your percentage for your trouble?" Jorge grinned.

"Maybe. Maybe not." Mike eased back with a devilish smile. Jorge was suspicious. And Mike needed him to be.

11

HOME SWEET HOME

The Vargas Estate was a sixty-acre enclave nestled away a couple of miles off Georgia Interstate 400, just outside the Forsyth County line. Opulent and well maintained, it was a hard earned five-million dollar gift that Jorge ceremoniously granted himself for his twenty-ninth birthday.

The main house was a stately, three-story Tudor style mansion built in 1922 by a sickly Pennsylvania steel tycoon who vacationed in Georgia to escape the harsh northern winters. The house bolstered twenty one rooms, seven bathrooms, half-timbering on its French-cut bay windows and upper floors, and a grand façade dominated by several steeply pitched cross gables. It was encased in earth-tone beige stone walls with large doorways, multi-paned casement windows, and large stone chimneys.

It was a picturesque, storybook home, better left in its original state. Still, Jorge saw fit to install an Olympic–size pool, red-clay tennis courts, and horse stables. In a clearing two-hundred yards from the main house, a white Bell Long Ranger III helicopter--with standard air-conditioning and cargo hook--rested quietly on the helipad. A large domed garage housed a spectacular collection of thirteen exotic supercars: three Ferrari Spyders, an Aston Martin Vanquish, four never driven Bentleys, a Lamborghini Mercialago and Diablo, two Mercedes Benz Maybachs, and a newly purchased Porsche GT. In all, there were just enough additions to make sure he had branded the historic estate with the modern day Vargas touch.

The ornate twenty-foot steel gate guarding the entrance to the compound parted slowly and the Chevy Suburban drove inside, traveling along a winding driveway that coiled for nearly a half-mile into the dense foliage like a black asphalt snake. Acres of towering pine trees lined the estate, hiding Vargas from the droves of sports stars, high-profile corporate executives, and celebrities that lived nearby.

A pack of snarling, champion pit bulls patrolled the grounds, barking profusely, circling the incoming car. Six security guards armed with AR-15 assault rifles took control, and corralled the yelping dogs, backing them down.

Mike despised the vicious animals. He had once seen Vargas feed the ravenous dogs human body parts scavenged from an unlucky Mexican courier who had been caught stealing. Barely conscious, the dying man was forced to watch in ghastly horror as the mutts feasted on his severed limbs.

Nearby, an overly nervous Tatiana Olazaban finally stepped out of her convertible Mercedes just as the Suburban arrived. Terrified of the rambunctious dogs, she'd been impatiently waiting in her car for thirty minutes.

"Those cursed dogs! They should all be put to sleep!" Miss Olazaban screamed, shaking her tiny diamond-laced fists. The jumpy dogs angrily barked at her, as if they understood her threat, and accepted the challenge.

The eccentric, but steadfast Miss Olazaban was in her early forties, graceful, articulate, a tenacious negotiator, and always dressed in designer business wear and Cartier jewelry. She was a prominent local realtor who was responsible for acquiring and maintaining the vast portfolio of Jorge's real estate holdings--residential and commercial, legal or otherwise. Ms. Olazaban greeted Jorge with a hug and followed him through the large, arched front doors of the mansion.

"Can't this wait, Tatiana? I just stepped off the plane. I'm tired. Really now, does it make any difference whether I spend a slow million dollars today or spend it fast tomorrow?" Jorge argued as his voice echoed from the vaulted ceilings.

"Jorge, of course it matters, I know you're busy, but I really need to get this paperwork finished by three o'clock sharp, the inspectors need to be paid off before we go to the zoning board, I have to make sure the county commissioner has his wallet taken care of, or none of this goes through," she answered all in a single breath. "Jorge!"

Surrendering, Jorge tossed his arms in the air.

"Fine, fine! The more I make the more I spend. Go with Manuel to my office. He'll cut you a check. You are a machine, Miss Olazaban! A greedy, persistent little machine!"

"That's why you love and trust me, Jorge!" Miss Olazaban cheered whimsically as she followed Manuel down the marble-tiled corridor. Adrianna kicked off her high-heels and shuffled into the large, stainless steel lined kitchen, digging into the refrigerator.

Meanwhile, Hector, Jorge, and Michael filed into the entertainment theater. There were rows of black leather chairs set against the stone-white carpet, and a giant, mirrored wet bar filled with top shelf spirits. Michael grabbed the universal remote and triggered the power button. The giant eighty-inch flat-screen television emerged from a wooden cabinet, and came to life, flaring its large HDTV image. Michael immediately turned to Channel 2 for the morning news.

"This guy and his local news," Hector laughed, pointing at Mike.

Jorge plopped down in a recliner and kicked his feet up. "You know, Mike, maybe you should've been a reporter. You seem to always know what's going on, and you always find the action."

"I'm a thinking man. I like to know what's happening out in the real world, that's all," Mike mumbled. "It's entertainment, ya know?"

"I'll tell you what's real in my world. Hey, Hector, how 'bout a drink?" Jorge snapped.

"You serious? It's barely noon and you drank the whole flight here," Hector preached.

"You get your day started your way, and I'll get my

party started my way," Jorge replied, clapping his hands.

"Suit yourself." Hector moved behind the bar, found two short glasses, and poured from a bottle of Jose Quervo tequila.

"Straight up...no chase," Jorge remembered. "For two days I've been force feeding myself those watered down Tequila Sunrises."

Mike smirked, "Since when did you start sippin' tequila fairy drinks?"

"I have a new mistress in Dallas," Jorge defended his manhood. "She makes them all the time."

Mike shook his head in disapproval. "You're gettin' soft, amigo."

Jorge countered, "What can I do? She's sexy, so I gulp them down, then I fuck her brains out. It's a small price to pay for the ride of your life."

Hector brought Jorge a glass and set the second one next to Mike. Confused by the generosity, Mike looked up at Hector inquisitively.

"I saw you lickin' your lips when Jorge mentioned the booze," Hector said smugly. "Alcoholism is contagious where we come from. So drink up and die."

So much for sincere generosity.

"Not only is our *muchacho* big and ugly, he's psychic too," Mike joked. "Cheers!" He tossed the shot of tequila down his throat.

The television blared an up-to-date report on that Hurricane Katrina. The menacing storm had finally come to shore with deadly rage with wave surges of twenty feet, and hundred mile-an-hour winds engulfing New Orleans. The aerial shots showed that several levies that guarded the residents from the sea were destroyed and entire sections of the city underwater.

Mike remembered standing on his balcony the night before, watching the heavy rain come down. He was suddenly sorry he'd wished for...*a storm to wash his sins away...to melt the dirt off this whole stinkin' city. God's really pissed off now.*

The TV anchorwoman promised more information on the storm as it arrived, then the screen flashed to another late breaking story. *Oh, shit!*

There it was--a small brick house that Jorge, Hector, and Michael immediately recognized. They rose to the edge of their seats, stunned by what they were watching, live and in living color. Coroners rolled covered bodies out on gurneys to waiting hearses.

In the sun-filled background, the ever vigilant 'Hat Squad'--seasoned Atlanta Homicide Detectives--casually prowled the crime scene wearing their trademark Dick Tracy style fedora hats and impeccable tailored suits. *They were too damn comfortable at a bloody murder scene,* Michael always thought.

"Alejandro...Cesar," Jorge whispered softly, the names of his nephews rolling loosely across his tongue. He stood up, teetering, his face frozen in stunned disbelief.

"We can't be sure it's them, Jorge. Maybe they got out alive." *Optimistic thinking.*

The news anchorwoman continued, *"...where neighbors discovered the bodies of three unidentified Hispanic males...All of them suffered multiple gunshot wounds...There were no apparent witnesses...Investigators also believe that the murders were drug related...Detectives say they found large bags of marijuana in the garage and...."*

"My God, Jorge!" her sweet voice came from nowhere. "I'm so...so sorry." Adrianna had been standing in the doorway. Not knowing what else to do, she rushed to his side, hugging him. Jorge stood motionless in her arms, his face cold, his body too numb to feel her.

"Do you still have friends at the morgue?" Jorge asked, his question seemingly directed toward no one in particular. An aching silence blanketed the room. "Well, do you?"

"Of course...I mean," Michael answered slowly, not sure if he should tell the truth. "Yeah, I still do."

"Call them." Jorge painfully lowered his head, pushed Adrianna away, and left the room.

12

TRAFFIC

The great state of Georgia, in all her southern majesty and charm is a vital destination point for major drug shipments. Concrete country highways, rusty rails, and dirty bus depots connect with international, regional, and private airstrips and salty sea marine ports, all working and playing together to supply her needs and feed her greed.

By the sheer grace of God, Georgia is a prime piece of real estate strategically located on the cursed I-95 corridor between rotten apple New York City and steamy hot Miami, the primary wholesale-level drug distribution and importation centers on the East Coast. Interstate Highway 20 runs directly into Georgia from entry points all along the southwest border and Gulf Coast.

As the largest, and most self-serving city in the south, Atlanta is a seductive location bordering tobacco row North Carolina, king cotton South Carolina, redneck Alabama, good ol' boy Tennessee, and alligator skin Florida.

From the coca fields of Peru and Bolivia, to the cartels of Colombia, through the beating heart of Mexico--so many miles, so many heartaches, so many dollars, so much death---and it's a dame shame that so much of it ends up here...

...Right here on a little strip of America called Bankhead Highway—where young brothers, costumed in dreadlocks and triple-X size white t-shirts, hold down every available corner,

hustlin' to get rich or die tryin.' From here, Bankhead's busy side streets bleed into the arteries of a wicked supply chain, feeding the heartbeat of sleepy Georgia towns, and hungry border states.

In 1995, the Atlanta High Intensity Drug trafficking Area (HIDTA) was established by the Office of National Drug Control Policy (ONDCP), with the Georgia Bureau of investigation (GBI) as the administrating agency. The Atlanta HIDTA's dual mission sought to target both drugs and violence in Fulton County, Dekalb County, and the City of Atlanta. There were thirteen agencies participating in the Atlanta HDTA--seven of which were federal agencies. All the trained manpower, and all that life paralyzing jail time still couldn't stop the million dollar tidal wave of money, death, and cocaine washing through Bankhead Highway. *God bless America.*

* * *

Officer David Alexander shifted his bulletproof vest beneath his starched, navy blue uniform shirt, adjusted his gun belt and slid behind the wheel of his Atlanta Police cruiser. Safe inside, he dropped a pair of Ray-Ban aviator shades from his visor, slid them onto his chiseled brown face, and smiled into his rearview mirror. "Damn, I make this uniform look good."

He cranked the blue and red marked APD cruiser and pulled out of the Zone One Police Precinct, cruising south on a congested Bankhead Highway. It was less than a three minute drive to Greenwalt's Garage where he pulled into an empty bay, parking next to the infamous black police cruiser.

Alexander popped the latch on his trunk and the lid flew open. "I see y'all had to get your hands wet last night," Officer Alexander joked with a wicked smile as he sat in the comfort of his front seat. Danny Diablo stepped from the office with a duffle bag slung over his broad shoulders.

"Yeah...shit's all over the news, huh?" Danny Diablo proudly mentioned with a gold and diamond grilled smile.

"News at noon and eleven," Alexander laughed.

"It woulda went down smoother, but them young ass wetbacks over there lost they heads...got all crazy with them tools," Danny admitted. "Everybody had to go then."

Alexander shrugged his shoulders, and wistfully said, "Two tears in a bucket...fuck it. All I need to know is where the money's at!"

"It was the lick of a lifetime, folk! Seven-hundred thousand in cash. All the *coke* a nigga could carry. Car got so packed we had to leave some o' that ol' bullshit Mexican weed behind," Danny Diablo beamed excitedly.

"Next time, I'll hook you up with this cargo van I got stashed at one of my restaurants," Alexander promised.

"We gonna need some dump trucks the way these amigos bringin' in this outta-state-weight," Danny Diablo joked as he tossed the duffle bag into Alexander's trunk and slammed it shut. "You got any mo' of these suckas lined up? I feel like puttin' in some overtime."

Alexander rubbed his chin. "I got a beam on these white boys up in Buckhead. They're supposed to have a couple of big money ecstasy labs that are ripe for the peelin'."

"For sho', folk. Just let us know where they at? Even if there ain't no cash layin' around we can still put them X-pills to work."

"Give me a couple of days. I've been talkin' to Mubarek about putting it all together. Supposedly, he already knows the crackers. Mubarek's been buying four...five-thousand pills at a time, shipping 'em back to New York," Alexander said.

"Mubarek? That greedy jungle monkey. We oughta hit him up. Ya know, word on the street, that African's pullin' millions with all them bootleg CD's and DVD's. I heard he got three mo' knock-off clothing stores down in Columbus and Macon, and one he gone drop in Miami."

"The trick with Mubarek is getting to his cash. Damn Africans are used to hiding shit so them lions and tigers, and gorillas won't eat it," Alexander laughed.

"We the gorillas 'round here, folk. Ain't no hidin' from

us. African betta get his shit together fuckin' wit' us."

"His time'll come," Alexander warned. "We'll let him think we owe him something for turning us on to these white boys."

"Don't make me no difference how, when, or where we gotta get-down with the get-down. 'Cause when he see them tools in his face, that African know what it is, ya feel a nigga?" Danny Diablo said, making a gun with his hand. "It's a robbery!" Danny mocked in an African accent. "Call Nelson Mandela! These Georgia boys are layin' me down!"

Officer Alexander and Danny Diablo chuckled, reveling in their treacherous sense of comedy. Alexander snapped his fingers when the memory hit him.

"That's what I wanted to tell ya. Listen. I was keepin' an eye on DeAngelo Woods last night while he set up a play for five bricks."

"That sissy still lettin' you extort 'em?" Danny reeled. "He ain't got no nuts."

"Drainin' the punk till his well runs dry," Alexander confided. "So I'm over on Ponce de Leon where I see one of yo' freak's partners...that Spanish chick with the ass on her."

"Adrianna. She turned my li'l bitch on to the Mexicans," Danny answered."

"Yeah, her. She hops outta the car with ol' boy with the Lamborghini. What's-a-face? Ya know who I'm talkin' 'bout?" Alexander fought to remember. "What's his name? Dre? Dex? He's supposed to be puttin' up good numbers in the street."

"What color Lambo'?" Danny frowned.

"Silver... sort of metallic like."

"Drake. Mike Drake," Danny Diablo recognized. "She's runnin' with him now. That's good to know."

"I seen Drake parked at the doughnut shop, waitin'. Adrianna's inside talkin' to DeAngelo and guess who else? Ahmad Lewis."

"The Steeler's running back?"

"The one and only," Alexander nodded.

"We all know Ahmad. He grew up 'round here. His NFL signing bonus was somethin' crazy like eight-million. We get some of that cheese outta his pockets and snatch up five bricks...shit, that'll work."

"I don't discriminate. You set his ass up. I'll knock him down," Officer Alexander assured. "Let me get outta here. I gotta deposit I need to make at the bank." Alexander cranked the car.

"The bank?" Danny Diablo smirked.

"I'm saving up for a rainy day," Alexander explained, rolling in reverse. "With what the city pays, man's gotta look out for his own future."

"Damn that!" Danny Diablo declared. "Ya better spend that shit, nigga! Let the muthafuckin' weatherman worry 'bout when it's gone rain."

13

COURTHOUSE CHAOS

I wanna go home. Ryan Ray Nichols stood impatiently in a prisoner waiting room at the Fulton County Courthouse. His dark blue Rice Street jail issue uniform pressed tightly against his muscular body. Iron shackles on his wrists and feet restrained his movements. Hovering around the tiny room, a single female sheriff calmly performed her guard duties.

Only one way outta here. Nichols could see the paneled door that opened to the courtroom just on the opposite side of the wall. *Out the front door.* He could smell perfume wafting in from the adjacent room. *Scent of a woman.* He inhaled the beauty.

"Time to get ready, Nichols," the lady sheriff said as she inserted the keys, removing his metal bonds.

Nichols sniffed at the sheriff's womanly perfume. *You want me to rape you too, don'tcha?* And he calmly began to dress himself for his court trial. *Anything's better than the shitty smell of jail. Anything better than going back to the seventh floor rapin', beating, screamin', stinkin', filthy...I ain't going back today.*

He slid on a tan pair of slacks, black socks, and dress shoes, then stretched into his pressed white shirt and sports jacket. The sheriff casually turned her back to him--her gun bulging from her hip. *I ain't going back!* Nichols swung a heavy fist, striking her across the temple. She moaned, crashing to the floor. Beastly instincts took over, and he pounced on her, kicking, and pounding her relentlessly until a river of blood spewed from her distorted face.

Ryan Nichols reached for her gun, chambered a round, and stormed into the courtroom next door. He whisked past the public defender who was seated, thumbing through case files.

Distracted, the court clerk sat at her post near the foot of the judge's bench, pecking away at a computer keyboard. Nichols briskly moved through the center aisle between the brown courtroom benches, where a few people waited for the trial to begin. No one noticed the gun pressed firmly at his side. *I ain't going back.*

He stepped out of the courtroom, tucking the gun into his pants pocket. Unfamiliar faces traversed the hallway as hastened steps pushed him toward the bank of elevators at the east end of the building.

Nichols shared the quiet elevator ride down two floors with a tall, stocky male sheriff and two chattering women who appeared to be court appointed attorneys. Desperation boiled and Nichols' heart quickened as he stood there watching them. *Ding!* The elevator doors parted.

Nichols exited, swiftly pacing across the brilliant white-walled atrium. Darting eyes glanced quickly over the array of courthouse direction signs...*Appeals...Civil Filings...Criminal Magistrate...Food Court...Sky Bridge...*until he found the one he thought he needed.

Nichols rushed across the sky bridge, where the glass walls gave him a breathtaking view of a bright, clear cast day-- his first view of potential freedom in months. The city was just a few feet away.

He quickly crossed the bridge, entering into the Old Courthouse Building. *Too many exits, too many ways to get caught.* He saw more wall signs with judges' names and courtroom assignments. None of the names meant anything to him in particular, so he made his fatal choice.

Nichols crept through two large, wooden doors into the private Chambers of Judge Gregory Barnes. He smiled coldly as he passed a secretary, and a part-time student aide, and ducked through an adjacent door. Stepping inside, Nichols' heart streaked. A robust male sheriff rose to his feet, dropping his morning newspaper.

"Sir, can I help you?" the sheriff suspiciously asked.

Nichols' pulse drummed. "I ain't goin' back." Nichols drew his gun, taking point blank aim at his target's head. The sheriff recoiled, throwing his hands over his face.

"Whoaa! Wait! Wait a..." the sheriff panicked, stumbling back against the wall.

"Don't die in here!" Nichols screamed. "Gimme your gun!" Nichols jabbed the gun barrel into the sheriff's chest, and with his free hand, unholstered the sherriff's weapon.

"Get down on your knees!"

The sheriff obeyed, slumping to the floor.

"Don't shoot me. What ever ya troubles, don't kill me."

Nichols swung the pistol down hard, cracking the defenseless sheriff across the skull. *I ain't goin' back!* Again and again he swung until his victim lay in a bloody, unconscious heap. Sweating profusely in an adrenaline rage, Nichols continued into the courtroom, entering from a private door directly behind the judge's bench.

The court was already in session. Judge Gregory Barnes sat at the bench presiding over the morning docket. Confused courtroom onlookers, defendants, plaintiffs, public defenders, and lawyers were the first to see the strange man standing behind the unsuspecting judge. *I ain't goin' back!*

Nichols raised his gun and fired!

Through shrieking screams of terror, God's Children trampled for cover, lunging for safety. Bloody chaos.

14

11:50 AM. It was another scorching hot country morning.
Hector manned the wheel of the teal green Mercedes Benz
Maybach, carefully navigating the giant, air-conditioned
automobile. Manuel sat next to him in the front passenger seat
as the car rolled through congested downtown streets. Michael
and Jorge sat in the rear, reclining against the supple
butterscotch colored leather interior, but even such opulent
luxury could not wipe away the misery smeared on their faces.

"We shouldn't being doing this right now, Jorge."
Michael shook his head. "It's too soon after the murders. At
least wait until the investigation's had a li'l time to die down."
Mike's warning fell on deaf ears, and a cold heart.

Jorge sat motionless, staring from his window. The
relentless sunlight burned through the lightly tinted rear glass.
Jorge wept in a quiet, dignified stupor. His eyes were bloodshot
and puffy. The stench of Jose Quervo tequila bled from his
skin, mixing with sweat and too much Armani cologne.

The gigantic Benz passed along Trinity Avenue, and
started a quick left turn onto Central when suddenly, Hector
slammed on the brakes, throwing everyone forward.

"Jesus, what the...."

Central Avenue was in complete chaos! Panicked bodies
streamed from the entrance doors of the Fulton County
Courthouse. There were billowing police sirens, their whines
screaming of danger. Ecstatic sheriffs and courthouse deputies
grasped for sanity, a few despondently crying in each other's

trembling arms. Banners of bright yellow, crime scene tape flapped in the brisk wind, dangling from parking meters and swaying trees.

"Turn on the satellite TV," Michael remembered. "See what's happenin'."

Manuel reached for the dash and powered up the Kenwood radio. Slowly an automated digital screen lifted from the radio face. As it glowed to life, the twelve-inch screens mounted in the rear of the seats flickered and came into focus.

"Late breaking news...A suspect due in court this morning has escaped from the Fulton County Courthouse...If you have any contact with the suspect, please do not confront him...He is believed to be armed and extremely dangerous...." Sound bites were all they needed.

"We're right in the middle of it," Mike said. "Hector, back up and take us 'round to Memorial." *This mayhem will work in our favor.* Police cars and motorcycle officers fought through the traffic, squeezing through whatever road space they could muster.

"The suspect has been identified as thirty-three-year-old Ryan Ray Nichols...Nichols was scheduled to begin trial today for rape, false imprisonment, and several additional charges, after a first trial ended in a hung jury...We have confirmed that Nichols has shot and killed Fulton County Superior Court Judge Gregory Barnes...There were two other fatalities...Court Reporter Julie Brandeis, and Sheriff's Deputy Sergeant Wyatt Teasley have both been pronounced dead."

For a five block radius, there were sheriff's cars, ambulances, fire trucks, and emergency response teams fighting to intersect in the hot zone. Nearly every street corner was swamped by satellite news trucks with mounted aerial antennas. Poised cameramen focused lenses on stoic reporters who held microphones up to their flapping mouths.

Hector followed Mike's instructions, floating along block-by-block, navigating through tight intersections, finally escaping the fray. Moments later, they slowed in front of the *Fulton County Medical Examiner's Office.*

15

"I'm not going to hide in my office while this lunatic runs loose around the city! And for the love of God will somebody please get Chief Harrington on the phone!" Mayor Cheryl Franco exploded. The first strains of the tragic news were just setting in as Mayor Franco circled her office, taking charge of her pooling staff.

"How do we not know where this man is?" Mayor Franco asked in frustration.

"The last confirmed sighting was in a parking lot stairway across the street from the courthouse," an Aide informed.

"A lot of good that does us if he's miles away by now. Contact MARTA authorities, and get them up to speed. We don't need this maniac taking any hostages on the trains and buses. Or worse."

"Momma, are you going to be okay?" Kylie whispered as she cusped her mother's shaking hand. She had been talking with her mother when their heated conversation was interrupted by the boiling situation. More staffers poured into the room behind them.

"No, but...we'll make it through this mess anyway," Mayor Franco answered.

"Alright, Momma." Kylie hugged her. "I'll call you in a few hours to make sure these people haven't driven you crazy."

"Kylie, I'd really feel better if you stay close to me. At least until we find out where this Ray Nichols is hiding."

"Don't worry, Momma. Todd's on his way to pick me up.

We were going to look at some new houses, but with all this happening...."

"Another house? What's wrong with the one you're living in?"

"It's just an investment," Kylie assured. "Todd's car dealership is doing pretty well. We were thinking of putting some of our extra money into more real estate just to avoid some of the taxes."

Mayor Franco grasped her daughter's arm, pulling her close.

"Kylie, I want you to be careful, alright. There's too much at stake for everybody."

"We can't finish this conversation now," Kylie frowned.

"I'm not talking about myself here. I've lived, baby. My track record will speak for itself. No matter what happens to me, you do whatever you have to do to protect yourself."

"Momma, Todd and I are fine. He's waiting for me." Kylie lifted her purse and waked out of the office.

As Mayor Franco watched her eldest daughter leave, she desperately wanted to believe that her son-in-law would take care of her baby. But the Atlanta grapevine had already given Mayor Franco the word that Todd Graham's business was not all that it appeared to be, and to compound that nagging burden, there was a psychotic killer loose in her city.

Just another day at the office.

Mayor Franco motioned to several members of her security team. "James...Kenny...walk my daughter downstairs. Make sure she gets to her car." They complied immediately.

"Mayor Franco!" an assistant burst into the office. "We have another problem!"

* * *

Kylie Graham rushed from the City Hall doors and climbed into a waiting Porsche Cayenne truck.

"I need you on point, Drake. Don't let me down. Later." Fat Todd finished the call, and leaned over to kiss his wife.

"Mayor Mom holding up alright in there?" he asked.

"As well as can be expected under the circumstances. You know how tough she can be. She's taking it all in right now, trying to figure out her best move."

"Her best move is to cover her ass," Todd said.

"She just gave me the same advice about us," Kylie worried.

"None of what I do ever gets back to her. That's the promise," he consoled. "So stop worrying. Here, look what I got you." Todd jerked open the glove compartment. With a gasp, Kylie reached for a blue, velour ring box stashed inside.

"What have you gone and done?" she asked.

"Why do I have to be guilty of something to show the love of my life how much she means to me? Women! Never frickin' satisfied. Just open the box."

She flipped it open, and a rainbow of light reflected through the diamond cluster set atop a gold ring, casting a prism of radiance.

"I love it! No...I *really* love it!" She dove into his arms, squeezing him as tight as her small arms would allow. "I love you."

"How could you not love me?" Todd sneered. "I'm the man with the plan." Kylie stared into the sparkling rays. Brilliant colors flared and died again, as she swiveled the ring in the sunlight.

"We have to be careful," she said remorsefully and snapped the box shut. "We're gambling with everything we have."

Behind them, a car horn honked!

16

FULTON COUNTY MORGUE

Michael scanned the street from corner to corner. He knew for certain that no one had called the morgue to identify the bodies, and even if there had been a few nosey detectives waiting to see who would show up, they were all running to the scene of the courthouse ruckus. *We'll be in and out like ghosts.*

Mike and Jorge popped out of the car, and crossed the street, moving with hastened steps. Mike's eyes fanned for undercover detectives, while Jorge simply didn't give a damn.

Inside the morgue, there was still a lingering reporter and a bored cameraman. The hapless media vultures were forced to stay behind, against their will, to scavenge any leads about the triple murders. To his left, Michael caught a glimpse of forensic technician Lathan Goldman in a chemical stained lab coat. Goldman sipped from a can of Dr. Pepper. They exchanged no pleasantries as Goldman silently crossed their path, and continued through a set of double doors.

"C'mon, Jorge. We follow him." They briskly traveled through an intricate maze of poorly lit corridors, Michael and Jorge trailing a few steps off Goldman's pace.

Along the way, Mike fought off the uneasy fumes of death. He could taste it on his dry tongue. He vaguely remembered that Aunts Irene and Marlene had been the ones to identify his father's body. The grizzly sight of their gunned-down brother crushed poor Irene's spirit, and her will to fight her own sickness, and she died nine months later of pancreatic cancer. A year after that, Marlene died alone from a broken heart.

It was in their honor that Michael had given his trusty guns their firing positions. *Irene* stayed in his left hand, while *Marlene*, the last to die, was always clutched in his right. Hopefully, she would be the last to falter when he needed her most.

The cadaver freezer room was icy cold; its frigid atmosphere mocked the stiffened bodies that had already dispatched warm souls. Goldman crumpled the Dr. Pepper soda can, fake dribbled it between his legs, posted up and made an animated jumpshot, firing the empty can into a nearby garbage bin. "Three-points at the buzzer!" Goldman cheered. Michael and Jorge weren't amused.

"We don't have much time. The rest of the staff is in a meeting with the Chief Coroner," Goldman stated as he yanked open a refrigerator door, and slid out the tray holding the naked body of nineteen-year-old Alejandro Castillo.

Jorge gasped, gnawing teeth grinded behind his tightened lips. Goldman stepped to his right and opened a second refrigerator door, revealing its human contents--a blood-stained, seventeen-year-old Cesar Castillo.

"No, pobrecito...," Jorge gasped in sheer horror as his shaking right hand traced over their discolored faces.

"These are my sister's only children. I tell her I take care of them...I watch over them. Look what's happened." Jorge's voice trembled, his eyes flushed with tears. "They were still little boys."

Jorge paced wildly, mumbling incoherent memories, swears, prayers. Mike shifted uneasily, hoping Jorge wouldn't erupt in one of his infamous outbursts. *This ain't the time or the place for a mental meltdown.*

Sandoval, where is he?" Jorge gathered himself.

"The fat guy? He wouldn't fit into one of these units. "They already got big boy on the slab. They're going to autopsy him first," Goldman answered too coldly. Jorge shot a fiery glare at him. Goldman melted and smartly took a step back.

"I should've sent them back to Mexico. They should've never been here with me." The words flowed from Jorge's lips in an agonized whisper. "They'd still be alive. This will tear my sister's heart out. Ay, fuck me. What did I do to these children?" Shock and fury bent Jorge at the waist. He buried his face in his hands, and expelled a painful, bloodcurdling howl.

"We should leave now, Jorge." Michael rested his hand on Jorge's shoulder, breaking the spell of desperation.

Gaining his senses, Jorge nodded and kissed both boys on their foreheads. "Alejandro, Cesar, I'll send you home to be buried in honor."

As Jorge and Mike turned to leave, Goldman cleared his throat loudly. Jorge stopped, then abruptly rushed into Goldman's face, and slapped him with a handful of hundred-dollar bills. Goldman slammed to the floor, holding his aching jaw as money floated over him like drifting snow.

Jorge and Mike left the morgue, walking beneath the unrelenting mid-day sun. Its brilliant glare burned on their weary, tequila soaked skin. *Damn, I hate the light.* Mike shielded his eyes with a pair of black shades. Hector soon drove the car around and they climbed into the back seat.

"This is a real sticky situation," Mike warned. "It's better that we lay low for a while."

"In Mexico there'd already be blood spilling in the dirt. *Mano y mano*...we take the war to them."

"Hear me out, Jorge. Everything we get away with...it's all because people either don't know or somebody allows it. We go upsetting the balance around here and we all get wrecked. Think. Is that what you really want right now?"

"I need to hurt somebody for doing this to my boys." Jorge punched the bulletproof window, his eyes flooding again with angry tears. "I want them to scream!"

For a very brief second, Mike allowed himself to feel a grain of sympathy for one of the most heartless men he'd ever known. *He was mortal. Just a man, that's all.*

And no amount of money, no luxury item, no payoff could make up for this loss. There wasn't a single trace of reason in Jorge's eyes, only rage. In Jorge's heart there was a large debt due. And somebody, somewhere, would have to bleed.

17

MANHUNT

The largest manhunt in Georgia history was under way.
Ryan Nichols sightings flooded 911 switchboards across nine Georgia counties. And a stunned Fulton County Sheriffs' Department wilted under the microscope of extensive national media coverage, as the City of Atlanta squirmed in the grips of a madman they could not find.

Ryan Nichols had entered the courtroom of Judge Barnes from a secluded door behind the unsuspecting judge's bench. In cold blood, Nichols shot Judge Barnes in the back of the head, then gunned down a court reporter, and a pursuing deputy. Nichols finally escaped the courthouse, where he attempted to hijack three different cars, and ended up pistol whipping a local newspaper reporter in a nearby parking deck, before disappearing into the city.

* * *

In the City Hall Atrium, droves of reporters, cameras, and hot lights focused on the press podium, bearing down on an assembly of Atlanta's top brass--Mayor Franco and Chief of Police Dale Harrington joined several spokesmen from the Sheriffs' Department, the FBI Atlanta Field Division, and the Georgia Bureau of investigations to field the pressing, hard-line questions of a besieged city and a shocked nation.

"We're going to have officers working around the clock in extended shifts. But we still have a responsibility to keep normal patrols to monitor crime in other parts of the city," Chief of Police Dale Harrington said at the podium, standing beneath the crush of lights.

As the former top cop of New Orleans, Harrington had been heralded for his success at cleaning up the thoroughly corrupt Police Force in the Big Easy.

"Once again, I emphasize that Nichols is our top priority. Please do not confront Ryan Nichols if you see him, do not attempt to make any contact," Harrington warned.

Chief Harrington had been courted to Atlanta in brewing controversy when Mayor Franco granted him a generous six-figure salary during a tense time when Atlanta City Police and Firemen were fighting for much needed pay increases. *Welcome to Atlanta, Chief.*

"We're still waiting from an official report from the Sheriffs' Department, but we believe that a single deputy was left to guard Nichols. And that in itself is a breach with normal jail operating procedures," the Chief finished and stepped aside.

Mayor Franco took her turn at the podium, squinting under the glare of lights, as a steady barrage of media questions flew at her.

"Are there any more confirmed deaths? Is the Sheriffs' Office taking any responsibility for this morning's shootings?" the inquiries darted in like machine gun fire. "When will the courthouse videotapes be released?"

"The City of Atlanta is offering a $60,000 dollar reward for any information leading to the capture of Ryan Nichols," Mayor Franco alerted. 'We ask if you have any information please contact the Atlanta Police Department or the Fulton County Sheriffs' Office."

Three years earlier Mayor Franco had cut jobs and funding to the Atlanta City Jail in an effort to trim the city budget. The shift led to a world where simple misdemeanors that normally would have taken an unlucky inmate through the city jail, now took him on a non-stop trip to the already overcrowded Fulton County Jail—and now the metropolitan strains on the facility and its employees were too much to contain.

Only a year and a half earlier, the former top sheriff at the jail was forced to resign after she lost some two-million dollars from a nine-million dollar Fulton County Jail fund that the she had somehow been allowed to invest. Only in Atlanta could a sheriff--with no financial expertise--legally get her hands on nine-million dollars of county taxpayer money.

God Bless America.

Then you toss in a nut like Ryan Nichols, trap him on the murderous Seventh Floor in cramped jail quarters, and disease ridden accommodations. It was a chain reaction that took years to erupt.

* * *

Early the next morning, tragic news broke again as the death of U.S. Customs Agent Daniel Wilhelm spread like wildfire over the AP newswire. Agent Wilhelm's body was found in a vacant home in the upscale, Buckhead section of Atlanta. The slain agent's badge, gun, and pickup truck were also reported missing. Ryan Nichols was now the prime suspect in a fourth brutal and senseless murder.

18

"9-1-1 Operator. What's your emergency?"
"Yeah! Uh...that man ya'll lookin' for that escaped from
the courthouse. He's in my apartment!"

In Gwinnett County, some twenty-five miles north of the
Fulton County Courthouse, the tired and frenzied gunman had
approached Madeline Smith in the parking lot of her
apartment complex. Nichols abducted her at gunpoint, forcing
her back to her apartment where he tied her up in the
bathroom. While the madman showered, she sat on the toilet
seat with a towel covering her head, and took the frightful time
to tell him about her four-year-old daughter, Paige.

Nichols asked for marijuana, but she told him that all
she had was crystal-meth. Miss Smith, a recovering addict
herself, had taken methamphetamines only a few hours before
she was taken hostage. Now she refused to join him in a drug
binge, but instead offered to read from the Bible.

Calmly, she had tried to convince her captor to turn
himself in. She told Nichols the heart wrenching story of how
her husband had bled to death in her arms after being stabbed
during a bar fight. The next morning she cooked scrambled
eggs and toast for her captor, and they watched some television
and prayed.

Finally, in a moment of compassion, Nichols allowed
Madeline Smith to leave her apartment to go see her daughter.
Given the window of opportunity, she immediately phoned in a
frantic 9-1-1 call. Minutes after the call, the Gwinnett County
SWAT team quickly surrounded the apartment, and awaited
the arrival of troops from the FBI, ATF, and the Georgia
Bureau of Investigation.

After a few hours, Ryan Nichols walked out of the apartment and peacefully surrendered. The bloody police standoff the world was waiting for never materialized.

"I'm surprised he turned himself in alive," said Police Chief Harrington. *God Bless America.*

* * *

U.S. Attorney David Namath straightened his tie, took a deep breath, and faced the buzzing fray of reporters and cameramen.

"We're ready whenever you are, Mister Namath," a cameraman signaled.

Namath cleared his throat and began, "My office and the Bureau of Alcohol, Tobacco, and Firearms has filed a federal criminal complaint against Ryan Nichols charging him with possession of a firearm by a person under indictment. This is basically a holding charge that will ensure Mister Nichols' detention while we prepare to bring additional federal and state charges against him."

"Where is Nichols right now?" a reporter loudly asked.

"At this time, Ryan Nichols is being fingerprinted and booked at an FBI field office," Namath said. "After that he'll immediately be escorted to the Sam Nunn Federal Building in downtown Atlanta for further questioning and psychiatric evaluation."

* * *

Two months later, Ryan Ray Nichols was indicted by a Fulton County grand jury on fifty-four counts including murder, kidnapping, armed robbery, aggravated assault on a police officer, carjacking, battery, theft, and unlawful flight to escape authorities.

Ironically, Nichols' former hostage Madeline Smith was under investigation for months following her ordeal because skeptical law enforcement officials believed that she was a prior acquaintance of Mister Nichols, and that she had been aiding and abetting him.

However, no culpable evidence of any prior relationship materialized, and the stubborn and stingy FBI finally relinquished the reward money. For her troubles, Miss Smith also got a two-book publishing deal, and a guest spot on the *Oprah* show. *God bless America.*

19

FIESTA DE LOS MUERTOS

Water spouted from a marble fountain, its crystal clear flow reflecting pure golden sunlight. The manicured lawn was lined with dozens of blooming, white and pink flowered dogwood tress. Pristine flower beds lay filled with scarlet leafed poinsettias, giant black-eyed Susans, red and white petal rose bushes, and gardenias. As it seemed, Senor Jorge Moreno-Vargas, in all his wealth and power, had built himself of virtual Garden of Eden.

There was a swarm of playful children racing across the courtyard. Today was his daughter Gabrielle's birthday. Jorge's wife Maria and daughter had flown back to Atlanta that evening upon hearing the bad news. If it were not for her love for the murdered boys, Maria wouldn't have bothered to come near her cheating husband.

Maria Vargas was thirty-one, gorgeous, outspoken and brash. She was a lot like her husband, which made their volatile marriage a case study in bedroom fist-fights, long-distance separations, superficial knife wounds, and telephone death threats.

Maria drew her skirt up at the thigh, and kneeled in the grass, joyfully watching Gabrielle celebrate her sixth birthday. Dozens of colorful balloons billowed in the hot afternoon breeze. There were three black ponies for the children to saddle up, while fluffy, droopy-eared rabbits ran amuck. A feisty, white swan arrogantly strutted about, fanning its giant plume of feathers. There were life-sized cartoon characters--Mickey Mouse, Donald Duck, and Spiderman—dancing and entertaining the young crowd. Jorge had spared no expense, but money is never as good a remedy for pain as time. As he watched them play, there was a sad sickness in Jorge's face that all his wealth and even the sight of gleeful children could not cure.

"Here you go, Gabrielle," Adrianna grinned as she handed over a big bow-tied box.

"Thank you, Aunt Adrianna. Can I open it now, Mommy?"

Maria took the gift box. "Not now. Wait until after you blow out your candles. Now go gather all your friends. We're about to bring out your birthday cake."

"Okay, Momma!" Gabrielle shrieked with joy and raced off. "Bye, Adrianna!"

"She's really turning into a beautiful li'l lady," Adrianna commented as she waved goodbye to Gabrielle.

"Don't think just because my husband is fucking you in his spare time that I want you around my daughter," Maria snarled and dropped Adrianna's gift. "You're nothing but hired help just like the maids, and all the other whores and pet dogs that Jorge likes to play with." Maria rudely brushed past Adrianna.

Nearby, Mike sat in a lawn chair, sipping from a crystal glass of brandy, watching the live soap opera between Maria and Adrianna unfold in front of him.

As Maria stormed off, Adrianna noticed Mike's nosey glare from a few feet away. "What's on your mind, smart ass?" she yelled at him.

"Go get your own damn man!" Mike chided and raised his glass in salute. Adrianna rolled her eyes in defeat and paced off toward the main house.

"Bring me another stiff drink and a TV dinner on your way back," Mike laughed at Adrianna. "This shit's better than *All My Children.*"

As he drank, Michael watched the gleaming children, trying to regain the vague memories of his sixth birthday....

* * *

There was a small chocolate cake, his favorite, that his mother baked herself, and decorated with six red candles. Li'l Mike squeezed his eyes shut, and made his wish, "Lord, please keep momma 'n daddy together...Don't let her make 'em mad...No more fussin' 'n fightin'...." He blew out the trick candles, and amazingly they flickered, only to defiantly relight themselves.

His father laughed at how mad Michael got when he couldn't extinguish the flames with another mighty breath. His son held his anger, his explosive spirit.

"That's daddy's boy right there!"

His piss-drunk father staggered out soon after the party began, even before the presents were opened. Momma raced into the yard after him, screaming at the top of her lungs about that, "...No good ass ho' you gonna go see on ya only son's birthday! You ain't shit!"

"Come, Michael." Jorge's voice splintered Michael's daydream. "Let's go inside. We need to talk."

Michael and Jorge walked across the courtyard, through the glass terrace, into the vast halls of the gigantic mansion where they finally resided in the confines of the Vargas library. The tiny giggles and joyous screams of the kids could still be heard; the echoes of their innocent voices permeated the French cut windows, and bounced from the vaulted ceilings.

"Remember how sweet life was at that age?" Jorge asked, staring from a sun-filled window. "Children run and play with no fear."

"Life's still sweet, Jorge. We just run and play with bigger and better guns."

"But we're no longer so innocent."

Michael strolled the floor, following the path of polished wooden bookshelves, reading the broad range of titles Jorge had accumulated in his collection. The twelve-foot bookcases were neatly lined with thousands of hardback novels, impossible to acquire first editions, and memoirs. There were books on political science, romance, war, psychology. In another life, Mike was an avid reader and the sight of the books was enthralling to a starved mind drowning in cash numbers, metric measurements, booze, and crime.

"You ever actually read any of this stuff?" Mike asked. "Or is this some kinda way to get women to think you're smart?"

Jorge smiled for the first time in days. "I read. I listen. I learn well. There isn't a single page in here I haven't read. A man should open up his mind whenever he can. It's the only way to be truly alive," Jorge said. "I was born the son of a poor mother whose love was devoted to a heartless man. He was a famous trafficker in Saloa, Mexico. My father only had visions of great wealth. The future was too far from his own needs. The good of his country, his people, it didn't matter. But my mind refused to stay so small. I grew in books."

"Which one of these books taught you how to be so greedy?" Mike joked as he pulled a leather bound edition of Henry David Thoreau's *Civil Disobedience.*

"Greed and ambition are acquired tastes. I don't do this only for the money. That would be senseless."

"Then why are we still on the grind?" Mike inquired. "We got everything we need. Too much money, too many women, and just enough power." Mike thumbed through the pages of the book, admiring its aged binding.

"Because we're forging history," Jorge exclaimed. "All the land you see from Texas, to Arizona, to California, it's Mexican land. The politicians can set up their barbed-wire fences and patrol dogs...they can hire all the *gringo* border guards they want, but America stole that land from my people." Jorge pumped his fist angrily.

"You do know if it weren't for American support, France would've taken over Mexico in those days. And you, my very rich Mexican friend, you'd be speaking French right now," Mike joked, knowing that it would completely piss Jorge off.

"Granted, but it was one battle in a series of many to come. We first had to rid our homeland of the French invaders. Then the American demons came to steal from us. So can there never be war again?"

"Not one that you can win, Jorge. Nobody's gonna move any more borders. It'd take too long to reprint all the maps."

"Victory is not always set, my friend. Times evolve. Situations change. War is always on the horizon."

Michael closed the book he was reading and focused on the intensity boiling from Jorge's argument.

Jorge approached him with clinched fists, pounding in mid-air, driving his point, "Now take you blacks. You also had to fight the oppression of Southern whites."

"But you Mexicans were never slaves," Mike ribbed.
Jorge dismissed the comment with a flippant wave of his hand and said, "Only reason you blacks were slaves is because you didn't have the balls to kill enough white people."

Mike laughed and nodded in agreement.

"Less than five decades ago, you couldn't even vote or sit in a restaurant with a white man. A hundred or so years before that, you shared no American freedoms," Jorge continued. "But your people waged their own war. They marched and protested until they had to be recognized. Now what scares you most is what you've learned from your captors. You've learned to dress, talk, and fight like him. You've acquired his tastes for drugs, his desire for power, and luxury. You have become him."

Michael stared at him blankly. The poor farmer's son had grown into an intelligent businessman with a killer's heart. Mike saw him in a strangely different light for the first time in the four years he'd been hunting the great Jorge Moreno-Vargas.

"War is an expensive pastime, Michael. It costs money to conquer. So while those bastards in Washington are distracted by Arab terrorists and gay rights, we're taking our country back. The cocaine, the marijuana are just commodities to fuel our rise. Like the Kennedy family. Jack senior was a bootlegger. His boys, John and Bobby got to the White House riding on dirty money. What about the Rockefellers and the mighty Vanderbilts--all ruthless thieves and barons of steel and railroads, no?"

Jorge placed his hands on Mike's shoulders and passionately said, "What you and I bleed for today will leave wealth and opportunity for generations, and they won't have to traffic in this poison as we have. Even your people have been smart enough, some of them, to pass on the lessons of your troubled past. One day our children will listen, and with our money, they'll control the lands that are rightfully theirs." Jorge gasped for air. In his fervor he had forgotten to breathe.

"What about the people who don't make it? The ones we drain with our product. What about the young soldiers who die trying to come up the same way we did?" Mike asked.

"Like I said, war is an expensive exercise. Good men die in all types of conflicts. The Civil War, Vietnam, Iraq, wherever. This is the way of the world," Jorge calmed. "My people have come to accept that, and yours should too."

A small hand suddenly knocked at the solid oak door.

"Come in!" Jorge commanded. The doorknob clicked and Adrianna peeked in waving a cell phone. "The plane's all fueled up. They're ready to go."

"Alright, we'll be down in a minute." Jorge's mood went dark again. He frantically rubbed his hands over his thick mane of hair, trying to shake off the insanity.

Adrianna started, "I know you're hurting, Jorge, but I want you to know that in time you'll be able to...."

"Vete!" Jorge snapped, ordering her away. *"No me vengas con tus pendejadas!"* Adrianna shot him the finger and slammed the door. *Don't come to me with silly stories.*

"A woman thinks she can solve a man's problems with silly emotional talk!" Jorge rubbed his aching temples, and paced the floor like a caged circus lion.

"Mike, I can't sleep at night knowing my nephews were slaughtered like dogs. Their killers are out their spending my money while our children rot in those caskets. God, I'm sending my sister's children back to her this way," Jorge strained for composure.

"I need you to find out who did this, Michael. Whatever it takes, I'll pay."

"Won't cost you a dime, Jorge."

"Can I count on you?"

"Of course you can...anytime...anywhere," Michael lied.

20

The autopsies were complete. Twenty-eight shattered bullets had been removed from decomposing flesh and sent to the Georgia Bureau of Investigations for analysis. A late night call from Renee Castillo--Jorge's younger sister and only sibling-- had identified the two bodies, and set in motion the necessary paperwork for release. Soon Alejandro and Cesar Castillo would board a plane for their final trip home.

Two metallic black coffins rose on a powerful conveyor belt, and disappeared into the belly of the DC-9 aircraft waiting on the tarmac. Jorge stood watch, leaning against the open Maybach Benz door as Adrianna climbed from the car, pushing billowing strands of hair from her face. Mike Drake had followed in the Lamborghini and still sat at the wheel, its motor ebbing with a low hum.

The turbine engines of the DC-9 exploded to life, the pilot signaled and Jorge waved in return. Young Alejandro and Cesar would make the return trip to Mexico without an official stateside escort. Their heartbroken mother would be there to greet them at their final homecoming.

The plane turned on its approach to the edge of the runway and radioed the air-tower for takeoff instructions. With clearance granted, the pilot throttled the plane forward, speeding down the bumpy runway.

Jorge watched the plane ascend into the heavens, its beacon lights flashing from lofty wings. "God, let me have my vengeance," he prayed as he thought of his poor sister waiting in the Mexico City airport. He had stolen her sons from her and had nothing to offer in return--nothing to ease a lifetime of a mother's grief. Their relationship would never be the same.

"Is there anything you want me to do, Papi?" Adrianna whispered. Ignoring her, Jorge angrily dove into the Maybach and slammed the door shut.

"Let's go, Hector," he barked, and the car left Adrianna standing alone on the tarmac. Michael watched her pose there, her hair billowing in the faint breeze. There was too much hurt in her eyes, and in turn, it made his heart ache.

She had wanted to share her remedies for pain...*Don't drink too much, cry too much, don't hurt nobody for it...*in hopes that it would bring Jorge a grain of comfort.

"Jorge!" she screamed out to deaf ears. Mike walked over and put his arms around her. *Jorge, don't hear nothin' but the devil screamin' in his ear.* Mike tightened his grip.

"Let 'em deal with it his own way," Mike said. "He's gotta dance with his own demons before we can help him."

She shook her head in pity. "I know what it's like to go cold inside. Even the sunlight hurts your skin. Jorge won't be so nice when he gets in war mode."

"Men like us live in the dark, lil' lady. This ain't nothin' we can't handle."

"People are gonna die for this," she said numbly.

Tell it like you smell it, sister.

"You wanna go sit down somewhere? Get somethin' to eat?" he mumbled, trying to change the grim subject.

"Not right now. I gotta go home and get ready for work," she declined. "But first...uh, you mind taking me somewhere?"

Anywhere, anytime.

21

Anywhere but here...Damn! Michael reluctantly parked at the quiet corner of Martin Luther King and Central Avenue, directly in front of the gray steps of the Catholic Shrine of the Immaculate Conception. Across the street, he could see the entrance to *Underground Atlanta* and directly adjacent from it, the glowing billboard of the almighty *World of Coca Cola* flashed brilliant red light over the entire block. *Even God's gotta have a Coke and a smile 'round here.*

The Catholic Shrine was a magnificent red-brick edifice that sat on holy ground in the heart of a blasphemous city. Ironically, it also faced the Fulton County Courthouse where days before a madman had gone on a murderous rampage. Adrianna climbed the grey concrete steps of the church while Mike unwillingly lumbered a few feet behind.

"Will you come on?" Adrianna fussed. "They're not gonna sacrifice you on the alter or nothin'."

Michael reluctantly followed Adrianna into the hallowed church halls, through grand wooden doors, past a white stone sculpture of some woman comforting a dying Jesus, and into the main sanctuary.

"You go on and do ya thing. I'll talk to God Almighty Allah from here." Mike sat down in a pew near the back row.

"Gun-toting heathen," she joked.

"I know you ain't talkin' stripper girl," Mike laughed as she walked down the center aisle, and disappeared into a confession booth. *You got the devil in ya when you're on stage, li'l momma.*

It wasn't that he was opposed to God, or religion, or human sacrifice, but Catholic churches rattled his spiritual nerves. They were too structured and formal it seemed--too many artifacts, carvings, candles, novenas, rules, clauses, by-laws, and regulations.

Mike's aunts *Irene and Marlene, God bless their souls* were divine, church-going women in fine suits, flamboyant Sunday hats, white gloves, and flesh-tone stockings. The deacons always greeted the grand ladies with respect, while the ever attentive *Reverend Doctor FeelGood* counted on their Sabbath day offerings to keep his shiny, brand new Cadillac running. In return, the good Reverend preached till fire melted his tongue and sweat drenched his silk robe, and the paying congregation was embroiled in a holy revival that threatened to shake down the pearly gates of heaven. *Hallelujah!*

Mike was raised in the fire-and-brimstone Southern Baptist tradition. *Sing, shout, and dance till the Holy Ghost fills the room!* You screamed 'til God heard you, and then maybe he'd pay you a visit down the road when you needed him the most--*right 'round tax time, bill time, hope you catch your period time, pray this pain in my chest ain't a heart attack time, put your grandma nanna's house up and post that bail time.*

In the Catholic Church, it felt like God was sitting there next to you the *whole* time, and if you made a loud sound or got out of holy line, he would call you on it. Mike stared at the ornate, circular stained glass that sat in an arched recess over the main alter. Its red inlay outlined an image of a man he thought was Jesus, while blue and yellow images he didn't recognize circled outward along its circumference, protruding from the radius. It was too much symbolism for a shallow man to swallow. *You gotta spoon feed a spiritually hungry man or he'll vomit like a good night on too much bad booze.*

And he'd heard too many stories about Catholic priests molesting little boys. *What the hell's that shit all about?* "Sorry, Lord. *So sorry,*" Mike apologized, unsure if curses could even be *thought* in church. Celibacy is one thing, but if the average priest could at least get himself an occasional piece of pussy, then he probably wouldn't be stalking little boys. *Too many rules.*

* * *

"Bless me father for I have sinned. It's been three months since my last confession," Adrianna began.

"Go on my daughter. God will hear your sins, and heal you," the Priest softly confided from behind the mesh screen divider of the confession booth.

"I've shown my body to men for my own profit. At night I strip for their pleasure. Not every night. I'm off on Sundays...and my birthday, and New Year's Day not New Year's Eve."

Aroused, the Priest licked his lips, and shifted his legs, getting more comfortable.

"Go on child. Tell me *more* about your work."

"The music plays, I get naked," she frowned. "You still need *more* details, or are you through *gettin' off* in there?"

The Priest checked his enthusiasm. His shaking hand wiped sweat from his brow. "Go on my daughter, let it all out."

"You can't imagine the type of men I sleep with," she continued. "Actually it's just two men, but neither one of them is any good for me."

"Do you feel that these men give you the love and respect you're missing?"

"Yeah, right," she laughed. "They don't love and respect nothing but money. And they still don't give me enough of that."

"And you...what do you worship?"

"Expensive clothes, and jewelry, and...and the pills. I guess I've been keeping myself sky high to get through work...just to be able to get up in the morning. I've been runnin' on fumes too long. I'm feelin' real empty."

"But you know in your heart that your carnal lusts are wrong?"

"Yes, father, I do. But some o' the kinky stuff is just *so hard* to give up."

"What are you doing besides your prayers and confession to rid yourself of these negative influences?" the Priest asked.

"I stopped smoking, and I threw away my vibrator, and...." Adrianna paused, her mouth flung open, but no words escaped. *I can't say it.*

"God will forgive you for anything you have done. Just confess it," he urged.

"I've betrayed good friends...lied to them. I had to take the deal." Adrianna dropped her head and forced back the tears. *How else am I gonna stay outta jail?*

"The only loyalty you must adhere to is your loyalty to truth and a godly life. Anything else is sin. And by living in sin, you are already rotting in death." A long, awkward silence fell over them.

"That's it?" she complained. "I spill my guts to you and that's all I get? A parable? I'm trapped in a world of despair, about to lose my *ever-flippin' mind,* and all you can give me is a riddle?"

"I don't know what else you want me to say," the bewildered Priest shrugged.

"You better come up with something!" she demanded.

* * *

Michael was pacing outside the church when Adrianna stomped from the front door. The cell phone was pressed to his ear, his free arm flailing. "Will you just hear me out?"

"I want answers, Mike! Not excuses!" Jorge's jagged voice rattled over the phone. "Give me what I want!"

"Jorge, I told you I'm on it. It takes time to get a snake to crawl out from under a rock! You think these guys are out braggin' about a triple homicide?" *Click.* The phone went dead in Mike's hand.

"What did God say?" Mike greeted her.

"He was busy. I have to schedule another appointment," she groaned back. "Or learn to decipher riddles."

"That was your Papi on the phone. Stubborn bastard's gettin' to be a pain in my ass," Mike grunted.

"He called me twice while I was in confession. Told me to ask God why his nephews got such a rough ending. Then he asked for a lifetime of church donations back." She shook her head. "Madness, honey."

"Jorge's going over the edge," Mike chimed as he lifted the butterfly passenger door of the Lamborghini.

"I like him when he goes psychotic. He tends to make a lot of money," she smiled and fell inside the car. "Sooner or later, you gotta find out who killed his nephews, or he's gonna ask me to get involved, and I really can't handle that pressure right now. So, we're all counting on *you*."

"Seems like the whole world's been counting on me lately. I ain't the Pope, ya know?"

"It's the burden of being on top," she said. "Now you know how I feel."

22

Jorge slammed his phone into the wall, blasting it into shards of plastic and circuit boards. His head feel back, and he gaped his open mouth beneath the Jose Quervo bottle spout, chugging until his alcohol irritated throat burned.

"Mierda...me mata la cabaza!" he cursed and grabbed his throbbing head. *More pain and punishment for not protecting my boys! "Me jodi,"* he whispered. *I fucked up.*

Manuel and Hector entered the living room and stood paralyzed. Jorge was unraveling at the seams.

"Steady yourself, *hermano*," Hector said, openly pained by the sight of Jorge in such a stupor.

Jorge Vargas was the closest thing the twins had to family, and the one man who had unselfishly given them pride, power, and purpose. Their blind loyalty to Vargas was *puro*, unconditional, and they would kill for him. *Quick.*

"I have Alejandro's phone records," Hector said, waving four printed pages. Jorge collapsed into a purple, velvet covered chair and drudgingly leaned his elbows on the long dining table. A large crystal chandelier glowed overhead--its dazzling white light cast a haunting glow across the room.

"I can't think straight," Jorge slurred, knocking the bottle of tequila over. Manuel picked up the leaking bottle and swigged the last ounces of spirits.

"Jorge, take it easy. Me and Manuel are here with you to the end. But if you can't keep your mind on business, let us take care of this, alright. There's so much *mercancia* on the way. Six-million dollars a month is on the line here," Hector calmly laid out the situation.

Jorge nodded like he understood, but his reddened face was blank. "Tell me about the phone calls."

"The night Alejandro died he received twelve phone calls between six P.M. and three A.M. We think these last couple of in-coming calls were made just to make sure they were at the house when it was hit." Hector paused to make sure Jorge was absorbing the details. With a wave of his hand, Jorge motioned for him to continue.

"Now here...a 4-0-4 area code...about five times, back to back." Hector ran his finger down the list of incoming telephone calls. Jorge strained to read the fine print.

"It's a pay phone in a pussy bar on Veterans' Memorial. The niggers call the street Bankhead Highway."

"Blue? The Blue Flame," Manuel added.

"A strip club you say?" Jorge asked before a bolt of deadly intuition hit him, driving him to his feet, filled with new life. "There's a chance Adrianna can find out who made those calls." Jorge was inspired. "I have someone to hurt."

Manuel and Hector glanced at each other awkwardly. Jorge noticed their hesitation.

"Whatever it is, tell me!" Jorge demanded.

"De nada...at worst it don't mean *no-thing*."

"There was another call made late that morning after four-A.M.," Hector said. "The last call."

Jorge frowned. "Who? Who was it?"

"Mike Drake," Hector wickedly answered.

23

Department of Justice
United States Attorney David Namath
Northern District of Georgia

Today marks the start of a new era for the City of Atlanta.

The city government run under the Administration of Mayor Russell Campbell was stricken with a deliberate corruption that infested the highest levels of office. Mayor Campbell has received a fair and impartial trial, before an honorable and fair judge. Today's guilty verdict also confirms that Mayor Russell Campbell was a criminal. He is now a convicted felon and will soon be sentenced to a federal prison. It is sad to see such a successful man with so many options take this life-altering detour down a path of crime. Ultimately, we will never fully know the extent of the civic, moral, and economic loss to the City of Atlanta caused by the crimes committed by Mayor Russell Campbell and his co-conspirators.

We proved that Mayor Campbell had no legitimate source for the sizable amounts of cash that he used to support his extravagant lifestyle. Furthermore, we have shown that he failed to report that income on his tax returns. Mayor Campbell was also found guilty of one racketeering predicate offense which involved mail fraud related to the misuse of his campaign funds. The investigation culminated in the conviction of more than a dozen City contractors and Senior City Officials on corruption-related charges, including Mayor Campbell's Chief Operating Officer, Deputy Chief Operating Officer, and Chief Administrative Officer.

Damaging evidence against Campbell included three individuals who testified that they had personally provided large cash payoffs directly to the Mayor. As well, other cooperating witnesses confessed that they had given sizable bribes directly to the Mayor's close allies with full knowledge that the funds were designated for Campbell's personal use.

* * *

Flanked by his prosecution team, U.S. Attorney David Namath bid the crowd farewell, managed to shake a few hands, and escaped the crush of reporters. The biggest trial of his career was finally over and now it was time to hunt bigger prey. Agent Cooper kept pace with Namath as they made the short victory march from the courthouse back to the Sam Nunn Federal Building.

"Can we get back to some real work now, or are you going to sleep on this victory for a while?" Cooper asked.

"Sharks don't sleep," Namath boasted. "Want to help me raid City Hall?"

"Not if I don't have to," she admitted. "I don't see the use in wrecking Mayor Franco's legacy this deep into her final term. It does more damage to the city than good."

"Is this an honest, professional assessment, or are you merely standing up for your home town."

"Neither."

"I want to get inside Mayor Franco's financials," Namath said; his purpose undeterred. "The daughter's and Todd Graham's too. Let's go through their bank records, mortgage statements, credit, tax returns, everything." Namath targeted with deadly precision. "But don't step on the DEA's toes on this one. If they still want Todd Graham, they can have him."

* * *

Former Atlanta Mayor Russell Campbell walked alongside his wife, their swinging hands clenched in an enduring bond. As they strolled to the lower courthouse parking deck, they were trailed by three exhausted lawyers and a small contingency of news reporters.

Campbell was tired of answering questions. The wear and tear of this six-year ordeal had grown dark circles under his eyes, and drained the youthful exuberance that had driven him into office and sustained him for two terms.

The invasive trial had uncovered shocking tales of marital infidelity, domestic abuse, payoffs, true lies, deceit, and pushed Campbell to his emotional limits. *The worst part about going to trial is not knowing the final outcome.* Today, a jury of his peers solved half of that unknown equation.

Arguably, things could've been worse. Harold Riggins, the city's former Chief Operating Officer, died from a heart attack before he was due to testify against Campbell. The juicy secrets that U. S. Attorney Namath really wanted went into the deep, dark grave with Riggins. Damien Ellis, Campbell's Chief Administrator, had already been convicted and sentenced to a fifteen month prison term, but never fully divulged all that he knew about Campbell's criminal activities.

Russell Campbell was an outsider--a North Carolina born lawyer who was invited into the Atlanta legacy with open arms. In return, he desecrated the honor and the sanctity of his office with sexual affairs, bribes, spousal abuse, fraud, and then there was that little argument with an infamous *titty bar* owner over a city liquor license. And along the way, Campbell spit into the wrong country people's faces. *That ain't Southern hospitality.*

So that same *titty bar* owner went downtown and told the Feds about all of his cash payments to the Mayor. *Now that's Southern hospitality.*

Campbell and his faithful wife left the courthouse commotion for the comfort of a Lincoln Town Car and were quickly driven away. The cameras were still rolling, but none of that mattered anymore. Campbell was going home to wait for the sentencing phase of his conviction. It would take another twelve weeks to find out how long he was going to be in prison.

Former Atlanta Mayor Andy Young, who testified at the trial, later said, "Mayor Campbell wasn't guilty of running the City of Atlanta like a criminal enterprise. But if you ask me if he's guilty of stupidity and arrogance...Definitely!"

24

*M*ach *Pichu* was nearly empty. In the background, soft music played beneath a floating Spanish voice. The quaint Peruvian restaurant was outfitted with simple but tidy settings. Nestled away at a small secluded table, Adrianna sat with Jorge Vargas.

"What is this?" Jorge sniffed the clear liquid and swirled it around in his glass.

"Try it," she encouraged. "It's called *Pisco.*"

"It's called piss?"

"I said *Pisco.* It's Peruvian brandy," she lectured. "Go on. If you can drink that God awful tequila, you'll love this."

Jorge tossed the drink down and winced.

"It's good, isn't it?" she said.

"Waiter!" Jorge tossed his hand up. "Come here, get this! I want it off my table. It tastes like dog piss." The apologetic waiter scurried away with the offending bottle.

"Bring me some real drink. Tequila!" Jorge barked.

"Jorge, why do you have to embarrass me?"

"I'm embarrassed you talked me into coming to this place. Next time, I know better. You Peruvians are good for one thing...the coca plant. Everything else...nada. Useless."

"Go to hell, Jorge!" she huffed, folding her arms like a spoiled brat. "You dumb Mexican peasant!"

"Ewww...she likes to attack me where it hurts! In my Mexican pride!" he laughed on, sending Adrianna deeper into her tantrum.

"Okay! I sorry I say that. Did I offend you, my little rose petal?" Jorge couldn't help but laugh. "I'm kidding, *mija.* I spoil you too much. You know what I'm going to do? I'm going to spoil you some more. You name it?"

Greed softened her face. "You could spoil me all the way to Italy.

"I don't like Italians," Jorge confessed.

"Naples is beautiful in the summer. Oh, and Venice. We could get so far away from that evil witch you call a wife. I could take your mind and your dick off everything that's happened lately."

"That's no good. My wife, she's still here in Atlanta. I have to spend more...how is it they say?...eh, *quality time* with her," Jorge joked. "I hear it's the only way to keep a marriage together."

"So you want me to keep me hidden for a little while longer?" Adrianna huffed. "You just get to bring me back out whenever it's convenient for you...convenient your wife?"

"Well...yes. That's pretty much the case. But this *is* what it *is.*"

"What this *is*...it's me sharing you with another woman."

"Mija, I love you more than you'll ever know. But Maria's the mother of my children...and you...."

"Me...I'm just your fuck of the month!"

"Yes, but that's never the point. You have special talents. The nasty things you do to me, these things my wife cannot do. Her lips kiss my precious daughter."

"Then make me the wife and you can treat her like your goddamn sex toy!"

Enraged, Jorge grabbed her by the wrists, pinning her arms to the table. "Watch your tongue, mija. Or I will cut...it...out...of your head and feed it to you!"

"Let me go, Jorge! Dammit! Let me go!" she demanded, her rage boiling as she struggled to free herself. She reached for a fork with an escaped hand and swung it down hard. As Vargas swiped his left hand away, the fork stabbed into the table. Glasses rattled and the table shook. The boisterous commotion brought wayward looks from the last customers.

"That's it, mija! That's the fire I like to see in those gorgeous eyes. Let it hunt for me. I need your rage to find my nephews' killers."

Adrianna calmed, her arms went limp. She paused searching for the proper words. "Jorge, I miss them as much as you do. They were like brothers to me, but I don't want to get mixed-up in this."

"I already know where to find them. They too dance the *hoochie-coochie* dance like you," he said. At this, uh...*Blue Flame*. Know this place?"

"I've danced there a few times. It was years ago."

"See now, it'll be easy for you to find these whores. You'll do this for me, for your brothers. This I know."

"I don't want any blood on my hands, Jorge."

"I don't care what you want...or fear!" Jorge pounded the table, forks rattling, a glass of water overturned. "They've spilled my blood...our *familia!* We'll all rot in hell before I let this go unfinished!"

"Please," she begged, "there's gotta be another way to ..."

"When you had no one, I saved you!" he interrupted. "Your mother, father...when all was dead to you, I found you. I lifted you out of the dirt. I protected you. Show me you remember!"

A waiter cautiously approached with a note pad and pen. "Are you ready to order now?"

Jorge smiled and opened his menu. "Go ahead, sweetheart. Order whatever you like," he calmly offered Adrianna. "Just make sure it tastes like...revenge."

25

No one noticed the white cargo van sitting in the parking lot of the Bamboo Luau Chinese restaurant on busy Cheshire Bridge Road. Its side door panels were painted with a picture of a dripping faucet beneath the moniker *Harvey's Plumbing & Supplies.*

Inside the rear cargo bay, two weary federal agents patiently waited for the latest installment of their uneventful careers to unfold. Agent Paul Crawley dawned headphones and adjusted the digital console facing him.

"I gotta go now, Kylie. I'm working. I'll call you later," Fat Todd's recorded voice bubbled in the headphones, causing the LED meters to register in low decibels. "I said I'll call you later, some business just rolled up. I'll take care of it when I get home. Bye, baby!"

Nearby, a chubby, slightly balding Agent Milner peered through a set of binoculars from the tinted rear van windows. "Somebody just pulled up in a silver Lamborghini. Nice."

"Jesus Christ." Agent Crawley groaned, adjusting his headphones. "Doesn't anybody in this town drive a normal car?"

"Why should they when they're running around with millions in tax-free loot," Agent Milner argued as he bit into a six-inch sub sandwich—its contents of tomato and soggy lettuce dripped into his lap. "Crap! Not on my new Docker's. My mother-in-law just bought me these pants!"

"Your wife's mother buys your pants?"

"Sometimes...for like holiday gifts. So what?"

"That's just sick, Milner." Agent Crawley shook his head and adjusted the treble on his sound console.

"I love my mother-in-law," Milner admitted and raised the binoculars back to his eyes. He chewed slowly as he watched Michael Drake climb from the Lamborghini's cockpit.

"I can never figure it out," Crawley commented. "All this money, and the entire world at their feet...you'd think these idiots would have the common sense to run away before it all goes down the toilet."

"Yeah, well you know what they say," Agent Milner mumbled through another hefty bite of food. "A fool and his money shall soon part. No doubt about it."

* * *

Across the street, Michael Drake dug through the trunk of his car, caught the strap of a large duffel bag, and hoisted it to his shoulder. *Somethin' ain't right.* Nervous, Michael peered around, sensing that he was being watched. It was seasoned paranoia mixed with pure gut instinct.

Fat Todd quickly unlocked the glass front door of his *404 EuroSports* car dealership.

"I don't like being out in the open like this," Mike warned and stepped into the building.

"Would I put us in any danger? I like my freedom just as much as the next man," Todd replied and quickly locked the glass door behind them.

"Let's go back to my office," Todd suggested as he led Mike through a small showroom past a polished blue Bentley Continental on chrome rims.

"If you're looking to trade up, I can get you great deal on a slightly used, but well pampered Ferrari Spyder," Fat Todd offered. "I got one that used to belong to that rich white chick from that reality TV show on Fox. You know the freak I'm talking about?"

"Nah, I'm satisfied with the ride I got. But I appreciate the offer anyway."

"Suit yourself," Fat Todd said, "but remember, Lamborghini's get you pussy. But Ferrari's get you a lifetime supply of head."

"I'll keep that in mind."

Fat Todd and Mike disappeared into a small private office where two men were wrapping rubber bands around piles of cash.

"You know my partners, Scott...and this is Ray, "Fat Todd introduced. Mike had briefly met them both the day he bought his prized Lamborghini.

Scott Duval was tall and heavy-set, with the body a defensive lineman. He shook Mike's hand with a crushing grip and mumbled, "What's up, Mike D.?"

"Ain't nothin'," Mike replied, feeling some resignation in Scott's demeanor.

The second partner, Ray Hackett, was dark-skinned, slimmer, and far more relaxed. "Let's get to it," he grinned greedily.

Wasting no time, Mike unzipped his bag, and piled the fifty air-sealed bundles of cocaine on the desk.

"Fifty even," Mike confirmed.

"We on point?" Scott asked with an unfriendly scowl.

"Everything's *fishscale*," Michael assured, as he stepped back, casually resting his hands on his hips, sure to keep his trigger fingers close to the guns hiding in his waistline.

"It's all good, baby. Your reputation precedes you," Fat Todd peacefully offered. Scott cast a suspicious gaze, rubbed his chin, and added, "It better not be none of that flex."

Mike took immediate offense and stepped forward, resting his hands on the grips of his guns. "Then again, maybe my name ain't so good," Mike interjected, frowning in irritation. The room tensed.

"Everything's cool, Mike," Fat Todd offered, trying to keep the situation at an even keel. "Ain't that right, Scott?"

"If you say so," Scott replied, sucking his pearly white teeth. "Makes no fuckin' difference to me."

Ray laughed and said, "Don't pay big Scott here no

attention, Mike. He's been watching too many gangster movies. He's always mean-muggin' folks like he's some kinda cowboy."

"This ain't TV, my friend," Mike warned as he waved his hands across his waist and peered coldly into Scott's unwavering eyes. "Shit can get hot real quick."

Ignoring the macho face-off, Ray and Fat Todd quickly stuffed the bundles of cash into Mike's empty duffle bag.

"Nah, ain't no prime time gangsters 'round here. This here's the real deal," Scott returned, still testing Mike for the slightest hint of weakness.

"Now are *you* on point?" Mike asked as he lifted the bag, making sure that he directed the question toward the testy Scott.

"Every penny's there. You can hang loose and count it if you want to," Ray said.

"Nah, we're good," Mike said. "Trust is all we got, ya know?" With the deal done, Michael walked out with Fat Todd at his side, apologizing for Scott's rude temperament.

Unapologetic himself, Scott strutted out to the main showroom, leaned against the Bentley, and tossed a toothpick into his mouth.

"What the hell's the matter with you?" Ray asked.

"Don't nobody check my nuts in my own spot," Scott replied as he watched Mike drive away. "I don't know, man," Scott said, gnawing on the toothpick, "something ain't right about homeboy."

"I'll tell you what ain't right...you pissin' off the man that just put us back on!" Ray said.

But Scott wasn't convinced that everything was in order. "That Mike Drake...he's too relaxed, like he ain't even worried about gettin' jammed up."

26

WHITE LIES & BLUE FLAMES

The *Blue Flame* was legendary for all the wrong reasons. In Atlanta's famed *titty bar* circuit it didn't carry the flash of *Magic City,* or the upscale flare of the white-man's *Cheetah Lounge*, but as far as sex, drugs, and money go, it didn't lack for anything else. Standing not far from the Interstate-285 and Bankhead Highway exit, it was conveniently located near a bustling truck stop and greasy spoon restaurant, and actually tried to cater to the passing over-the-road truck driver crowd.

The shadowy inner space was littered with gold-grilled hustlers draped in extra large white-T's, fitted baseball caps, and thousand dollar throwback sports jerseys. It was a hideout for Bankhead's finest young soldiers and the few old timers who were still dedicated to the spot, and the occasional redneck trucker whose commercial driver's license guaranteed him free entrance anytime during operating hours.

Cloaked behind the tinted glass of the VIP booth, Danny Diablo leaned back on a black leather sofa, as a dancer undressed in front of him. Miss Starr was draped in a platinum blonde wig and fire red stilettos.

"Is that her?" Danny Diablo asked. Miss Starr danced around in stride and bent over. When she lifted her head, she could see Adrianna entering the club.

"Yeah, that's her," Miss Starr answered.

"I oughta go over there and thank the bitch for makin' me rich," Danny sneered.

Miss Starr backed up, pressing her ass in his lap, grinding feverishly against his body. "Fool, you betta not.

You're gonna get us all messed up."

"Fuck them Mexicans. They can't kill me no faster than I can kill them."

Out in the main room, a buxom, chocolate-skinned vixen named Pleazure danced on center stage, swinging around the brass pole. In the middle of her raunchy routine, she too noticed Adrianna moving toward the bar.

Pleazure finished her set and climbed off stage, making her way through the thick crowd, oblivious to the needy hands groping at her sweaty body.

"How ya doin' girl?" Pleazure greeted with a diamond encrusted smile.

"I'm holdin' it down," Adrianna answered with a forced smirk, her bottom lip trembling as she bottled up the rage that the mere sight of Pleazure had ignited.

"Here you go." Adrianna pulled her hand out of her purse, passing Pleazure a book of matches. "The hotel room number's inside," Adrianna said. "They'll be there when you get off work."

"How much they talkin' 'bout?" Pleazure asked as she popped the bubble gum in her mouth and slid the matchbook into her panties.

"Twenty-five-hundred a piece," Adrianna answered.

"Wheeeww, child! That ain't bad for one night!" Pleazure gleamed.

"Better than giving the ass away to these bums in here," Adrianna returned.

"Girl, I ain't never gave away a *free* piece o' pussy in my life. But hey, hold up. They ain't into no kinky shit, are they? I mean, I'm down with gettin' roughed-up, tied-down, ate-out, or fucked in the ass...whatever. But all that beatin' me with chains and leather whips, or pissin' and shittin' on me, that ain't what's happennin'!"

Adrianna shook her head. "It's just some straight up suck-and-fuck. They're these two bald-headed, beer-bellied diamond salesman from up in Roswell. They just snuck outta the suburbs long enough to get their chocolate pussy fix. All you gotta do is show up and get 'em off quick. Ya know they gotta be home before their li'l Martha Stewart housewives wake up."

"Good lookin' out girl," Pleazure thanked her and backed away. "I owe you one. Anything you need, anytime, anywhere girl...I *gotchyou!*"

No, baby girl...I got you, ya dirty, lowdown bitch. Adrianna didn't bother to finish her drink and immediately walked out the front door.

I'm so cold. Adrianna huddled her folded arms closer to her chest. The crisp night air was frigid. But it had nothing to do with the chills running through her shivering body. There would be no repentance for this one.

"God forgive me," she whispered as she fell into her car.

Back inside the *Blue Flame*, the sultry pitch continued with no end in sight as Pleazure rushed into the VIP booth.

"I got us another job, playgirl!" Pleazure cheered and grabbed Miss Starr. "And the money's sho' nuff right!"

"When?" Miss Starr asked while climbing back into her bikini. Danny Diablo leaned forward to listen.

"Tonight. And check this shit. I hear these lames sell diamonds. Ice, ice, baby!"

"They carryin' any rocks with 'em now?" Danny asked with a seed of treachery.

"Nah, not that I know of. But still, we could get 'em to fall in love with this good pussy and set 'em up later," Pleazure plotted.

Danny Diablo leaned back and crossed his hands behind his head. "You sure you can still trust her?" he asked--his mind calculating the double-cross from all angles.

"Hell, yeah!" Miss Starr said. "She don't know we the ones that set Alejandro and Cesar up. Matter o' fact she ain't even say nothin' 'bout them."

"That's what I'm talkin' about. She *shoulda* said something," Danny Diablo reasoned.

"What does she care anyway? She foolin' around wit' that nigga Mike Drake. He's the one with all the real paper," Miss Starr noted and walked off, happily pulling Pleazure with her.

"Y'all be careful and keep ya shit together now," Danny chimed as he swigged straight from a half-empty bottle of Martel, and summoned another naked dancer. "Best believe...'cause if my fuckin' name comes up in this bullshit, everybody dies."

27

It was a quiet evening just before dawn at the Econo Lodge on Fulton Industrial Boulevard. Breaking the silence, a pearl white BMW 5-series rolled into the lot, its bright halogen headlights glaring and radio pumping.

"Where is it girl?" Miss Starr asked as she banked the steering wheel and turned the radio down.

"It's on the back side of the hotel, uh...room 468." Pleazure fixed her makeup in the visor mirror. "I need to powder my nose, child. I hope they got some good shit to snort."

"Are you sure this is the right hotel?" Miss Starr asked.

"Hell yeah, I'm sure. I can smell the money, honey. There! That's gotta be their car. Park next to it."

Miss Starr slowed down, turned, and backed her BMW into a parking spot next to a black Porsche Carerra 4.

"Set your cell phone for speed dial just in case these tricks got any diamonds with 'em. We can call up them Diablo boys if there's some real work," Miss Starr plotted as she straightened her hair and climbed from the car.

"Sho' ya right, girl." Pleazure smiled at the idea, locked Danny Diablo's direct number into her phone, and dropped it into her knockoff Fendi purse. As the two of them wiggled in high heels toward room 468, the curtains slid back and a large frame peered out.

"Damn that white boy is kinda big!" Pleazure noted. Before they could knock, Manuel opened the door with his head thrown back, gulping down a cold Heineken. He finished the last drop, belched with a gaseous growl, and threw the empty bottle crashing into the parking lot.

"Come in *mamacitas*. The party's waiting for you."

Miss Starr and Pleazure slithered into the room, draped in skintight mini-skirts. "It sho' smells good in here, shawty! Whatchy'all smokin' on?"

"Mexico's finest. There are plenty of party favors, *senorita*. Go ahead treat yourself." Manuel fanned his large hand over a collection of goodies laid out on the counter next to the blaring television set. There was a smorgasbord of ecstasy pills, lines of coke, and a liter of cognac.

"Now that's what I'm talking about. Let's get high then get fly!" Miss Starr moaned as she scooped up two pills and dropped them on her tongue.

"Let's get some music going, amigo!" Hector turned on the radio. "Get you sexy things some tunes to dance to."

"Who wants to get sucked off first, huh?" Pleazure asked as she let down her hair, and moved closer to Hector, licking her lips, "Ummmm...you look like you taste good."

Hector smiled, then shot a vicious backhand slap that sent Pleazure reeling backwards, flipping over the bed!

"What the fuck is...," Miss Starr barked as she attacked, but found a thick leather belt looped around her neck, tightening as Manuel clinched his powerful fists behind her head!

"Slow down, mami," Manuel breathed into her ear. "We're going to be here all night." Manuel lifted her from the floor, her high-heeled feet kicking for dear life. She could feel herself slowly blurring out of consciousness. Dazed, Miss Pleazure stumbled to her feet, blood trickling from her swollen mouth. She tried to scream.

"Callate!" Hector charged, wrapping his massive hands around her throat, throwing her across the room. Her limp body slammed into the wall, crashing to the floor.

Hector snapped on a pair of latex rubber gloves and stood over her shivering body. "Tonight we will show you ladies what it's like to be in a real Mexican hell. Even the devil don't want to watch this." *And the propane torch ignited with a searing blue flame.*

* * *

Magic City. The rumble of music from the party going on upstairs reverberated through the roof. Down below the carnal ruckus, bikini clad dancers shuffled in and out of their lockers.

Straddled in a chair, Adrianna rifled through her purse as her missing cell phone clamored. "Hello? Tell me somethin' good," she answered the call. "Hello?"

She could hear deep *moans* of pain, muffled by duct-tape covered lips. In the background, a strip of tape was ripped away, forcing a bloodcurdling *scream!* Adrianna dropped her cell phone and sat there shivering nervously. She was certain the torture being delivered on the other end of the line was all her doing.

"Adrianna. girl, stop day dreamin'," a voice warned from the other end of the dressing room. "You're on stage next."

Adrianna swung open her locker to face her reflection in a mirror mounted inside. *God forgive me.*

She turned away, unable to look at a woman she could no longer recognize. She slammed the locker, gulped down a pill, and headed upstairs.

28

"*V*aminos! Can't you see the sun's about to come up?"

"I'm trying, eh! I can't get this stupid cell phone to work." Finally, Manuel managed to hit the speed dial.

"Hello, is this Danny Diablo?"

"Yeah, who the fuck is this?" Danny grumbled as he awoke in a sleepy haze.

"This is the man that's going to hunt you down and cut your throat, you fuckin' nigga cunt! You think you can rob us?"

"You 'spic mutha fucka who you think you talkin' too. This is my city, nigga! I say what you get to keep! You live or fuckin' die when I say so!"

"I'll see you in hell!" Manuel finished and tossed the cell phone into the river. Hector locked the BMW into gear and the two of them shoved against the trunk. The unmanned automobile rolled down an embankment, crashing through a thick wall of foliage, sage bushes, and kudzu vines, snapping and crackling branches. The car gained momentum, its front tires ripping through damp mud as it disappeared over the river bank.

"Adios, muchachas."

* * *

Where am I? Miss Pleazure woke up in pitch blackness. Her heart was throbbing. She cried out, mumbling frantically

through sour duct tape that burned, tearing at the soft skin on her lips. She could smell gasoline fumes. Her steel coffin was tumbling. Metal tools rolled around near her bruised thighs.
God help me. Sharp pains shot from the tips of her burning fingers, up her arms, and into her palpitating chest. Then she heard the *splash! Icy, cold water slowly pooled around her aching body as she kicked frantically, snorting for air...sinking.*

29

"There are problems brewing in Colombia," Jorge worried. "It looks like we may have to move our schedule up a few weeks."

"What kind of problems?" Mike asked, taking a seat.

"There's infighting between Diego Sandoval and Danielo Marela, the two acting heads of the Norte del Valle."

Mike pondered the situation. The *Norte del Valle* was the Colombian cartel that moved into the vacuum left after the dismantling of the former Cali cartel regime. And more importantly, they were Jorge's main suppliers.

"There are hundreds of bodies lying dead in the streets of Colombia as we speak," Jorge continued.

"What does all of this mean for you?" Mike asked even though he had a pretty good idea.

"Hopefully, they'll come to a truce and I won't have to take sides. I don't want my shipments interrupted over all of this senseless bickering." Jorge lit a Cuban cigar, puffing huge plumes of smoke. "Cigar? They're fresh from Havana."

"No, thanks." Mike stood and headed for the bar. "But I will lubricate my liver, if you don't mind."

"The United States has offered a five-million dollar reward for Diego Sandoval," Jorge continued. "But they can't get to him. Smart bastard's under the protection of a right-wing paramilitary organization in Colombia--guerilla fighters called the United Self Defense Forces of Colombia." Jorge twirled the cigar in his nervous fingers.

"Yeah, the AUC is what the news calls them. I saw a CNN report on them the other day," Mike said, pouring a glass of cognac. "The Columbian government is scared to go after them. They're a pretty violent bunch of *hombres.*"

"And Diego Sandoval is on the FBI's ten most wanted list next to Osama Bin Laden," Jorge added proudly.

"So what's all the infighting about anyway? Isn't their enough coca and money to go around?" Mike asked.

"It seems that Sandoval tried to cut a deal with American officials."

"A deal? Is he crazy?"

"Apparently so. He offered to surrender himself to jail time in the United States if he was promised a reduced sentence and allowed to keep his drug profits."

"There's no way in hell the Feds are gonna give him that kinda deal," Mike assured.

"Well other members of the Norte del Valle though that it might have been a possibility and now they consider Sandoval a traitor to the cause. But our problems are only beginning to...." Jorge stopped abruptly. His flirting attention turned toward the door.

Hector and Manuel casually entered the room and sat down. Jorge quickly fell into a seat and anxiously asked, "Well, what did you find out? Who did this to Alejandro and Cesar?"

"They are a crew of thieves. In the streets, they go by the name *Diablos*," Hector said.

Mike cringed. *They knew too much too fast.*

Jorge frowned and muttered, "Diablos? Devils. Then are they Mexican, or...?"

"No, they're black men. Locals operating somewhere near this Bankhead. We also know that they run a couple of drug houses set up on a street they call Boulevard."

"Where's this Boulevard, Mike?" Jorge asked.

"Old Fourth Ward. It's near downtown."

"See, Mike. You see how you can get my information when you set your balls to it," Jorge snidely remarked. "If I didn't know any better, I'd think you were holding out on me."

Jorge moved face-to-face with Mike. "I don't sense no hesitation on your part...do I, Mike?"

Mike stood his ground. "Yeah, you do. "Mike shook his head in dismay. "You just lost two kids who meant everything to you. Now you ain't runnin' on nothing but pure emotion, ain't thinkin' straight. So until you get ya mind right, I gotta do what's best for you, me, and our business. If that means keeping you outta some bullshit war with a bunch of small-time locals, then that's exactly what it gotta do." A tense silence fell over the room.

Jorge's rigid frown melted into a hearty laugh, and he grabbed Mike by the shoulders. "I love this guy...*Si,* I do. Sometimes, Mike, he thinks too much, but he's a smart man. Me...I am a simple man who lives by his gun and his balls." Jorge patted Mike's cheek. "Blood in, blood out...let's see who lasts the longest, you or me!"

Jorge turned to the twins. "So how's our revenge moving?"

"The heroine is ready now. All you have to do is give the order and it's on the first big-rig out of Texas."

"Tell Uncle to send me the purest black tar heroine he has to offer. No cut. Nothing but *puro,"*Jorge schemed.

"What do you think you're doing?" Mike asked.

"I'm charging this city the debt that it owes me!" Jorge's voice cracked with rage.

"You can't let that poison hit the ground runnin' uncut, " Mike warned. "You're askin' for an outbreak of overdoses."

"You tell me, what would you do in a time like this? Wait? Do nothing? Or mourn like the women?" Jorge jeered.

Mike moved closer, easing his tone. "I'd keep a cool head and not let emotion outweigh common sense."

"That's why you'll never be a king," Jorge said. "You can never make the decisions that maintain your power."

"So how many people get knocked down before someone tells them where it came from? You'll get our whole operation hot within a week," Mike laughed. "You fool."

"I like heat, my friend. It warms the heart. Makes a cold man feel alive again. There's only one way to punish them all. Bring me my poison." Jorge waved his fist, sending Manuel and Hector off to put their deadly work into action.

"You'll see, Mike. People will suffer and we'll all feel much better in the end," Jorge smiled and cusped his hands around Mike's face. "My cautious compadre, you'll take my nephews place in the family. You'll handle all the cash collections for me now, okay? Okay, Mike. We're locked at the hip like Siamese twins now, brother. Let's eat, sleep, and kill together as brothers!"

Jorge staggered off in a stupor, singing a solemn Spanish ballad.

PART II

LIVE FAST & DIE YOUNG

Every morning in Africa, a gazelle wakes up. It knows that it has to run faster than the fastest lion or be killed. Every morning a lion wakes up. And it knows that it has to outrun the slowest gazelle or it will starve to death. It doesn't matter whether you are a lion or a gazelle. When the sun comes up, you better be off and running.

--African Proverb

30

EMERGENCY ROOM

"Could you turn that down, please?" Adrianna begged as she buried her face beneath the covers.

"Sorry, Miss Hangover," Michael apologized and lowered the television volume.

"If you hadn't hung out all night, you'd be in a better mood," Mike mumbled with a toothbrush jammed in his mouth.

"It's a nine-to-five job, player," Adrianna huffed.

"Nine-to-five in the A.M. Those are factory graveyard hours. A classy lady would work in respectable daylight before the vampires and freaks come out at night."

"What the hell would a classy lady want with a criminal like you," she fired back.

"And where were you last night? I stopped by Magic City," he asked.

Adrianna smiled beneath the sheets. He was jealous and it made her feel needed.

"I was with Jorge. We went to dinner at *Pricci's.*"

Your lies, woman. Michael had been with Jorge for most of the evening.

Mike saw a news flash and immediately turned the television volume back up.

"Mike, please kill that noise! I'm havin' a mental meltdown right now!"

"Hush woman...I wanna hear this." Mike sat on the end of the bed, shoving Adrianna's feet out of the way.

The anchorwoman reported, *"The tortured bodies of two black females have been found in the trunk of their car...The vehicle is submerged in shallow waters just beyond a muddy embankment alongside the Chattahoochee River near Mableton Parkway...The two women are popular dancers at the Blue Flame Lounge on Bankhead Highway...Fulton County Police say that the victim's fingertips were severely burned...The cause of death...Point-blank gunshot wound to the head of one of the victims...In what appears to be an execution style double homicide....*"

Stunned, Adrianna rolled over in bed and closed her eyes.

"You believe this shit?" he said.

"Yeah, I believe it," Adrianna moaned as a rush of anxiety flooded her veins. Shivering, her skin went clammy. Beads of nervous sweat formed all over her tingling body and waves of nausea overcame her.

"It's a crazy, crazy life we lead," she winced in disbelief, her mind spinning in despair, vomit boiling at the base of her throat.

"What's done is done," she whispered, trying to stop the easy flow of salty tears.

"You gotta get outta them strip joints," Mike warned. "Too many sick perverts runnin' around gettin' their rocks off torturing women."

Adrianna wiped her face and slid from beneath the covers, forcing her weary soul from the bed.

"I'm going downstairs to kill myself," she said.

"Well, fix me some breakfast before you do."

Draped in a black silk nightgown, she took the seemingly endless, barefoot walk downstairs to the kitchen. The kitchen floor tile was cold beneath her feet, sending chills up her ankles along her calves. Her distorted shadow wafted across the stainless steel surfaces. It was all too surreal. Adrianna could feel herself leave her own body and stand next to the empty shell that was staggering around this lonely kitchen.

"Adrianna! Where's my black shirt?" Michael's voiced boomed from upstairs. "The linen one!"

"In the hall closet!" she yelled back. All of her

frustrations, fears, regrets boiled to the top, spilling over. She dug into a counter drawer, shuffling through its contents of spoons, forks, and knives. *Where are they?*

More determined than ever, she ripped open the cabinets, slapping boxes of cereals and canned goods out of her way. *Still nothing.*

Adrianna slid a stool from the corner of the kitchen, across the cold floor, and propped it against the refrigerator. She climbed up, reaching for a porcelain apple that rested above the refrigerator. She lifted the apple's lid and dug inside until she found a half-empty prescription bottle.

I'm tired of running.

Adrianna climbed down, shaking the bottle of pills. The tiny capsules rattled against the plastic container, echoing in her mind. "*Rattlesnake*...your poison's gonna put me outta my misery," she sang. Adrianna twisted the top from a fifth of Grey Goose Vodka. *It hurts to breathe.*

She slammed a handful of pills and gulped from the bottle of vodka until her throat burned. *This shouldn't take too long. Can't hurt no mo' than I hurt now.*

Adrianna turned to the sunlight beaming from the large, living room window pane. She closed her eyes, feeling the warmth of rays coating her face. She slowly began to turn in a circle, her arms outstretched--a tired martyr on the cross, her body rotating in the sunbeams....

All I want to do is sleep.

31

Mike traced down the steps, tugging away at his shirt sleeves, trying to fasten a rebellious button. "Adrianna? I can't get this stinkin' button to...." He stopped, his mouth gaped open.

"Adrianna? Shit!"

She was collapsed on the floor, her limbs posed haphazardly across her torso. "Adrianna!"

Mike frantically raced into the kitchen, kneeled, and scooped her in his arms. "Get up, Adrianna!"

There was the empty prescription bottle and two loose pills on the floor next to her feet. *Shit, woman!* He lifted her and trudged to the front door, praying to God, wishing he had come downstairs sooner. Out in the hallway, the lights mocked his blurred vision. The elevator took an eternity to drop twelve floors. Downstairs, he raced crossed the lobby, Adrianna cradled in his tensed arms. *Stay alive, woman. You're all I got now.*

* * *

"Get outta the way! Run!" Coffee cups flew. The startled crew of ambulance drivers scattered like flies, diving for cover, as the silver Lamborghini skidded into the emergency entrance of Grady Memorial Hospital. The car's bumper stopped inches from the front door. Michael raced inside screaming for *HELP!*

A young triage nurse rushed from her desk, alerting two orderlies who swiftly helped Mike lift Adrianna to a gurney.

"Sir, what happened to her?" the nurse calmly asked.

"She's had an overdose!"

"What was she taking?"

"Them goddamn pills...them lousy fuckin'...."

"Calm down, sir. What kind of pills? Was it prescribed medication? Sir?"

"Uh, it...it was ecstasy," Mike answered, his mind nearly going blank. "And a shit-load of Vodka." A team of nurses and orderlies whisked Adrianna away as Mike watched her limp hand dangle lifelessly. *Don't die on me, woman. God, please.*

Waiting at the nurse's station, Mike shuffled impatiently, his nerves on edge. There were all those insurance forms to fill out, names, dates, addresses, and telephone numbers, too many forms.

"Sir, what's the patient's full name?"

Mike fought to remember what it was in this world of aliases. "Adrianna Joyce Guevara." *At least that's what I been told.*

"Patient's date of birth?"

How the fuck should I know? "She's twenty-eight." He never really knew for sure.

"And what's your relationship to the patient, sir?" Mike was lost, his mind rolling into darkness.

"Sir, are you her husband?" The nurse's voice was relentless.

"Yeah, I'm her husband," he finally admitted without realizing that he had. His thumping heart flooded with old emotions, while his mind replayed buried visions of...*His father in a casket...but not before Slick Poppa found Momma unconscious in the kitchen one cold December morning...Aunt Irene and Marlene taking li'l Mike by the hands, leading him to church...Military tanks rolling along a dusty road in Kuwait City...Gunshots echoing at a firing range on a hot summer day in Quantico, Virginia.*

After the vivid flashbacks subsided, he eased his breathing, sat down in the waiting room, and stretched his legs. He was exhausted. His shirt, damp with sweat, cooled in the sterilized air until he felt a nervous chill run through his body. He sat in that crowded waiting room for nearly three hours, slumped over in that uncomfortable chair. His cell phone buzzed relentlessly--customers that needed his supply more than they needed him. *Fuck 'em all!*

He swallowed hard, trying to rid his parched tongue of that ugly taste. It was a sour hate. He hated every street corner pharmacist. He hated every client who insisted that he provide them with the poison that would make them rich. He hated every junkie, singer, rapper, lawyer, doctor, for wanting this goddamn poison. He hated every liberal and conservative politician that smiled into CNN cameras with cheshire-cat grins, promising to save us all from ourselves; and every fashion designer, and car maker who made the expensive products that poor men wished for and would do anything, sell anything to get. He hated the useless women, whores, the sluts who creamed in their panties to be with the type of man he appeared to be.

"Michael Drake?" A gaunt-faced, Swedish woman asked.

Mike exhaled. *Here we go.* And nervously climbed to his feet.

"Yeah, that's me," he said, finally noticing that she was wearing a white overcoat.

"Hi, there. I am Doctor Bjourn," she kindly said, extending her cold, wrinkled hand. Mike shook it reluctantly.

"What's happening with Adrianna? She's alive, right?"

"Don't you worry now, she's good. She's stabilized within the last forty-five minutes. We're still having a little trouble trying to get her body temperature down, but...."

"What kinda trouble? Serious or what?"

"You see, in high doses, MDMA can interfere with the body's ability to regulate temperature. This can lead to a sharp increase in body temperature."

"Hyperthermia?" he blurted out.

"Yes, exactly. Now we're still trying to cool her down another degree or two, but she's going to be fine."

"There's no brain damage or paralysis is there? I mean,

she wasn't breathing for a minute," Mike rambled.

"We won't know if there was any type of physiological or mental damage until she wakes up, but so far she seems to be somewhat responsive."

"I'd like to be able to sit with her, if I could."

"I'm afraid she's going to need her rest right now. But if you want, you could come back first thing in the morning. Visiting hours start at ten."

"I'm waiting here," he said before he could even think about it. He couldn't stand the thought of going home to the comfort of his bed only to come back in the morning to find out that she had passed away in the middle of the night. There was no one else to care for her and he would not let her die alone.

"You tell her to be more careful. She has so much more to think about than herself now. Let her know that she must protect the little one too," Doctor Bjourn lectured sternly.
The words took a second to soak in.

"The little one?" Michael asked with stunned lips.

"From the looks of it, about two months pregnant. Are you the father?"

"I don't know."

Doctor Bjourn patted him on the shoulder. "Well then, I suggest you find out."

32

Her sleepy eyes opened painfully. The first beams of light were blurred strobes of panoramic color. The next shards of light pierced her glazed pupils and shot sharp pains along optic nerves, burying the torment deep in her brain.

This ain't heaven. Sure ain't hot enough to be hell. Dammit, I'm still kickin'.

Mike came into focus. He was sleeping in a chair in the corner, his feet propped up on the air conditioning vents. Adrianna raised herself in the hospital bed.

"Ouch!" She accidentally pulled the sticky gauze holding the IV tube steady in her arm. "Mike," she whispered just to hear herself say it. She smiled knowing that she had not died alone. "Mike, that's just like you. Ya couldn't just let me die in peace."

Mike heard her voice in his dreams and shuffled his feet until they dropped haphazardly from the air vent, waking him abruptly. He shivered into consciousness, realized where he was, then sprang to his feet. Adrianna was still staring at him. He went to her side, sliding onto the bed, one foot propped on the floor.

"What were you thinkin', woman?" he asked with care and anger trailing every word.

"I killed them, Mike," she broke down. Tears formed in glistening pools. "I told Jorge about the girls that set Alejandro and Cesar up. You know how impatient Jorge gets. He thought you were stalling, so he had Manuel find out where they worked."

"At the Blue Flame?"

"Yeah," she said, "since I used to work there, they sent me to set them up."

"The girls they found in the trunk?" he asked, dreading an answer he already knew. Adrianna nodded slowly, then buried her face in her hands, sobbing.

"They tortured them to death, Mike. I heard them screamin' on the phone!"

"It's okay, baby. You did what you had to do," Mike tried to console her. "You didn't have a choice."

"I did have a choice, Mike. I was the one who introduced the bitches to Alejandro and Cesar in the first place!"

"Ya shittin' me," Mike frowned as he stood and tossed his arms in disbelief. *This really ain't good news.* Adrianna watched a wave of worry drown Mike's face. Then it hit her too.

"What if they told Hector and Manuel that it was me that turned them on to Jorge's nephews. This ain't happenin' right now." Adrianna collapsed on the bed.

"All I know is the twins killed them real hard. Those poor girls would've told them anything they wanted to know just to get them to stop," Mike figured. "If they did give you up, we could always just say they were lying to save their necks. I just hope Jorge goes for it."

Adrianna stared at the ceiling light and huffed, "I gotta get outta here. Maybe if I go talk to Jorge and tell him..."

"Are you crazy?" he interrupted. "You don't tell Jorge nothing until we find out exactly what he knows. Besides, you're not going anywhere. That doctor still wants to run some more tests on you to make sure you didn't roast your brain, or hurt that little bun you been hiding in the oven."

Adrianna's head whipped toward Mike with a look of utter confusion. She slowly asked, "Who's gotta what in a where?"

"You actually don't know, do you?" he grinned.
Adrianna raised from the bed, propping herself on her elbows.

"You're pregnant, woman. Knocked-up. With child. Fertilized."

"No way." She sat stunned, her hands clutched on top of her head.

"Yes, way! Why would I make somethin' like that up?"

Adrianna cupped her hand over her belly, rubbing along the sides, trailing down to her waistline. She had not only tried to take her own life, but that of an unborn child she would have never known.

"How far along am I?"

Mike shrugged, "Two months...so they say."

Instantly, her eyes sparkled and a radiant smile formed across her lips. She leapt from the bed, wrapping her arms around his neck. "I can't believe it! I'm having a...I mean *we're* having a baby!"

Then suddenly, sensing his apprehension, she backed off. "What's wrong?" she joked. "I know I may not be the perfect housewife...but, c'mon...I can learn to be."

"Nah, woman. It ain't that. I'm just wondering who the daddy really is before I break out the Cuban cigars and sign up for day care."

Adrianna burst into laughter and pounced on him once again. "Ahhh, you're so cute when you're jealous," she mocked. "But you'll be happy to know that Jorge Vargas hasn't touched me in almost six months. You do the math."

"He's gay, isn't he?" Mike inquired.

"You wish. He has a new mistress in Dallas that he's been breakin' in. I'm just a toy doll that he can't throw away. Jorge thinks I don't know about her, but the twins can't keep a secret."

"Then that makes me...," he paused, too stunned to finish.

"Yeah, that makes you a...."

"Daddy!" they both yelled in unison as he lifted her from the bed and danced around the room.

"Mike, what have we done "she softly whispered in his ear. "He'll kill us."

Not if I put him under first.

"Sooner or later he's gonna find out when you blow up

like a hot air balloon." Mike filled his cheeks with air.

"You ain't funny," she groaned. "You still don't know Jorge like I do. He's going to look at this baby as an assault on his personal property."

"I'll smooth it out with him. Right after I tell him you tried to knock yourself off."

"Dear God, whatever you do, don't you tell him I got admitted to the hospital! He'd lose his raggedy mind."

For a second Mike considered telling Jorge about this little hospital visit anyway. *That's the sure-shot way to get you off them damn pills.* The mad Mexican would get the point through her head, but it meant a death sentence for whoever was supplying her with the pills. Mike hoped this baby would be her reason to give them up. *Yeah, she'll do that for us.*

"Promise me, you won't tell Jorge about this whole ICU, trauma, near-death soap opera," she softly demanded. Mike nodded and she smiled reassured that everything was settled.

"On one condition," Mike requested, "you gotta turn me on to the cats that sold you the *beans*."

"Why?" she whined.

"That's the price you pay for almost dying on me." Mike's face went course, the wrinkles in his forehead stiffened.

"Count ya blessings and let it go," she said knowing that Mike had more sinister reasons for wanting her to introduce him to her ecstasy supplier.

"I wasn't asking," Mike rumbled, deadly serious.

33

GAMBINO WAS HERE

Damn, I miss the good ol' days! During the raging 1990's, Atlanta's *Gold Club* was one of the most lucrative and well known strip clubs on the entire East Coast. Big money was abundant and the champagne flowed like water. All was well until the ever resourceful FBI discovered that the rambunctious owner Stephen Kaplan was affiliated with soldiers in the Gambino crime family. The Bureau hound-dogs sniffed out the money trail and soon deducted that the clubs $40 million dollars in annual revenue was being funneled back to organized crime syndicates in New York city.

The extensive four-year fox hunt culminated in a sensational trial that captivated national media attention in the blistering summer of 2001. But when detailed witness testimonials about sexual favors for celebrity athletes appeared, suddenly the trial became the center of one of the biggest sex scandals in professional sports history.

The entire country tuned into *Court TV* as a colorful parade of trial witnesses--strippers, bouncers, bartenders, disgruntled customers, doormen, and valets--spun erotic tales, describing a seedy, high-flying world of $200,000 bar tabs, private sex rooms, and regular club visits by well known celebrities such as NBA stars John Starks, and the ever eclectic Dennis Rodman, NFL running back Terrell Davis, multi-platinum singer Madonna, and actor Stephen Baldwin.

Dozens of high-paid, professional athletes eventually appeared on the stand, including Gold Glove centerfielder

Andruw Jones of the Atlanta Braves, and New York Knick Patrick Ewing--both candidly testified to receiving "special treatment" from loving strippers at the now infamous Gold Club.

Still, despite the lurid testimonies, and countless hours of sanctioned harassment by good ol' Uncle Sam, Stephen Kaplan's connection to the Gambino crime family was never confirmed. *You want justice? How much justice can you afford?*

Mighty Uncle Sam even had detailed surveillance and audio tapes of Kaplan meeting with the Mafioso family heir apparent, John Gotti, Jr., and they had solid proof that Kaplan was present at a New York nightclub in 1988 when a prominent Gambino family member was shot and killed.

Additional charges of credit card fraud, prostitution, money laundering and tax evasion were also never proven.

Still, after the sensational and rather candid testimony of Jones and Ewing, Kaplan agreed to a plea deal, a $5 million dollar fine, and a prison sentence of three-to five-years.

And that was that. The great era of the *Gold Club* was over. The morning after the going out of business party, FBI agents were chaining the doors as drunken strippers, bartenders, and sad employees stumbled home.

Now in the winter, during the cold holidays, they sell Christmas trees in the old Gold Club parking lot. *Now what did I tell ya bout Atlanta dealing with legends?*

But Atlanta is also a very, very resilient town. And the erotic void left by the world infamous Gold Club was immediately filled, for better or worse, by a cadre of sultry hideouts.

34

ECSTASY COWBOYS

Instead of falling into extinction, the sin and decadence of southern nightlife simply swarmed to the fast growing midtown area. And it was here in the elegant *Cheetah Lounge* that upwardly mobile, red-blooded, upscale white men found, or amply rediscovered, their source of urban erotica.

Michael tossed his keys to a smiling valet who was relishing the chance to get behind the wheel of a brand new Lamborghini.

"Not a single scratch on her, or I'll scratch ya ass," Mike warned the valet. Adrianna slid from the car, her tanned thighs protruding from a short, green Dolce & Gabanna skirt.

"Don't be such a dick, Mike. It's a car!" she chastised.

"That's easy for you to say. You get to ride in it without paying for it."

"You're not gonna do anything crazy in here, are you?" Adrianna worried, as she tightened her grip on his arm.

"Crazy is a relative concept."

Beneath the fluttering lights, and pale shadows, it was every red-blooded, meat-eating, terrorist hating, horny white man's fantasy. *Silky haired, Asian petites in plaid, Catholic school girl min-skirts. Gaunt, pale-skinned Swedish swimsuit models. Tall, slinky, flat-assed Russian imports. And those All-American, bleached-blonde, Barbie Dolls--their tanned titties pumped so full of clinical grade silicone that they looked like they might explode.* Wall to wall, there were thirty-two or more international flavors to satisfy every single one of your carnal taste-buds. *God bless America.*

Marco Nobles was sitting in an elevated section near center stage, gawking at a busty, sun-tanned brunette nurse sliding out of her white overcoat. Nobles was twenty-eight, Japanese, and a hair shy of being a genius. He was styling in designer glasses that reflected the flashing strobe lights. Next to him sat an odd, skinny looking white dude in a black, ten-gallon cowboy hat. The man was an anorexic John Wayne trapped in designer clothes.

Adrianna greeted the odd couple with friendly hugs.

She began, "Marco...Wild Bill this is...."

"The one and only Michael Drake!" Wild Bill interrupted as he goofily sprang to his feet, towering to a lanky six-foot-four. "The pleasure's all ours!" the animated cowboy said with a deteriorating Dutch accent as he waved an outstretched hand. "They call me Wild Bill. Care to beam up?" Wild Bill pulled a gold cigarette case from his pocket and opened it, revealing a multi-colored collection of ecstasy pills.

"*Mercedes, Double-stacks, Vampires?*" Bill rambled off his hefty menu, "*Heartstoppers, Smiley faces, Scooby snacks?*"

"*Poppa Smurf, Cloud Nine, Blue butterflies?*" Marco chimed in with equal fervor.

"Nah, I'm good," Mike refused. "I'm a professional alcoholic by trade. It's family tradition." Everyone sat down.

"Cool, my man. But when you wanna touch heaven and kiss the lips of angels...all you gotta do is let me know," Bill boldly proclaimed as he put his pills away.

The strobe lights brightened, shifting the sultry shadows. Mike noticed the rugged scars that ran along Wild Bill's hands, forearms, and along his neck trailing up to his lower left cheek. *Burns maybe or possibly some birth defect.*

"I hear you're lookin' to extend your product line," Marco noted. "Pillsville's where the money is today."

Wild Bill hooted, "Pills are the thrill, dude!"

"Possibly," Mike returned, "but I can't afford to fuck around with no amateurs. I gotta know you can handle the volume. Nothing pisses off my clientele more than when they can't get a refill when they need it."

"I feel you my brother!" Wild Billed yelled and slapped Mike on the back. Mike grimaced. *Y'all ain't none o' my brothers.* Adrianna sensed the abrupt mood swing and calmly placed her hand on his lap.

Mike's face relaxed. "I need a good ticket on at least seventy to a hundred-thousand a month...pills and capsules."

"My brother, if you got the cash, we got the stash!" Will Bill laughed and slapped an awkward high-five with Marco.

Now these dizzy mutha fuckaz are rhymin' to me? Mike wasn't in the mood to deal with these two jackasses, but... *Business is business.*

"How long will it take to ship 'em in?" Mike asked. Wild Bill and Marco gazed at each other and exploded in hilarious laughter. *These crackers are zooted outta their minds!*

"Ship 'em in?" Will Bill hooted. "My guy, we manufacture these babies off the assembly line like Toyota. Why shop in New York, L.A., or Amsterdam when you can come straight to us?" Wild Bill leaned in close, his liquor-laced breath seething in Mike's face.

"You do business with good Ol' Wild Bill, and Madman Marco here, you automatically cut out the middle-man, the shipping and handling costs, and you get rich! I guarantee it! YAHOOO!!!"

An hour past as the drinks flowed against the pagan backdrop of carnal music and naked flesh. Soon, Mike was distracted by the sights and sounds, too consumed by the spiraling complexity of the mission he had to complete. He was so distracted that he never noticed Will Bill nod toward an approaching waitress. She registered the signal and adroitly cracked a capsule over a glass of brandy, spilling the powdery contents into the brown liquid.

The waitress delivered the next collection of cocktails to their table. Mike instinctively reached for the glass of brandy, while Wild Bill and Marco Nobles grinned like spoiled kids up to no good.

"Welcome to our Candy Land, Mister Drake!" Marco shouted as he raised his glass in salute. Mike gulped his drink down--his tongue too numb from the previous rounds to notice the tinge of chemicals lacing his taste buds.

For another psychedelic hour Mike sat and watched the freak show as the drugs breached his bloodstream, racing out toward his synaptic nerves, the heightened sense of euphoria rushing smoothly over his body, until suddenly his vision blurred a degree more than it should have.

Sonnuva bitch, Mike cursed to himself. *They laced up the drinks.* He was furious and...*Boy, I'm high as a kite.* It was a volatile combination. *Be easy, man. Making a hasty, violent move right now gonna's be more trouble than it's worth. I'll reach out and touch these idiots later...hurt 'em when your mind clears.* The ecstasy rush spread through every inch of his body, pleasuring him more than he wanted to admit.

"Open sesame! Open says me!" Marco chuckled.

Mike hazily watched Adrianna close her eyes and stick out her tongue. Marco Nobles reached out slowly, and dropped a pill on the tip of her tongue as she curled it back.

"Spit it out," Mike slurred. He was in no condition to stop her.

"Last one." The warmth of her breath caressed his ear, soothing his mind. "After the thrill is gone...my body, my child belongs to you," she promised. Adrianna threw her head back and swallowed.

Wild Bill howled, "Tell me how that tickles your G-spot!"

Mike and Adrianna glared into each other's eyes, falling in a chemical haze, and dove into a deep kiss, their tongues locked in a tingling embrace.

"Do it for the love! Do it for the love!" Marco cheered, and clutched a passing dancer, pulling her into his lap. "Dance for me, my lady!" Marco tossed a handful of hundred-dollar bills into the air. "Dance till the pain melts away!"

35

GHOSTS WRITE YOUR NIGHTMARES

Summer 1992. A young and vicious Jorge Vargas twisted the hand-crafted silencer over the muzzle of his Walther pistol and crept into the bedroom through a squeaking door. He could see the snoring, gray-haired man sleeping peacefully next to his plump wife. She was an aged picture of her beautiful daughter. Jorge watched their chests move up and down.

Blood in...Blood out.

Jorge triggered bullets into their skulls at point blank range. As their puffy cotton pillows filled with blood, he leaned in close to examine the looks on his victim's faces. Satisfied with his work, he tucked his gun away, and left the room.

A pale beam of light intersected the hallway, and he stopped to look at her one more time through the tiny crack in her open bedroom door--her smooth, teenage face rested against a tan satin pillow. She was beautiful just like her mother used to be. He wanted to taste her lips. Now, Jorge would take her as payment for the debt her father still owed.

Adrianna's brown eyes opened slowly as her deep sleep disintegrated, and she thought she saw a shadow float past the crack in her open bedroom door.

"Daddy? Is that you out there?" she asked and rose sleepily from the bed. A door slammed! Adrianna peeked out of her room into the dark empty hallway. Her parents' bedroom door was lodged open.

Timid steps carried her the length of the passage way to their door and she pushed it open wider. Her heart wrenched in

*pain, and her lungs burned as she inhaled the horror of seeing
her mother and father posing in a bloody, lifeless portrait. Run!*

Adrianna screamed, ripping from her nightmare! Her shriek
pried Mike from his sleep. It took a hazy moment to realize she
was in his arms. She was drenched in sweat, her damp lingerie
clinging to his skin.

"Same dream?" he asked.

She nodded. "Can't shake it."

"Everything takes times to heal. Especially
nightmares," he offered.

"Fifteen years should be long enough." She buried her
face into his chest. The dampness of her tears was cold against
his bare chest.

"You gotta replace the nightmares with some o' the good
shit you remember about your folks," he began. "Like whatever
birthdays, or vacations...and the holidays you spent together.
You keep replaying that one night... it's gonna wreck ya."

"I've tried to...but it...it's still killin' me inside. I got way
too many ghosts to fight."

Don't we all, sister.

Shivering, she laid back in his arms. After her parents
death she had been homeless on the streets of Atlanta for
almost two years before she started dancing at Magic City.
Jorge Vargas, a young associate of her father, had raised her
sporadically in a cycle of cold cash, lukewarm love and then
complete denial. She was always important until Jorge found a
new mistress to adore or a bigger shipment to deliver.

"Everything's changed. If we don't get outta here
soon...," he mumbled as he imagined a tragic ending to both
their stories.

"No regrets. We set our plan. Make our move. We never
look back," she finished for him.

"Where do ya go when the world's yours?" he asked.

"What do you mean *we?*" Adrianna perked up, lifting
her head. "I work alone, playboy."

"There are three of us to look after now," he stated

firmly, rubbing her stomach. "One more person I'm responsible for."

"Li'l kid ain't gotta chance in the world if his father's a two-bit hustlin', dope pushin' thug."

Mike's chest swelled. "I ain't no thug. Children are thugs. I'm a businessman," he stated with a noble air.

"We're about to bring a brand new life into this world of insanity. Don't seem fair to the baby, does it?" she moaned.

"Uh uh." *Nope, just don't seem right at all.*

36

His cell phone wouldn't stop ringing. Officer Alexander
dragged the handcuffed suspect in the white T-shirt and jeans
from the back seat of the squad car. They were just two black
folks lost on a stroll down a rocky, dirt road that snaked deep
into a dense tapestry of pine trees. Still under construction, the
naked timber frame of a giant, residential home sat on a hill
far off in the distance

"Hey, folk! Whatcha doin'? Ain't no jail out here!"
the frantic man screamed. "Help!"

Alexander rammed the pistol into the suspect's bleeding
mouth. "Shut up!"

Alexander's cell phone chirped relentlessly, until he had
to answer, "Mubarek, I'll call you back! I'm protecting and
servin'!" The call ended as Alexander kicked the suspect in
the stomach, knocking him flat on his back in a puff of dust.
Finger trigger itchin', Alexander racked his pistol and fired a
shot that exploded in a cloud of red clay dirt, inches from the
suspect's head.

"Are you crazy, man!" the suspect rolled around in
horror..

"Everything sold between South Marshal and Jones
Street, you pay tribute to me," Alexander demanded and
sneezed. "I hate this damn pollen. I'll see you every Friday from
here on out to pick up my paycheck. We understand how this
works?"

The suspect nodded respectfully. "We got it."

* * *

Officer Alexander pulled his squad car into his driveway. It was a modest two-story brick house, settled in Southern suburbia. As soon as he unlocked his front door, a frisky black Rottweiler barked loudly, and playfully rushed him.

In the back of his walk-in bedroom closet, he dialed the combination and popped the safe door. Inside, he neatly stacked the piles of money and slammed the safe shut.

"Another deposit in the policeman's retirement fund."

His house phone rang. Alexander peeked at the caller I.D. box. "What's this fool want now?" he muttered, snatching up the phone.

"Mubarek, what I tell ya 'bout callin' me at my house?" Alexander blasted into the receiver.

"I told you I don't trust cell phones. The white man can just pull your talk right outta the air," Mubarek's thick African voice rumbled back.

"And I don't want my home number poppin' up in your phone records. So don't ever call me here again. Now what do you want?" Alexander growled.

"I want to know that I'm safe, that's what I want. I see the news. There was too much blood last time," Mubarek worried. "Now I hear some crazy Mexican is out for revenge."

"You keep ya mouth shut and let us handle the rest. I talked to my people, and as long as nobody gets outta line, then nobody gets hurt on this one. You just make sure that there's plenty of pills and cash when my crew shows up."

"It's already done," Mubarek said confidently. "Them rich white boys, them trust me. And they're greedy. Them want to sell me as much ecstasy as I can take."

"And this's the last time I tell ya not to call my house!" Alexander said.

"Fine...fine!" Mubarek ended.

"Crazy fuckin' African," Alexander grunted and hung up the phone.

37

WEIRD SCIENCE

Mike rang the front door bell and waited in the humid night air, dodging angry bugs that circled around the glowing porch lamps. Mike swatted at one overly persistent Georgia mosquito. Moments later the door opened and Mike shoved the barrel of his pistol into Marco's gaped mouth.

"Whooa there cowboy!" Wild Bill appeared in the doorway--his hands raised in surrender. That's when the dark barrel hole at the killing end of the second .357 pistol targeted Wild Bill's forehead. The tense trio backed into the foyer of the house.

"I'll say this one time. If either of you two retards ever spike another drink of mine, or get slick and come short with the dope, if you ever get outta line in any kinda way, I swear I'll kill ya!"

"Peace, Mike! Peace and harmony, Daddy-O!" Will Bill stuttered. "It was just a gesture of love."

Marco Nobles mumbled his apologies with the gun barrel still wedged in his mouth. He waved his hands and shrugged his nervous shoulders.

"If you ever give Adrianna another pill...I'll kill ya again!"

"That's our way of sealing our communal bond, brother!" Wild Bill spewed. "Can I get an Amen? We get high together, we get rich together...like hippies on a magical tour, Daddy-O. It's just chemical love, dude!"

"The only thing I love is the money," Michael spoke from lips still curled in rage. "You've been warned."

"Mister, your gun-toting rage and your unwarranted physical and verbal abuse have been duly noted." Bill astutely remarked as Marco drooled around the gun barrel and mumbled in affirmation.

Michael wiped his gun on Marco's sleeve and tucked the pistols away. Marco and Wild Bill exhaled short breaths of fear and relief.

"Now that we've come to terms on *that*...let's do business," Marco said as he rubbed his sore lips.

They walked into the spacious, three-story home. Nestled in the heart a secluded Alpharetta neighborhood, it was well worth the two-million dollar price tag. Mike counted *seven, eight* more employees, whirling in motion, *nine* dudes running the enterprise.

Marco strolled the lab like Willie Wonka giving a tour of his great chocolate factory. *"Ecstasy, Adam, Big E, hug, beans, X-T-C,* or the *love drug*...whatever you want to call our tasty little treats, we are the number one source of quality product in the southeast," Marco proudly noted.

"And one day the biggest manufacturers in the world!" Wild Bill exclaimed grandly.

These white boys got no sense of reality. Michael was amazed by the efficiency of the operation. There were a dozen busy bodies moving room to room, focusing on the intricate manufacturing and distribution process--forty-gallon drums of chemicals stored in the dining room, sorting and shipping operations in the living room, and a cash accounting office in the kitchen.

"Mikey boy, are you still with us?" Wild Bill asked.

"I like what I see. I'm just wondering what all goes into the *love drug?* I'm sure it ain't all a bunch o' healthy FDA approved ingredients," Mike joked.

"Methylenedioxymethamphetamine," Will Bill skillfully enunciated.

"That's a big word," Mike shrugged. "Big words don't mean shit to me."

"Or MDMA for short," Marco added. "It's a synthetic,

psychoactive drug similar to methamphetamine and the hallucinogen mescaline. In actuality it's no more dangerous than king cocaine or any of your other garden variety amphetamines," Marco said.

"Well, we do use a few more secret ingredients...but I don't know...." Wild Bill tapped his chin. "Should we tell him?"

"It's a trade secret," Marco admitted.

"If you don't fill me in, then we don't do business," Mike interjected. "And since we won't be partners then...well...I'm gonna kill both of ya for spiking my drink."

Wild Bill relented, "It's a rather ingenious mix. On top of our base we add a dash of ephedrine, a pinch of dextromethorpan..."

"A pinch of what?" Mike asked.

"DMX...it's a cough suppressant. And for good measure we add a little caffeine, cocaine, and top it all off with a drop of ketamine."

"Ketmanine?" Mike frowned. "Hold up. Ain't ketamine some kind of anesthetic? My vet used it on my dog once."

"And a fine anesthetic it is too!" Marco chimed.

"This shit's wild, man! Where the hell are you cats gettin' these ingredients from?" Mike asked in amazement.

"It's not so hard when you know a doctor here, a veterinarian there, and when you have few old college roommates working at research labs for major U.S. Pharmaceutical companies," Marco said proudly.

"Yep, partner. We know people who know people," Wild Bill continued. "So, Mike, are we partners in crime? It's time you grab ya saddle and *cowboy-up* to the greatest rodeo on the planet!"

Mike paused for effect, staring around the room. His final decision had been made years before he ever met these two idiots, and now their fate was about to be inextricably sealed by his next few words.

"Are you both sure you wanna get down with me. I only play for high stakes. Anything less is uncivilized," Mike offered, graciously providing them a mirage in the dessert.

"Can we do business or *can we do business?*" Marco anxiously asked, rubbing his pale, greedy hands in anticipation.

Too bad white boys, ya had your chance to run.

"Let's get to the money," Mike said with no remorse.

*T*he large front doors of the house burst open! Screams followed! *"Get the fuck down!"* Guns targeted.

Mike backed up. His first instinct was to reach for the pistols hidden in the small of his back, but the sight of the banana clip hanging from the belly of the AK–47 being aimed at him said otherwise. *Be easy. They ain't cops.*

Four masked sheriffs circled the room, barking orders. From nowhere, a cold pistol slammed against the back of Mike's head. He buckled, tumbling face first to the floor. He could feel the trickle of blood flowing out of his hair, streaming along the back of his neck. Faring no better, a screaming Marco took the heavy butt of a Mossberg shotgun directly to the jaw and he landed nearly unconscious.

Through blurred vision, Mike watched two masked gunmen handcuff Bill and drug him away, kicking, yelling, pleading for mercy. *Shit! Robbin' crew.*

Mike rolled to his knees in a foggy haze, the concussion distorting his sense of depth and space.

"Get down on the ground, Drake!" the third sheriff ordered as he raised his Mossberg shotgun. *He knows my name.*

"You thieves gonna rob me, then rob me and let me go. I got plenty mo' money." Teetering, Mike rose to his feet in a stupor. The sheriff moved a step closer, his trigger finger running out of patience.

"If not...," Mike coughed out and patted his chest. "...I'll die on my feet."

BLAM! The thundering hot blast struck Mike mid-chest, lifting him from his feet, tossing him fifteen feet across the room. Mike crashed through a table stacked with shipping boxes. Landing face down, Mike hit the floor with numbing force. A gasp of air shot from his lungs, razor pains racked his body, and the pitch-blackness engulfed him.

"What the fuck's wrong with ya, Drake? Get down means get the fuck down! The sheriff kneeled and scoured through Mike's pockets, taking a wad of cash. He quickly slid the Rolex timepiece from Mike's left wrist and rushed out of the room.

For thirty minutes, terrifying screams emanated from a distant room in the house. They were working Wild Bill over, blow by painful blow. Marco Nobles could hear the howls of pain as he waddled, hog-tied on his stomach, fading in and out of reality, mumbling incoherently, shivering in a tide of fear.

Don't move ya scary shit, Marco thought.

We can make it outta here alive! Marco watched the scuffed black heels of the two armed watchdogs trace back and forth across the floor. The other two accomplices ran back into the room with a suitcase and boxes in tow.

"Let's dip!" one of them ordered and the four sheriffs exited quickly, slamming the front door.

38

*S*tay *Alive. Now, inhale...*

Mike sucked in a bolt of air and rolled over on his back, spitting blood. His chest was on fire. Shotgun shrapnel scarred his throat.

Mike heard a car engine ignite. It was the familiar growl of a Chevy motor. Marco was sobbing, whimpering like a small cowardly dog, waddling in his own urine.

Hell bent on settling the score, Mike cusped his Sig Sauer .357 tools from his waist, and crawled to his feet. Staggering to the front door, he stepped over Marco, and aimed his guns. From the porch, he could see the police cruiser rolling into the street.

With steady hands, Mike squeezed off, and the crackling thunder of gunfire pierced the night, echoing through the calm cul-de-sac. With deadly precision, the back window of the police cruiser burst into shards of razor-sharp glass, as the shocked occupants ducked for cover.

"Sonnuva bitch!" Danny Diablo yelped from the rear seat. "Stop the fuckin' car!" Shards of bloody glass dripped from his face.

I ain't stoppin' shit!" The driver yanked the steering wheel, veering, and punched the gas.

"I'll kill that muthafucka!" Danny Diablo jammed the steel muzzle of his AK-47 through the fractured window, vomiting hot flames. The rapid spray of automatic projectiles riddled the earth, rattle-snaking toward Mike, spewing clouds of red dirt and gravel. *Ahhh shit!* Mike backed off, clamoring for cover, still triggering. He raced for his life, diving over the hood of Marco's Benz, crashing to the opposite side, as hot bullets punctured the pricey, metal car frame. *Be patient.* The gunfire paused.

Mike rose again, triggers clicking, until his gun chambers jammed empty. "Shit!"

The sleepy suburban neighborhood woke up as bedroom lights flickered and nosey, frightened neighbors timidly peeked from behind drawn curtains, trying to get a glimpse of the aftermath. *Your high-priced mortgages didn't save ya from a good ol' fashioned American gunfight, now did it?*

"Go back to bed!" Mike raged into the black sky and raced for his car. He dove inside, reversed out of the driveway, and peeled off in pursuit.

* * *

"You alright?" the driver asked and stomped on the gas. The police cruiser shot through the residential neighborhood.

"Glass cut my fuckin' face," Danny Diablo muttered from the back seat and swiped the blood from his tattered cheek.

"All the cash we got, we'll get ya a facelift."

Suddenly, the driver peered into his rearview mirror and squinted at the glaring, low slung set of halogen headlights, bearing down on them.

39

GETAWAY

Mike's heavy arms struggled to guide the steering wheel. His head was pounding, ears ringing, and his swollen ribs and sternum pulsated with every heartbeat. Beneath his shredded silk shirt lay a Kevlar bulletproof vest, splattered with metal pellets from heavy gauge shotgun shells. *Stay Alive.*

Mike dug two extra ammunition clips out of his glove box, and fed them to *Irene* and *Marlene. You hungry, ladies?* Behind the passenger seat, he found his pet MP5 submachine gun and rested it in his lap. Up ahead some two-hundred yards or so, he spotted the black sheriff's cruiser. Mike dropped the clutch and slammed into second gear.

Danny Diablo swiftly spun to his knees and rammed the AK-47 through the gaping hole in the shattered back window. The Lamborghini growled, closing in rapidly as both cars raced through busy four-way stop signs, cutting off skidding mini-vans, and luxury coupes.

"Heat his ass up," the driver grinned.

The AK-47 clicked off, spitting flames in a staccato rumble. The Lamborghini swayed from a fiery trail of bullets that traced across the fender, splintering the fiberglass body. Mike triggered a rapid, thunderous volley of shots that punctured the police cruiser's trunk, crumbling what little glass still dangled in the back window. The sheriffs frantically ducked down in their seats, as deadly metal projectiles, ricocheted inside the car's metal frame. Two hot missiles ripped through the driver's seat headrest, whistling past the sheriff's right ear, puncturing the front windshield. The tires screamed as the shell-shocked driver swerved dangerously into oncoming traffic, facing off with a blinding pair of headlights from a bulky Hummer H2.

"Watch it!" The driver yanked back into the right lane, scraping across the front fender of the Hummer. Two sheriffs raised bulletproof vests, stuffing them in the back window, and the AK-47 erupted again, accompanied by the heavy thump of a Mossberg shotgun.

The Lamborghini skated away from the slashing line of fire, losing traction, fishtailing in a screaming skid. Mike countered the wheel and corrected, slamming on the gas.

Bolting away, the police cruiser, gained some distance as it climbed the next hilly street and leaped over the incline, landing roughly.

"Brakes! Brakes!" The driver stood on the brake pedal, throwing them all forward. Hot tires squealed and brake pads burned as they slid uncontrollably for ninety-feet, and stopped inches before crashing into...

Friday night traffic. Peachtree Street. Bumper to bumper chaos. Car horns. Bars. Clubs. Ladies in skirts. Legs everywhere. Fags in drag. Neon lights and shiny cars.
The black police car inched into the crawling traffic.

"Not here. Put the chopper down," the driver ordered and gassed the police cruiser ahead. Danny Diablo lowered the AK-47.

"Where is he?"

Seconds later, the Lamborghini roared to the corner, and slowly turned right, wading into the river of cars.

"About six cars back, far right lane." Danny Diablo locked on the halogen headlights.

* * *

Mike could just see the top of the police cruiser as it moved a few cars ahead. Suddenly, a four-pack of Friday night party girls pulled up next to him in a red, convertible VW Beetle. The drunken, twenty-somethings bobbed and danced to a Top 40 pop tune blaring from the radio.

"Can I ride in your Lamborghini?" the bubbly brunette passenger slurred and leaned from the window, jiggling her sun-tan parlor painted boobs as an incentive.

"Not right now, sweetheart. I'm in the middle of a high speed chase." The traffic slowly inched forward six more feet and Mike rolled away.

"What kinda lame ass excuse is that?" the spurned brunette screamed from her car window. "If you was gay, all ya had to do was say so!

"Good Lord," Mike moaned and lunged the car forward. A few moments later, the red party VW evened up with Mike again in traffic.

"What, you think ya cute n' all o' that just 'cause you got a Lambo'!" the brunette ranted on and on. 'You ain't shit!"

VROOOM...VRROOM! Mike gunned his engine, drowning out her nagging voice.

"What the fuck are you doing? We're supposed to be the police!" Danny Diablo complained from the back seat.

"Damn, that's right. The driver flipped a switch on the dashboard, and the red and blue flashers mounted in the car's front grill ignited. The police siren wailed to life. Obediently, the cars in front of the police cruiser began to pull out of the way.

"Nah, nah nah! C'mon!" Mike pounded the steering wheel as he watched the police cruiser slowly get away.

* * *

The police cruiser turned right on 10th Street, forcing its way into the turning lane entrance to I-85 South.

"We lose 'em?" the driver asked.

"I think so." Danny Diablo answered as the car descended the ramp to the interstate and jetted into the fast lane. Suddenly, there they were again; those low-slung halogen headlights reappeared, tearing down the highway ramp.

"He's back on us!" Danny Diablo announced. "Drake's startin' to piss me the fuck off."

Streaking steel torpedoes chased each other, jetting into a sharp curve, passing the *Williams Street* exit, diving into the belly of the city, running beneath the grey, concrete overpasses....*Freedom Parkway...Georgia State....* Tunnel lights ripped by at nauseating speeds as glowing skyscrapers towered over the dangerous race.

The police cruiser shot from the HOV lane, skated hard right, slicing across slower cars into the I-20 merge lanes, just past Grady Memorial Hospital. Two car lengths behind, the Lamborghini weaved through traffic, bobbing inches from speeding bumpers. Sixty-yards ahead, I-20 would soon split.

"Where we headed tonight, fellas? East side or West side?" Mike asked maniacally, and downshifted, sliding into a tiny space between two cars, waiting for the police cruiser to decide. "I got plenty o' gas and all the ammo I need."

"Let's take this shit back to our side o' town!" The police car jerked to the right lane, I-20 West, digging into the deep curve, lunging from its apex. The Lamborghini squealed through the turn, running inches from the police cruiser's rear bumper.

The chase broke the crest just after *Lee Street &
Atlanta University Center*, and raced across the path of an
Atlanta Patrol Officer clocking speeders with a radar gun.

The gun flashed...105 MPH.

Tachometers climbed and speeds rose...*110 MPH*...as
the two bullets stormed past *Langhorn to Cascade*...highway
signs whipped by in green blurs, reflecting bronze sunlight at
115 MPH...M. L. King Jr. Drive, nearing the *Hamilton Holmes*
exit...*120 MPH*....

As the police cruiser closed in on an eighteen-wheeler
truck, Danny Diablo aimed the AK-47, blasting shots from the
rear passenger window. The bullets shredded the truck's
massive back tires, and sheer speed peeled them from the
metal rims like rubber potato skins. Wide strips of rubber laced
with sharp metal fibers slammed across the Lamborghini's
windshield. Mike swerved right, but alertly jerked back
avoiding a skidding passenger van packed with screaming kids.

Instinctively, Mike punched the gas, swerved left into
the fast lane, running inches from the concrete divider wall.
And barely shot past the swinging trailer.

"Fuck!" Mike clinched the wheel. A green Toyota
blocked his path. In his rear view mirror he saw the jack-
knifing truck's long trailer swinging forward, chasing down the
Lamborghini. Mike gunned the car forward, slamming into the
rear of the Toyota, shoving the slow, green turtle forward.
Inches behind them, the big rig's trailer collided with the
concrete highway wall, exploding in giant strips of metal.

Silent flashes from the AK-47 sparked in the distance!
Bullets ripped through the Toyota, stabbing chunks of concrete
debris from the highway divider. Mike ducked, and yanked the
car hard right, evading the gunfire. The rear tires lost grip, and
the Lamborghini spun wildly, scraping across four lanes,
missing honking cars, shooting into a grassy recess next to the
highway.

The black police cruiser escaped, quickly merging onto
I-285, and streaked a short mile to the very next exit, ramping
off at Bankhead Highway.

40

After thirty-one frustrating minutes of squirming, Marco Nobles finally wiggled his legs free from the plastic straps, and wobbled to his bare feet. He heard the rumble of the Lamborghini as Mike returned.

"Where...where's Wild Bill?" Marco stuttered, snot bubbling in his nostrils as he drooled on himself like a spoiled toddler. Mike untied Marco's hands.

"Is he dead? Did they..." Marco exploded in tears, mumbling promises, *"...To change my dirty life...get outta this business...gotta go to church more...gonna pay my child support....call my mother first chance I get!"* Marco rubbed his sore wrists and wiped the blood from his forehead.

As Mike searched the house, the smell of chemicals wafted past his nose nauseating him. The bathrooms were empty and each bedroom had been untouched.

They were thorough...knew exactly what they were looking for. Mike admired the work of intelligent, organized criminals.

Rat bastards could've used the same balls and intelligence to run corporate America. A mind is a terrible fuckin' thang to waste.

Mike found five more employees gagged and bound in the kitchen. He freed the thankful young white boys as they hugged him in gratitude.

In the master bedroom, Mike heard a slight murmur coming from a walk-in closet. He reached for the handle and paused, "Wild Bill?" The mumbles quickened as they got louder. Mike ripped the door open, his trigger finger ready. *Ahhh, look at the naked li'l baby.*

The sight threw Mike into laughter. Wild Bill was stripped naked and hog-tied. His bloody face was swollen and horribly distorted like he had just gone twelve rounds with Muhammed Ali.

Better off disfigured than dead, Mike grinned as he untied Wild Bill.

These are the rules, kids. You only get to keep the product and the cash if you got the balls and the muscle. The strong survive, the weak surrender.

Welcome to Atlanta white boys.

41

2:56 AM. Marco Nobles sat nervously in the Emergency Waiting Room at Grady Memorial Hospital. Wild Bill was still in surgery; his cheek bones were shattered and his soul was a little weary, but he would survive.

Mike had reluctantly taken twenty minutes to let a spunky nurse from Nigeria remove the shrapnel from his neck and bandage him up. He thanked her with a crisp hundred-dollar bill that she never thought twice about taking. *Last time I was here I was savin' Adrianna's life. Tonight, I'm here with the men that almost killed her. Karma's a bitch.*

Marco Nobles rocked back and forth, contemplating his near death experience. Mike plopped down beside him.

"Marco, stop rockin' like that. You're messin' with my nerves," Mike ordered. Marco stopped moving altogether.

"Who could've tipped that crew off tonight?" Mike asked. "Who've you been dealing with from my side of town? Anybody new?"

Marco searched the corners of his mind, but the fear that remained wouldn't let him concentrate. "Wild Bill usually brings in new clients. He's the talker, not me. I'm a chemist, a scientist. I graduated with top honors from Georgia Tech. I'm not built for this shit, dude." Marco broke down in tears, sniffling.

"Pull it together, Marco. You're embarrassing me." Mike looked at the other people taking notice of Marco's hysterics. *Everybody knows everybody in Atlanta, and dangerous ears are everywhere, even in crowded hospital waiting rooms.*

"I don't care dude! I just had some fuckin' Russian

machine gun pointed at me like I was in a third world country!
That shit ain't American, dude!"

"Hell, if it ain't American," Mike joked. "Good Lord,
what's that smell?" Mike sniffed his arm pits.

"That's me. I pissed on myself," Marco admitted.
Mike slid over one chair, trying to escape the stench.

"Now think back. Did Wild Bill talk about anybody you
cats didn't really know? Was he working on any new deals?
Anything outta the ordinary?"

"Not really. Well, he was thinking about trading a
couple thousand pills for some recording equipment?" Marco
remembered.

"What?" Mike puzzled. "What are you sayin'?

"Wild Bill, he always wanted to run his own record
label. You know how everybody around here either wants to be
a rapper, a singer, or some big-time producer. He was gonna
trade some of our *skittles* for these heavy duty CD decks. You
know the ones that can burn a couple hundred CD's at a time.
He was gonna manufacture his own product, sell 'em on the
internet, and cut out the middle man."

"Middle man whooped Bill's ass tonight," Mike mumbled
as he pressed his hand against the loosening bandages covering
his neck.

"Wild Bill wanted us to go legitimate with the music.
We'd finally be able to rinse our money clean. Doesn't sound
like a crazy idea now."

"Who was Bill gonna make the swap with?"

"I met him once. He was a deejay at this rave in Little
Five Points. He's Jamaican or African. He buys a lot of pills
from us, but he really makes his money selling bootlegs." Marco
stopped talking as his mind wandered from the question he
thought he answered.

"Marco. A name?" Mike asked, breaking Marco's trance.

"DJ Afrika is what he goes by in the clubs. Wild Bill
calls him Mubarek."

The name pulled Mike from his seat.

* * *

3:52 AM. Auburn Avenue. High atop the steeple of the
Ebenezer Baptist Church, a fluorescent cross and "Jesus Loves"
sign glowed in blue neon lights. It had been a long time since
the Reverend Doctor King had been around here to preach the
good gospel.

It was Friday night at the *Royal Peacock*--a legendary
nightspot that had hosted the careers of legends like Ray
Charles, Gladys Knight, and Stevie Wonder. Mike Drake
legged up the steep, wooden stairs to the club's entrance where
he was searched, before he stepped into the pounding darkness.

Inside the small, crowded nightclub, Mubarek manned
the spinning turntables, skillfully driving the ethnic ebb and
flow of the crowd with his musical craft. The dance floor
whirled in a tribal swarm, driven by soulful drums, reggae
chants, and break beats inspired by the severed bloodlines of
the African diaspora.

Mubarek looked down from the DJ booth and spotted
Mike milling through the crowd. Stalling for time, Mubarek
cued another record and the crowd went wild. A rhythmic
frenzy washed over the dance floor, trapping Mike inside the
tide of dancing bodies.

Mubarek removed his headphones and shouted into the
ear of a broad shouldered bodyguard posted at the booth door.

As Mike neared, the bodyguard blocked the path to the
DJ booth. Two wiry-eyed, dark skinned goons clamored closer,
also offering support.

"Tell Mubarek I need to talk to 'em!" Mike shouted over
the blaring music."

"And who are you *muddah fuckah*?" the giant bodyguard
arrogantly asked with a rumbling African accent.

"Tell 'em, it's Mike Drake. He'll know the name."

"DJ Afrika is spinnin' the good vibe now. He'll talk to
you tomorrow, or maybe the day after that, *I dunno.* Maybe, he
won't see you at all."

"Let him know he talks to me sooner or later, whether
he likes it or not. And I'm talkin' to *you* now. The next time I

come for Mubarek, if you or anybody else gets in my way...then you gotta fuckin' problem on your hands, brotha."

Mike walked off.

"I no scared of no soft ass American niggah!" the African bodyguard growled and pounded his chest. "Fear is for cowards with no God and no heart."

* * *

8:00 AM. *Candler-Smith Warehouse.* One of Mubarek's largest manufacturing plants was buried inside a loft-style complex in southwest Atlanta that housed an eclectic set of artists, mechanics, and musicians in a Southern Bohemian lifestyle.

Mike kicked the large African guard directly in the stomach, sending the man crashing through the warehouse door. On the plant floor, packs of African employees turned from their production jobs and trained on the ruckus.

Rushing to assert his control, an angry African supervisor yelled and ranted in some language Mike completely couldn't understand.

"What?" Mike frowned, racked the chamber of his MP5 submachine, and triggered. The bullets ruptured the walls of CD duplication trays and computer monitors as dozens of African workers scurried for cover.

It took ten minutes for Mike to pick out a selection of free items, and another twenty for the African supervisor to load the Lamborghini's trunk with designer knock-off purses and clothes, bootleg CD's, and DVD's of all the latest movie releases.

"Be sure to tell Mubarek, I'm comin' to get my watch," Mike ordered. "Today!" And he slammed the car trunk.

42

Mike parked at the Bankhead Flea Market and opened his stuffed trunk as a crowd of ghetto kids circled the strange looking Santa Claus in the sharp, silver Italian sleigh with a 400-reindeer-powered engine under the trunk.

"Take these purses home to ya mommas. Tell 'em Mike Drake said Merry Christmas." Mike carelessly passed out bootleg records, clothes, and movies—all free contraband from Mubarek's warehouse.

"It ain't Christmas till it gets cold," a snotty-nosed little boy complained as he took a pile of CD's.

"Well give it back then," Mike answered. "Li'l ungrateful nigga."

* * *

Across the parking lot, the *Street Life Record Shop* rested in a busy corner of the strip mall.

"Mubarek that's him! He's the one that shoot up the warehouse this morning," the skinny Nigerian lookout said, pointing into the parking lot.

Mubarek stood in his shop doorway, watching Mike pass out gifts. "Is that my things, he's giving away?" Mubarek furiously asked. Mike looked over and waved. Mubarek stepped away from the door, dialing his cell phone.

* * *

Ten minutes later, the free gifts were gone, and Mike entered the record shop. Stepping inside, he walked past the skinny Nigerian lookout who suddenly whistled out loud, warning of the unexpected visitor's arrival. Kneeling behind the glass counter case, Khalid Mubarek thumbed through a cardboard box crammed with neatly aligned CD's. Alerted by the signal, Mubarek calmly closed the box hiding its contents and stood up smiling. Mubarek was a tall, gaunt Nigerian, with coal black skin, and piercing eyes that always seemed to glow with a yellowish tint. Never short of words, his dominant accent drowned every syllable he spoke.

"Mike Drake, my man," Mubarek greeted Mike with his arms spread wide open as if he expected to be hugged.

"What's the deal Mubarek? How ya been?" Mike asked as he leaned over the counter.

Mubarek shook his head and let his arms drop, his hands slapping his hips. "I'm just a poor boy from the slums of Lagos tryin' to make an honest dollar in America. You know how I do, eh?"

"Yeah, the whole city knows how you do." Mike glanced at the shelves lining the wall behind Mubarek. There were dozens of bootlegs CD's and DVD's lining wall racks--always the premiere releases. In the back room there were thousands more. Mubarek was one of the biggest bootleggers in the state and had become a multi-millionaire in the process.

"I need some help, Mubarek." Mike leaned in close and dropped his voice. "You heard anything about a robbin' crew? Four cats, well armed, wearin' Fulton County Sheriffs' gear?"

Mubarek rubbed his chin, trying hard to look like he was searching his mental data banks. "No, Big Mike. I haven't heard *no t'ing* like *dat.* You sure they're from this hood?"

"I couldn't be any surer."

"Young men got no respect for hard work. Them want to take what them want. It's no good for business. Bad spirits for *e'rybody,*" Mubarek said. "Them get you for something?"

Mike slammed his pistol through a glass CD glass, shattering it into a thousand fragments. Mubarek never

flinched. The boisterous calamity brought three heavy-set Africans from
the back storeroom.

"You gotta problem out here, Mubarek?" one of the Africans asked in a deep growl. It was the same muscle-bound bodyguard from the *Royal Peacock Club.*

BLAM! Mike fired a shot that gashed the wall inches from the giant African's head. This time the entire room flinched.

"Big Zulu, what I tell ya the other night?" Mike waved his gun at the giant African. "Don't interrupt me again."

"Put the gun down, Mike. If the heart attack knock me down, nobody gone give me mouth-to-mouth resuscitation." Mubarek laughed awkwardly, trying to ease the tension. He wasn't so relaxed now. The skinny man guarding the door chimed in with a chirping, bird-like giggle. Mike's second gun targeted the thin man and the laughter halted.

"Like I was saying, they got a time piece o' mine. Be sure to let 'em know I want my shit back."

"Calm down, brethren," Mubarek said as he waved his goons off. "Calm yourself too, Mike."

Very few people on the street knew that Mubarek would take stolen high-end jewelry, large karat diamonds, gold, silver, platinum, and convert the contraband into cash for enterprising local thieves. Mubarek still wasn't convinced that Mike knew this, but he wasn't taking any chances. "I sell the music. That's all I do."

"Don't fuck with me, Mubarek! I ain't in the mood." Mubarek's face went limp.

"I'm truly sorry. If I could help you, I would." Mubarek smiled with a toothy white grin—the type of smile slick, smart asses reserve for slave masters and people who they think are dumber than them.

"Robbin' me is gonna get you killed, Mubarek." Mike promised as he walked to the door. "And nobody sleeps till I get my watch back."

"And I wish you a good day too, my friend!" Mubarek

cheered halfheartedly, all the courage drained from his body. As he watched Mike climb into his car and drive away, Mubarek hastily grabbed his cell phone and punched in a number.

"Yeah, this is Mubarek. I don't care what you say about callin' you. It's Mike Drake. He just left my shop!"

* * *

"What the hell you mean Drake's still alive?" Officer Alexander asked excitedly with his cell phone firmly pressed to his ear. "Alright, where's he now? I'll take care of it, Mubarek."

"Hold up," Danny Diablo said as he stood nearby, listening to the call. He turned, yelling into the garage. "Yo, Tank! Didn't we kill Drake the other night?

"I hit him chest high with the Mossberg," a voice chimed from an adjacent office. "That oughta done it. But remember he chased us."

"Then you caught 'em with some good shots when we was on the highway," admitted a second deep voice. "He musta crashed at 'bout a hundred miles an hour."

"There it is," Danny said.

"Mubarek's seeing ghosts then," Alexander brewed, "He says Mike Drake just trashed his shop, and shot up one of his CD plants just flush us out in the open." Officer Alexander dropped into his patrol car.

Danny Diablo gnawed on his bottom lip as he filtered the boiling scenario through his head. "That was my girl Pleazure and one o' her partners they found dead in the Chattahoochee River. We was all at the *Flame* the other night when Drake's girl shows up with an easy play," Danny Diablo remembered. "Next morning early, I get a call from some Mexican threatening to get us for robbin' 'em. I'm like, which Mexican is you? I done robbed plenty. Now the more I think about it, the more I know it was a set-up." Danny Diablo shook his head as he made his final decision. "We gone have to see about Mike Drake."

43

From the flea market parking lot, Mike turned right back onto Bankhead Highway heading south toward Interstate 285. In his rearview mirror, he could see a disgruntled Mubarek leaning in the doorway of the record shop, talking on a cell phone.

Further down the street, Mike noticed patrol officers starting to gather along the strip. The Lamborghini purred into the main entrance of Bowen Homes. There were Mercedes Benzes, Porsche Cayenne wagons, and even a Ferrari in the projects parked along the roadway. Why? *'Cause concrete business is good in the city.*

Mike didn't come back often. There were too many memories around here that refused to go away--the yellow exterior walls; the fading painting of a young black child alongside the words, "*Care...Watch.*" A haunting warning that has served as a constant reminder of the dozens of black children, boys and girls, slain during the *Missing and Murdered Children* ordeal of the late 70s and early 80s--an unimaginable time when a serial killer stalked the city and held an entire nation's attention.

On a lone path midway down Shiver Street, Mike spotted the man he was looking for.

"Mister Whitfield!" Mike greeted with a smile.

"Li'l ol' Mike Drake, junior! Look what the cat done dragged in. Whatcha you doing 'round here, boy?" Mister Whitfield grinned back. "I heard ya had finally made a life for yourself in the Army."

"I did for a while," Mike said, "then they ran outta foreigners for me to kill."

"Give them crackers in the White House some time. They'll find some other poor country to raid," Mister Whitfield said sarcastically.

"I need to know about a robbin' crew that's been putting their muscle down around here lately," Mike said.

"How come? They been causin' you some trouble?"

"Something like that."

"There's all kind o' troubles 'round here, son." Mister Whitfield removed his fishing hat, and wiped the sweat from his wrinkled forehead. "We gotchya dirty cops, murderers, pimps, junkies. Then there's them ungrateful ass *young-uns* runnin' 'round here with all *'dis* dope and money, flashin' them guns. Damn fools don't know where they come from, don't care where they going."

"I need to find them," Mike said.

"I can't rightly say who they are. But I can get ya close. All you gotta do is keep an eye on this Officer Alexander. David Alexander, I hear."

"Alexander's with the APD?" Mike asked in disbelief.

"Sad ain't it?" Mister Whitfield shook his head in dismay and traced his loafered foot across the dirt. "A black cop bleeding his own people is worse than the devil himself. A brother like that don't deserve nothin' but death. Back in my day we'd a done away with 'em."

"What's he got to do with these robberies?" Mike asked.

"I hear my nephews and all complaining about how Alexander is extorting everybody, controllin' things. Now who a criminal gonna run to when the law's the one doin' the stealin'. Officer Alexander even givin' crews the heads up about police raids if you're payin' enough."

"He's one helluva law man, ain't he?" Mike pondered.

"Go talk to the *Plant Man*, he can help you better than I can. If ya in some real trouble, he can sort it out for ya."

Mister Whitfield placed his straw hat back on and tried

to focus his squinting eyes. "You lookin' a lot like yo daddy, boy. But you ain't foolin' me. You ain't nothin' like him." Mister Whitfield's brow arched over a discerning eye.

"I don't get ya old man?"

"You ain't who they *think* you is, Mike Drake. You got something real slick goin' on. I just pray you run it slicker and faster than the way me and yo' daddy did."

"That's strange advice comin' from a man standing out in the projects in a two-thousand dollar pair of Louis Vuitton loafers," Mike noticed, staring down at the inconspicuous, tan shoes on Mister Whitfield's feet. "My daddy told me 'bout the money you had stuffed away. Aunt Irene and Marlene said, twenty years ago, you had to be a millionaire," Mike said.

"*SHHHH!* Don't be talkin' foolishness like that 'round these cutthroats." Mister Whitfield whipped his head around scouring for prying ears. "What's my business is my business." He winked at Mike, and whispered, "I'm still rich!"

"Why don't you move out to one of them high-rise old folks' homes?" Mike asked. "Enjoy the money."

"Money or no money, I can't leave the ghetto," Mister Whitfield said. "I do that and there won't be nobody left to lead the children outta here. Some listen to me. Some don't. Either way, I gotta spit the truth."

"You could give your money away."

"Like the billionaire that built that big ol' fish tank downtown?" the old man growled.

"It's an aquarium."

"Crackers will spend *bookoo-millions* on a giant fish tank, but won't spend a dime on nothin' to help the poor man out." Mister Whitfield was on a roll. "There's a giant white fish that billionaire cracker keeps shippin' over here too. He kills one of them every few months or so, then has to order another fish from that China man."

"It's a giant tiger shark or something," Mike shrugged in bewilderment. "You going somewhere with this or is this just senile, old folk crazy talk?"

"Don't get smart with me, boy! You know why them fish

keep fallin' over dead?"

"Why old man?"

"How'd the damn fish get from China-man town to here? Tell me that!"

"They put it on a truck, drove it to a plane, and flew it over."

"Aha! Whales don't come outta the water and drive trucks. Hell, you ever seen a whale fly a plane! That's what I'm gettin' at, boy! Keep your ass where you belong and don't do nothing you ain't got no damn business doing! That's the secret of life!"

"Yeah...old man, are you on some type o' medication?"

"Don't mock me, fool!"

"Thanks for the word," Mike said and turned, walking back to his car.

"You see them NAACP folk on TV, tryin' to bury the N-word. They even had a real funeral. Silly niggas!" Mister Whitfield waddled along, slowly chasing Mike. "Go on then, walk away. You ain't gotta listen to me, I just want somebody to shoot the shit with."

"Get outta the heat, Mister Whitfield. You're cookin' your brain," Mike warned.

"Your daddy died way too young, boy. You gonna die the same way if ya don't change your ways," Mister Whitfield warned, still straddling along.

Mister Whitfield removed his hat again, fanning himself with it. "I done paid ten years in prison for my troubles. Then I come home and tried to do right by folk. That was my price for living the fast life. *Whatchyou* done paid, boy?"

"Nothing...old man. Nothing at all," Mike's voice faded in the distance.

"Hell...not yet, young nigga. Not yet!" Mister Whitfield laughed until his chest erupted in a hacking mucus filled cough, and he spit into the dirt. *"Whoooo,* boy! I crack myself up sometimes!"

44

As he drove from Bowen Homes, Mike mulled over the sage words of wisdom Mister Whitfield had planted on him. Mike was nothing like his father and in every way the very same man.

Suddenly, blue lights flickered in his rearview. Mike veered the car into a gas station parking lot. In his side view mirror he watched an Atlanta Police Officer step from the car and casually dawn a pair of aviator shades. As the officer approached, Michael dropped the power window.

"This here's a pretty nice piece of machinery. What did this cost you?" Officer Alexander asked as he ran his hand over the car's roof.

"A quarter-million and change," Mike said.

"Lamborghini Mercialago, eh? These things still have that overheating problem like the Countach, and the old style Diablos."

"Not really. They reworked the whole cooling system. She can run top haul over longer distances like it ain't nothing," Mike played along calmly. "What can I do for you officer?

"You can't do shit for me. You know who I am?" Alexander asked.

"Should I really give a fuck?" Mike returned the disrespect. The corners of Alexander's mouth instantly curled up.

"Get outta the car," Alexander ordered. As Mike climbed from the cockpit, Alexander twirled him around, and cuffed his wrists so tight the metal bands cut into his skin.

"Owww! I gotta sweet Spanish bitch like it rough just like you," Mike laughed. Furious, Officer Alexander threw a vicious punch into Mike's rib cage. Gasping for air, Mike laughed through the pain. "That's the American way!"

Alexander whispered into Mike's ear. "You know you can't cruise 'round my town like you own it. No, sir. You gotta pay taxes before you get to flex up and down my strip like you the boss."

Alexander shoved Mike into the backseat of the patrol car, and he tumbled inside, his head slamming against the opposite door. As he painfully sat up, he watched Officer Alexander walk back to the Lamborghini and reach inside. The illegal search went on for a few minutes until Alexander emerged from the car with a small wrapped packaged in his hand.

"What the hell's that?" Mike whispered. Then he dropped his head, realizing that the *set-up* was in full effect.

"Not bad, Drake. I figure this is 'bout a quarter-brick of *coke* and I also found a gun in the dash. The serial numbers been filed off. That my friend is a federal offense."

"You're makin' the biggest mistake of ya life," Mike warned.

Alexander radioed in the traffic stop again and began to fill out his paperwork.

"What's wrong big timer?" Alexander asked, peering into the rear rearview mirror. "You ain't talkin' so slick now."

"I'm a patient man. I'll take care of you later."

"Now is that a threat? Don't you know the penalty for making terroristic threats to an officer of the law."

"Do whatcha do. I'll be back on the street before your shift ends."

"Ohh, I doubt that very seriously."

Mike leaned back and closed his eyes. "You just remember I warned you. This was the biggest fuckin' mistake you ever made in ya useless life."

"Could be. But I don't worry too much about them

Mexicans you're dealing with, Mike. See to me, they're just visiting our hometown on borrowed time. Besides, I'm a cop, nigga. They come after me and this whole city heats up on them. Most of 'em illegal any-fuckin'-way. You think for a minute a bunch of wetbacks is gonna go toe-to-toe with the whole Goddamn police force?"

Officer Alexander went through Mike's wallet taking his Visa and American Express Cards, then he typed the driver's license information into the data terminal. The screen showed no priors. Alexander frowned. "You gotta pretty clean record here, Mike. At least you did. I figured a heavyweight like you would've had a couple of knocks...misdemeanors...a felony here and there."

"It costs to be this free. I gotta cop-eatin' shark for a lawyer and he spits with a million dollar mouthpiece."

"Good, 'cause you're gonna need him when I'm done."

Mike knew there was more going on than he could tell so far. Alexander was too confident about the charges sticking. With no prior arrests and less than a kilo of soft white, there was a solid chance that Mike would get off. *It's the gun,* Mike realized.

"Them 'cuffs fittin' you okay?"

"They're perfect," Mike returned. The handcuffs were so tight he couldn't feel his fingers anymore. Still, he refused to put his pain and suffering on display for Alexander's personal entertainment.

The dispatcher squawked back on the static filled radio, reeling off a full name, date of birth, and confirming that there were no outstanding arrest warrants for the suspect. Fifteen minutes later the tow truck pulled up and a grease stained driver quickly hoisted the Lamborghini onto the flatbed.

"Not one fuckin' scratch!" Mike yelled from the back seat. It was then that he noticed the small crowd of black kids forming around the parking lot. There were young wide-eyed boys in white T-shirts, with dreaded hair flowing from beneath fitted baseball caps, and little fast ass girls in tight, cut-off jean shorts, and tank tops and flip-flops. The children were stunned by the sleek design of the Lamborghini, hoping to one day be able to ride one.

As he watched them stare in awe, Mike realized that he was their dream. They were willing to risk everything he was going through just for a damn car. *These kids probably know a lot more about Officer Alexander than I do.* But how many actually knew how far this cop would go to get them out of his way. Any one of these neighborhood boys and girlies could be in the back of this police car with a pure bag of dope and a hot weapon planted by a rogue cop, but they wouldn't have a tenth of Mike's resources to rescue them from this sticky situation.

These kids are why I do who what I do for a livin'...I'm hunting killers to save them.

Mike watched the tow truck roll away with his Italian supercar riding piggyback. As he passed by, the grinning tow truck driver honked his horn and waved with grimy hands.

"Say *bye-bye* to the Lamborghini fuckhead," Alexander chuckled and cranked his car. "Next stop...Rice Street Blues."

Alexander pulled onto Bankhead and headed due north toward downtown. It was a beautiful sun-coated afternoon, Mike noticed for the first time. It took losing his freedom to finally feel the sunlight. Alexander checked his rearview where his eyes met Mike's icy stare.

"You got something to say to me?"

"What makes you think I'm gonna let you get away with some shit like this?"

"Who's gonna stop me?" Alexander arrogantly huffed. "What? You expect me to risk my life everyday, chasing after these young fools for a measly thirty-two-thousand a year while niggas like you pullin' down six and seven figures tax free? You're cruisin' up and down my block. My fuckin' block! Pushin' a Lamborghini, flaunting it in my face."

Mike knew he had a point. "There's other ways of gettin' it. You're wearing a badge, man, coming down on your own folk."

"You wanna lecture me now? You got a pair of nuts on you, Drake. Gotta love that about ya. But niggas like you never know when you're ahead. Just too greedy to know when to fuckin' quit, so you grind until you get caught, or your dumb asses get killed. Me, I put myself in a position of power so that it's damn near impossible for me to ever get caught. And as far as killing me? Well...shit if you can touch me before I touch you, then so be it."

Peering from the window, Mike saw more uniformed officers on motorcycles, whirling like striking eagles, their blue lights flashing, pulling other drivers over. It was an afternoon sweep in the neighborhood. Half a dozen automobiles were being searched. Mike wondered if there were police roadblocks going up in Buckhead or Roswell, or any of the other upper-income white enclaves across the city. *Hell naw...White folks wouldn't have it.*

This was where Atlanta officers, good and bad, were most likely to catch struggling poor folks driving with no insurance, suspended licenses, and improper tags—all probable cause for a legal search to find cash and drugs, most of which never made it to the police evidence room. Underpaid and overworked, some Atlanta cops had discovered that the easiest way to get a raise was to take it from the pockets and trunks of their local neighborhood dope boys. *It was better than winning the Georgia lottery.* Further still, each arrest, jail bond, and subsequent court fine would bring much needed money to the city coffers. Atlanta was making an honest earning from breaking the poor man's back. Taxin' niggas.

God bless America.

45

901 RICE STREET

It was known to the locals as simply *Rice Street*. Only TV reporters and lame newcomers, out-of town visitors, lawyers, judges, and Feds called it by its full name--*Fulton County Jail*.

It was an impressive dungeon of horrors expanding over 450,000 square feet, fourteen-stories, and seven levels of terror for your displeasure. Opened in 1989, the 1,280 bed facility now housed, stored, and tortured more than 3,000 inmates daily. *God bless America.*

Officer Alexander pulled into the prisoner drop-off zone, and opened the rear door. Mike stepped clumsily from back seat, jerking his arm away from Alexander's helping hand.

"Be nice nigga, before I taser yo' ass," Alexander threatened.

"I'll see you in the streets," Mike cursed. "Don't forget to duck."

Alexander's face shrunk in fury. In his mind Mike was better off dead. *But there's always a better time and place for murder.*

"Don't count on it, player. This is your *last* stop," Alexander whispered into Mike's ear. They moved into the staging room and Alexander removed the handcuffs. Mike rubbed his stinging wrists where the metal had left a ringed bruise.

Inside the white, brick walled room a tall, muscle-bound sheriff popped on latex gloves. "Face the wall, take off your shoes. Empty your pockets," the sheriff commanded.

Mike obediently turned, kicking off his loafers, and dropped his wallet on the floor. The sheriff searched the shoes, then thumbed through Mike's wallet, looking for small hidden weapons, or any undiscovered contraband. "Okay, grab ya stuff and head that way," he pointed.

Mike lifted his scant belongings and stuffed them back into his pocket. His sore ribs throbbed in sync with the beat of his heart. He was escorted through two glass doors to a large waiting room where rows of uncomfortable, dark blue plastic seats held other inductees. The polished white floors reflected the pale light cast from aged fixtures hanging above.

"Head count!" a voice rang out. The blue chairs emptied as everyone stood. Guards corralled the prisoners into a large holding room with green walls and another polished white floor.

"This shit's real fucked up, *homes*!" a frustrated voice blasted out."

"I know it's fucked up," a less than concerned sheriff said as he stepped into the room, fanning a clipboard. "The problem is ya'll decided to get locked up on the weekend. Processing is gonna be real slow. We're working with a skeleton staff. When you get outta here make sure you tell somebody about it. Maybe things'll get right around here. Until then, welcome to the world famous Rice Street, where getting in is a whole lot easier than gettin' out. And the only way to get outta here *quick* is if ya know somebody. Now when I call ya name, just let me know you heard it." The officer traced down his clipboard, harking names as their owners chimed back.

Twenty minutes later, they were all herded like cattle back to their blue seats in the outer waiting area.

Fingerprinting process was two-fold: there was the time-honored, old school way with criminal hands rolled in slimy black ink, then there was the modern high-tech method where fingers were digitally scanned into a computer. Not since Herbert Hoover inducted fingerprinting to the National Crime

Information Center (NCIC) has the system been so thorough.

Tired men stared at a small TV mounted on the wall. Below the TV, a doorway opened to the nursing station where overworked technicians provided blood tests for AIDS, HIV, tuberculosis, and whatever scourge of germs had been wrangled inside this cramped building.

Mike rested his hands behind his head and got comfortable. *Why not? There's plenty of entertainment.* There were maniacs screaming for God to come and post bail. Men peered from a small glass panel, locked in the quarantine room--their battered bodies harboring some infectious diseases that no one wanted to acquire.

"Martin Luther King's turnin' over in his grave the way y'all niggas down here actin'!" a grey-haired schizophrenic preached at the top of his mad lungs.

"You gone sit down and shut up," a lady deputy warned. 'Don't make me have to tell ya again!'"

The mad man shook his crusty fist at her.

"You ain't that crazy," she said and rolled her eyes.

Homeless nomads scoffed down trays of bad meat, waiting to be *dressed-out* and taken upstairs to bunk down in a concrete suite for the weekend--a vacation spot from hot summer days and frigid winter nights. The City had recently passed a law against vagrancy and apparently the jails were the cure for clearing the downtown business district. In years past, it was just a misdemeanor charge that would have sent a man a few blocks away to the Atlanta City jail, which was now underutilized with plenty of space to spare.

"Shit! Goddamit! God's gone come down on ya. Gone kill us all!" the same gray-haired schizoid cursed at high volume. *"Treatin' a man bad like this! Quick to lock a nigga up! Real quick! Sho'-nuff slow to let a nigga's ass outta here!"*

Annoyed officers charged the crazy man as he ranted on. The guards fought hard, securing his kicking legs.

Maybe he's crazy. Maybe he's a prophet.

The officers dragged the screaming prophet into a small room just out of sight of everyone. Mike heard the sparked *buzz* of an electric taser-gun, and in the corner of the door he saw the prophets legs shaking in spastic kicks as 40,000 volts of electricity ripped though his nervous system.

The blood's gotta heat up...his heart could stop.
Mike rubbed his own chest, feeling the prophet's pain.

"C'mon, Miss Lady! Please, Miss Sarge," begged a saggy pants inmate already dressed in county blues.

"Boy, don't try me now! Y'all know me better than that!" she yelled back, letting him know that he couldn't press his luck--not on her shift. "Give me a minute and I'll get everybody to the phone. Just hold on," Miss Sarge promised. Her voice was reassuring like a mother's breath on a child's face.

Miss Sarge was a tiny black woman, not an inch over five feet, regal in her brown sheriff's deputy uniform, with nothing but a can of mace and a bad attitude to defend herself. She demanded respect because she gave it to those that deserved it.

On the opposite side of the waiting room, women prisoners were kept secluded in their own world. Mike studied the assortment of ladies waiting, longing for freedom. A middle-aged white woman sat sobbing and shaking in utter disbelief that she of all people could end up in a place like this. She was too scared. This was here first time.

She's probably in on some silly misdemeanor.
Failure to appear. She ain't no virgin no mo'.

Three seats away, a young black woman, twenty-five at the oldest, blanketed in a satin Donna Karan dress, and designer pumps, sat with her arms folded and her legs crossed neatly. Her silence was hardened and polished. *This ain't nothin' knew for her. Identity theft. Third Offense. Forgery in the first degree. Looking at a year easy.*

Mike snickered and rubbed his tired eyes. The sad, patient women reminded him of another Rice Street saga. A few years back, a female inmate escaped from a maximum security wing while guards were serving as extras during the authorized filming of a rap music video. The lady escapee was a convicted forger jailed on a parole violation. She was wearing the same blue medical scrubs she had on when she entered the jail. She simply strolled out an employee entrance. Luckily for the jail administration, she was caught at a gas station some six hours later. That same escapee is now suing the jail under allegations that deputy sheriffs were so embarrassed by her escape that, upon her return, they severely beat her until she was unconscious. *Ouch!*

This was the volatile soup. Vagrants, criminal trespass, armed robbery, murder, sodomy, and child molestation all mixed in one pot. *Blue* arm bands signified misdemeanors. *Red* bands marked the felony charges. And too many inmates sat smiling and laughing comfortably. *Some of these cats are way too used to this. Just another day on the grind.*

Inmates in orange jumpsuits, shackled hands-to-waist-to-ankles walked inside. They were being transferred in from neighboring Dekalb County to satisfy pending jurisdictional warrants, fighting through the paperwork, trying to tread water in this muddy system. As time passed, other suited inmates entered the waiting area in various colored jumpsuits: Henry County, Cobb County a once white-enclave, Clayton County, and that dirty Douglas County where a first offense could get you maxed out --*ten, fifteen, twenty years to the door*-- depending on how bad you'd crossed that Dixie Line. Redneck judges proved with a gavel and an ink pen that niggas couldn't get away with that stupid shit in their jurisdiction.

No forgiveness. Jail was the new slavery. And second chances only come after you get paroled. *Strange fruit dies real slow in here,* Mike worried. A white man didn't have to lynch you anymore. *That would be too easy on you niggas. We'll just let y'all hang yourselves now.* All he has to do is wait until he catches you disobeying the laws of his land and sentence you to so much hard time that you wish they would hang your sorry ass from a tree. *Death penalty's waiting if ya got the balls to reach the electric chair. Last nigga to die turn out the lights.*

Mike remembered a bitter story told so sweet by Aunts Irene and Marlene about their cousin Aubrey. He had died in the Georgia electric chair in 1954 and to this day still holds that claim as the only family member to have done so.

Cousin Aubrey, never a bright man, had been riding with a crazy Jew named Hiccup who killed another Jewish store owner in downtown Atlanta on the site where the Sam Nunn Federal Building now stands. Aubrey admitted that he was in on the robbery, but it had been Hiccup who pulled the trigger. Mister Hiccup never confessed otherwise, but every time Irene and Marlene saw that *"...murderin', back-stabbin' Jew..."* in public they made sure they showered him with the country curses he deserved.

Then it occurred to Mike that '*Old Smokey*', Georgia's fabled electric chair, had been ceremoniously retired a few years back. Lethal injection was the new state-sectioned method of human waste disposal.

Live by the sword...die by the needle.

Mike's attention darted from one scene to another. Jailhouse street lawyers consoled new inmate clients. Jittery, wanted men sitting on alias names waited, praying like hell they can post bond before the NCIC data search brings back their real identity. *Don't give up hope though. Fingerprints don't lie, but this is Rice Street and shit happens. They mighty just let you out by mistake anyway.*

"I see you done calmed your nerves down," Miss Sarge said to the once screaming schizophrenic. The man shuffled to a seat, calmly crossed his legs, and grinned crazily.

"When I call ya name, I want you in cell 367! And move like you're tryin' to get outta here in a hurry!" Miss Sarge called out and began reading from a list, "Lockhart, Eckersley, Drake...."

Mike chuckled at the comedy and rose from his seat, heading for his designated holding cell. Thirty captured men huddled into the smelly space designed for maybe fifteen. There was one aluminum toilet that no one was allowed to use. The lingering smell of urine and musty breath clogged your nostrils. The benches along the wall filled up fast, while others took refuge on the nasty concrete floor.

The musty funk of dirty men coiled in an obnoxious cloud as Mike stood against the wall, leaning his heavy head against the plexi-glass window, looking to the outer waiting area. Behind him, a white business man mumbled, "I can't believe this. I can't believe she did this to me...I just can't believe...."

"Believe cracker...*BELIEVE!!*" the same schizo bum screamed at the dumbfounded white man. "You're a guest of the county, *CRACKER!* Now move yo' rich ass over and let me get comfortable!" The laughter exploded as black faces smiled in a moment of sheer comedy. Even the white man had to grin. He was still safe, at least for now.

This shit is better than TV, Mike smiled.

Killing more time, Mike stared blankly at the white business man from head to toe. The man was neatly dressed in khaki pants, and a sky blue Polo shirt. He didn't belong here. Hell, nobody did. *Well, maybe some of these folks do.*

"I can't believe she called the police," the white man said out loud, his fluttering tongue running under its own power.

"My bitch called the folks on me too."

A dozen or so men joined in the jailhouse rally against domestic violence. Their home troubles were the unifying reasons most of them were there. "Goddamn O. J. Simpson got us all fucked up!"

There were tales of girlfriends, wives, and baby's mammas that they didn't hit, punch, or slap, but the ladies called the fuckin' cops anyway.

Stupid dudes dating stupid broads; the flashing thought startled Mike. The situation was far more complex than that. He'd seen a sweet woman drive a bad man to complete rage. He remembered hiding in a dark kitchen corner, crying while his irate mother followed his father through the house screaming, cajoling. Looking back, he knew his father deserved it. But every man has his breaking point.

Still don't make hittin' momma right.

Momma's mouth was full of blood when she fell over the sink, spitting, crying, her face swelling. Li'l Mike would bring her a washcloth packed with ice cubes. "It'll be okay, momma." The front door slammed as Mike's father left for the arms of his young mistress. "Fuck ya, pops. Rot in hell ol' man."

Mike glared at the black faces around him, storing this jail drama for future reference. He'd never realized how so few of these scared little boys had been equipped with the mechanisms to ward off a woman's scolding. Then when unfocused rage mixed with romance the result was explosive.

A man coughed and buried his face in his hands. It was a cable repairman still in his work uniform. *What the hell's that all about?* Mike shook his head in wonder.

Wasting more time, Mike scanned the ceiling, looking for vents. He'd heard stories of microphones in the roof.

Loose lips sink ships.

A gold-toothed smile joked about the motorcycle chase across Maddox park that had ended in his arrest. The animated storyteller was part of a Bankhead crew that robbed a trainload of expensive four-stroke dirt bikes and four-wheelers when the *World of Motorcross* hit the Georgia Dome a few years back. Mike remembered the case.

A million dollars worth of machinery raced away in the middle of the night and vanished into the ghetto. Two years later, there were still dozens of stolen motorcycles still on the street.

Six more hours slowly crept by as Mike waited for his reprieve from the Rice Street gallows. He'd made his one obligatory phone call and set the wheels of his release in motion. All he could do now was wait it out.

Where the hell are they?

46

COUNTY BLUES

"Drake!" The seated sheriff yelled from behind his desk. Mike dragged himself from his seat and walked to the table.

"You got any money you wanna turn in?" the sheriff asked as he lifted a large, gray plastic container from the floor.

"Y'all got it," Mike sneered and shook his head. "One of ya dirty cop buddies just robbed me of every dime I had on me."

"Tell it to your pastor," the sheriff grunted and checked for the next name on his clipboard. "Turner!"

Mike picked up the container and walked off with a group of prisoners to the dressing room.

"Keep your item slips. You'll need it to pick up your money and your stuff on the way outta here," a sheriff instructed as a dozen inmates stripped down, replacing their civilian attire with dark blue Fulton County uniforms.

"Y'all bullshittin'!" a mouthy inmate jeered. "I ain't tradin' in my silk *draw's* for no county underwear!"

"Take off *everything* you came in here with and place it in the plastic container," the frustrated sheriff ordered.

"Fuck that. I'm already locked up! What else you gone do?" the inmate lipped off again.

"Always a jackass in every bunch. That's how you loudmouth niggas got in here in the first place," the sheriff said angrily.

Dressed for the occasion, the troop was shackled together in a human train of twelve men and herded off through a series of sliding doors. They escaped into a long, white-walled hallway. "Stay to the right," the voice ordered. The chained slaves pushed over, leaving the left side of the hall clear for passage in the opposite direction.

The *clinking* of the steel restraints echoed from the drab concrete walls. *There are ghosts in this building.* Mike imagined what it must've been like to walk into the gallows of a slave ship. *What if I was facing five, ten, twenty years to life and this was day one?* Mike could feel his soul trying to escape this cursed building. *Ray Nichols should've killed himself instead of comin' back here.*

The cattle drive ended in a staging area where the slaves in blue were released from their bonds and granted their county issued, tax payer funded amenities--gray bed mats and a laundry bag stuffed with a toothbrush, toothpaste, complimentary inmate T-shirt, sheets, soap, and a fresh roll of toilet paper.

First Class accommodations.

* * *

6th Floor South. Silver metal tables and benches filled the bottom floor of the two-tiered dorm. As Mike and five other men entered, the present residents eyed the new visitors to the neighborhood. A few inmates stood at a bank of phones that lined the wall just past the front door of the dorm. A female sheriff muttered through roll call and cell assignments.

Mike moved his belongings into a cell on the bottom floor and dropped his mat on the naked metal bunk frame. He snickered at the sight of a single wash basin and a toilet. *Plush.*

Mike crashed to the mat, finally resting, folding his tired arms over his chest. *Just a matter of time.*

* * *

3:06 AM. "Drake!" the sheriff yelled from the open cell door. "Grab ya stuff."

"It's about time," Mike yawned and stretched his arms. He climbed from the bunk, grabbing his bed mat and laundry bag, and trailed the sheriff out of the dorm.

What time is it? Mike glanced at the watch protruding from the sheriff's swinging wrist. *3:09 AM.* It was a strange hour to be released even for Mike's people on the outside.

They climbed into an elevator and the sheriff punched the floor button. That's when Mike knew he was in trouble.

We should be going down.

47

7th FLOOR: TERRORDOME.

Someone wants me up here. He had reached the seventh floor. The steel dorm doors parted, giving way to the sounds of fighting, rowdy taunts, and violent curses. The sheriff shoved Mike inside the snake pit.

"Which cell am I supposed to be in?" Mike turned to see the sheriff walking away as the steel door banged shut.

The dorm was dangerously overcrowded with bad souls, *just waitin' to get shipped down the road so they can get the hell up outta here.* Their wrists were choked by nothing but red name bands--*all felons.* Some were carrying life sentences on their backs, while others rotted away, waiting on state trials for murder, arson, aggravated assault, armed robbery, rape, kidnapping, trafficking, and too many were about to find out what really happens to convicted felons who get caught with firearms. *Men with nothing to lose and every reason to take their pain out on your ass.*

3:20 AM. The concept of lock down was irrelevant. Up here in hell, the demons tortured each other all night long, and there wasn't a sheriff in the building that could do a damn thing about it.

I gotta get outta here. Mike dropped his mat and laundry bag near the bank of phones. Stooping, he dug into his bag, and palmed the toothbrush, securing his only weapon.

Above the dorm, a guard's observation deck overlooked the swarming prisoners. Behind the booth's tinted glass panes, two sheriffs sat watching the dorm start to boil.

"Fifty bucks say Tank kills this guy in under two minutes," a sheriff offered.

"It's a bet, Mister!" his partner matched.

Back down in the dorm, Mike reached for the telephone.

"No phone calls, nigga!" A giant hulk dressed in bright orange federal jail garb barked from the top tier. "Where the fuck you thank you at? This ain't ya momma's house!" Tank was six-foot-four and three-hundred pounds of country trouble. He rushed down the steps, and closed in on Mike, hovering over him.

Ignoring the monster, Mike dialed the phone and pressed the receiver to his ear.

"You stupid or just fuckin' deaf?" Tank asked.

"Both."

Mike struck with cobra-like quickness, smashing an open palm into the hulk's wide nose, crumpling frontal cartilage. Blood spewed from his crushed nostrils. In a blind rage, Tank threw furious punches that whipped past Mike's bobbing head, tossing gusts of air. Mike shot a powerful low kick into Tank's right knee, ripping ligaments, sending the hulk slumping to the floor. Mike swooped in, crashing a knee into Tank's skull, blasting him unconscious.

Ahhh, shit! A sea of black bodies rushed Mike as he backed off, jabbing with combat-trained precision; the pointed toothbrush handle protruding from his clenched fist gouged a prisoner in his eyeball. The wounded victim howled and collapsed in excruciating pain--his bloody hands, pressed over the leaking socket.

Weaker hearted inmates cringed at the gory sight of the one-eyed bandit and cowardly fell from the fight. But the next vicious wave of predators attacked as Mike threw a ferocious flurry of fists and elbows, smashing fragile cheek bones, and knocking teeth from broken jaws—the trained strikes felling an attacker just as the next appeared.

Heavy knuckles popped across Mike's temples, knocking him to the ground hard. *Get the fuck up!*

A kick slammed into Mike's ribs, knocking the wind from his churning lungs. Mike rolled with the force of the blow, spinning to his feet as another kick swept toward his face. Mike blocked the foot, securing the outstretched leg, and stabbed the man in the crotch. As the victim fell holding his balls, another hapless soldier swooped in too fast.

Mike side-stepped and spun him, locking him in a choke hold, using the captive's body as a shield from the onslaught of punches.

"Y'all thank y'all got the heart to fuckin' kill me!" Mike challenged. *I'll kill all of ya!* Mike tightened his bulky arms in an anaconda's grip, and lowered his head, biting the man's ear. The prisoner let out a bloodcurdling shriek as gnawing teeth sliced into rubbery flesh, tearing the ear from its perch. Mike released his choke hold. The victim hit his knees, screaming, clutching his hands over the wet, burning skin peeling from the side of his head.

Mike spit the dangling ear from his bloody lips. "Next!"

"Goddamn! That mutha fucka's *crazyyy!*" an old prisoner shouted. "Y'all betta let that fool alone 'fore he kill one of ya!" Heeding the old timers warning, the once scrappy prisoners backed off slowly. Even in 7th Floor hell that kind of cannibal brutality had to be respected, if not appreciated—but only for a little while.

Exhausted, Mike wiped the blood from his mouth and stepped over the moaning victims scattered on the floor, as he staggered back across the dorm. Bleeding from the forehead, and drenched with sweat, Mike slid to the floor with his back pressed securely against the wall of phones. He exhaled and dropped the deadly toothbrush in his lap.

Another twenty-four hours in here... I'm dead.

48

FBI Press Release

Atlanta, GA – More than two hundred friends, associates, family members, and law enforcement personnel from around the United States joined today in a heart felt dedication of the "Daniel G. Wilhelm OCDETF Task Force."
The multi-jurisdictional drug strike force is named after the slain U.S. Immigration and Customs Enforcement (ICE) Assistant Special Agent who was slain by Fulton County Courthouse shooter Ray Nichols.

The idea for the Strike Force was developed by the Special Agents in Charge of the federal law enforcement agencies here in Atlanta, and in conjunction with the United States Attorney's Office. The force was compiled to combat the growth of Atlanta as a major hub for narcotics distribution and money laundering. The new Atlanta OCDETF Strike Force will join nationwide efforts and capabilities with comparable task forces in New York City, Florida, Dallas, and Houston.

U.S. Attorney David Namath spoke today, commenting, "The Wilhelm Strike Force assembles the strengths of federal, state, and local drug enforcement agencies into one cohesive weapon. The Task Force is designed to find, investigate, and prosecute high-level members of international trafficking cartels with operations set up in metro Atlanta, and the rest of the country. The Atlanta Strike Force will not only dismantle the local branches of these cartels, but will also aggressively seek the arrest and extradition of the organization's top leadership.

We will seek forfeiture of all property and assets gained by illegal drug activity. The Atlanta office will use the memory of Daniel Wilhelm as a special way to motivate our efforts. He was a great law enforcement agent."

Attending today's dedication were U.S. Homeland Security Secretary Jeremy Chertoff, ATF Acting Direct Tony Sullivan, and other senior officials who spoke of the increased need for investigation, prosecution, and longer sentences for the people who poison our communities with drugs.

The day was highlighted by a ceremonial "fly over" by aircraft from the DEA, and a soulful rendition of the national Anthem sang by David Wilhelm's brother, also an ICE Special Agent.

The media was also given a tour of the training and support facilities used by the Strike Force.

* * *

Agent Cooper rushed from the ceremony stage. David Namath remained behind with the Secretary of Homeland Security and the senior dignitaries, conversing in a huddled circle.

Cooper had noticed Agent Stanton trying to get her attention near the end of the task force dedication, but was unable to leave until she made her brief speech. She could see Stanton's head weaving across the sea of heads in the crowd. They fought to reach each other in the fray.

Once they met, Stanton handed her a sheet of paper.

She glanced over it. "How long has he been inside?" Cooper snapped impatiently.

"About forty-eight hours now," Stanton admitted sheepishly.

"Two days! And you're just getting in touch with me?"

Agent Stanton stammered, "He'd been there for about fifteen hours before he called. Then the message sat on our desk for another day and a half while we were out on surveillance."

"What are the charges?"

"He's been arrested for possession of cocaine and one count for possession of an unregistered firearm," Stanton read from a flapping sheet of paper.

"Unregistered?" she asked surprised.

"It was an old .45 caliber Smith & Wesson. The serial numbers were etched off. The arresting officer was David Alexander."

Agent Cooper tensed at the mere mention of Officer Alexander. "I'm going to make a few phone calls to make sure that we gain jurisdiction," she fired into action. "I need you to get over to Atlanta Police Property and get a hold of that gun. You may meet some resistance, but don't take no for an answer."

Agent Stanton nodded in compliance.

"No more screw ups, Stanton, or this time next year you'll be a security guard at the Smithsonian."

49

"Drake! Mike Drake!" Miss Sarge's voice boomed from her tiny body. "Time's up!"

Mike looked up and sighed in relief. He had been forced to stay up all night, with both eyes open. As he breached the dorm door, Mike turned back to the collection of brown and black faces, any of which at any given time in the universe could have been him.

"You stupid fucks do whatcha gotta do to get outta here," Mike unconsciously growled back at them.

"You too muthafucka!" a voice mocked back.

"Yeah, keep hope alive, nigga."

"You can keep that bullshit, nigga! I need bail money!"

Downstairs, Mike dressed again, pulling items from the grey plastic container that housed all his worldly possessions. Once he was ready, a sheriff placed Mike back in handcuffs.

Mike was escorted through a corridor where a metal door released to the front waiting area. Just beyond the door, Mike could see the tired *baby's mommas, aunties, grannies, nannas, and girlfriends* waiting on their incarcerated loved ones. The sheriff carried Mike beyond that exit to a secluded cell where he quietly sat alone for another forty-five minutes.

Suddenly, the metal door slid open. Two white men stood by the front door, their stiff professional demeanor creating its own aura.

Fuckin' G-men. Mike smiled for no apparent reason. He'd never been so glad in his life to see two white boys in a pair of cheap gray suits. *What the hell took you so long?*

50

BACK ON THE FARM

The Sam Nunn Federal Center is the cornerstone of the FBI's stronghold in the southeastern United States, and houses over 5,000 employees for more than a dozen interrelated federal agencies. The facility was named for the former U.S. Senator from Georgia, and is one of the largest federal office buildings on the East Coast.

It encompasses 1.9 million square feet of space, including a ten-story mid-rise section, and an eight-story bridge that lurks over Forsyth street connecting to a twenty-four story high rise tower.

The behemoth Federal Center was designed for continuous occupancy--twenty-four hours, seven days a week-- to accommodate the complex missions of the various agencies housed in the facility. But it now stood tall on a foundation of loftier goals—to be the right hand of God, the fist of Uncle Sam, and keep law and order in the tragic city of Atlanta.

* * *

7:00 A.M. A darkly tinted Chevrolet Caprice sped down the service ramp that disappeared below Forsyth Street. The car rolled up to an innocuous security guard who flagged them down and checked the driver's credentials. A barricade arm rose and the car drove on, circling around to a rear service entrance. Yawning, Mike stepped from the back seat as he stretched his cramped arms. The morning air was fresh and crisp; a relief to stifled lungs that had been sucking in contaminated jail fumes for almost four days. Jail instantly forces a man to appreciate the minute details of life--sights, sounds, smells, tastes, fears and all.

Mike followed the grey-suited G-men up a cracked concrete ramp to a polished silver elevator door. An Agent swiped his ID card, the scanner *beeped*, flashed a green light, and the elevator doors parted. Mike and his two escorts stepped inside the cabin. Annoyed by the jailhouse odors wafting off Mike's body, the two Agents politely backed away. At the ninth floor, the elevator doors parted again and the men stepped into the corridor. The two Agents walked on without him.

"Appreciate it fellas," Mike said thankfully.

"Just watch your ass out there," one of them stated.

Mike detoured to the employee lounge and grabbed an ice pack from the freezer. *Man, it's been one helluva week.* The soothing coldness helped ease the storm of thoughts brewing in his mind. He dug into his pockets looking for loose change for the soda machine. *Dirty stinkin' cop.* He'd forgotten that Officer Alexander had robbed him for every dime he had.

With labored steps, Mike walked out to the office suite. There was a cadre of stoic-faced agents, carrying on with their official duties, oblivious to the man with the ice pack and dirty, wrinkled designer clothes. A maze of workers rushed through a bullpen of desks and computers, while phones lines buzzed constantly.

"Have you seen Cooper?" Mike asked Agent Stanton as he passed.

"Wheew!" Stanton exclaimed, fanning the musty odors away from his nose. "She's in the briefing room with a bunch of Senators and reporters from Washington. You're welcome to join them if you like, but I really suggest you watch from the observation deck. Save them the agony of having to deal with that putrid smell coming off your body."

Mike gave him the finger and continued on.

"And by the way Mike, you look like shit!" Agent Stanton finished with a chuckle.

Mike disappeared into the observation room and crashed into a metal chair. The bag of ice felt like heaven on his throbbing skull. In front of him a large two-way mirror gave him a view of the briefing room on the other side of the wall. From his seat he could see the outlines of half a dozen bureau heads, politicians, and news reporters sitting around a mahogany table; their silhouettes highlighted by the flashing glow of a digital projector.

Mike could make out the graying, well-cropped hair of U.S. Attorney David Namath. Special Agent Angela Cooper was leading the discussion.

Mike leaned back in his chair, closed his eyes, and focused his ears as Agent Cooper continued, "There are eight-point-three million legal residents in the state of Georgia, of which Hispanics account for over five-percent of the population. The growth of the Hispanic population has been bolstered by an influx of undocumented immigrants, mostly from Mexico. Our latest intelligence currently indicates that as the Mexican immigrant community has expanded, so too has the presence of Mexican traffickers."

Agent Cooper paced slowly. "This is especially true in the metro Atlanta area. Cocaine seizures have increased dramatically as a result of the Mexican cartels moving into Atlanta as have methamphetamine and marijuana seizures."

"More significantly, in recent years, the Atlanta Field Division has seen a drastic change in the drug trafficking patterns in and around Atlanta. Now historically, cocaine, marijuana, and methamphetamine have crossed the country from the southwest border through Houston, McAllen, Corpus Christi, and other Texas cities along Interstate-10 through Louisiana to Atlanta. But recent investigations have shown that traffickers are using the route less frequently in favor of traveling north using state highways. This phenomenon is attributed to increased monitoring and pipeline seizures on the interstate highways...."

* * *

Agent Stanton walked into the observation room bringing Mike a cold Coca-Cola and a bottle of aspirin.

"Thanks," Mike offered as Stanton left. Mike swigged the entire Coca-Cola and burped. "Would've been better if it had some liquor in it."

* * *

Back in the conference room, Agent Cooper continued, "Mexican drug cartels are the preeminent threat faced by the Atlanta Field Division and half of all our drug investigations target Mexican trafficking organizations. Recent intelligence revealed that a large scale trafficking organization in San Antonio was responsible for importing kilogram quantities of cocaine, marijuana, black tar, and methamphetamine into the metro Atlanta area. The Birmingham, Alabama regional office reported that a business front in Augusta, Georgia was importing cocaine and heroin into the U.S. and Atlanta. We later discovered that the business had ties to a very powerful Colombian narco-terrorist group."

"Cocaine and crack cocaine remain amongst the most widely available drugs in Georgia. Traffickers utilize numerous transportation methods including the use of private or rental vehicles and tractor-trailers with increasingly sophisticated hidden compartments, safer travel-routes, and highly advanced counter-surveillance techniques. Colombian cocaine traffickers use the ports of Charleston, South Carolina and Savannah, Georgia as cocaine importation points. These locations are major shipment centers for cocaine destined for Atlanta, other East Coast drug markets, and Europe. During the past year, Mexican and Dominican organizations have delivered major shipments of five-hundred to eight-hundred kilograms of cocaine or more to Atlanta for local consumption and distribution to other sectors of the region."

* * *

Bored and completely drained, Mike laid his head on the table. As he drifted off to sleep, Agent Cooper's regional status report swirled in his head, mixing with images of all the cold hard cash he had seen in the last four years...

He remembered the night he meet Adrianna...and the morning she introduced him to the grand Jorge Moreno Vargas...and the trap was set....

Agent Cooper rattled on..."Atlanta is a destination city for ecstasy from other major U.S. cities. The *date rape drug* GHB, MDMA, and Ketamine, also known as *Special K,* continue to be popular and readily available. Unfortunately, we're seeing increased appearances in gyms, college campuses, and associated teenage haunts. Now, LSD is usually found in school settings and is imported to Georgia from the West Coast via U.S. Postal Service Packages or commercial express mail. The wholesale cost of ecstasy, depending on location and quantity purchased, varies between $3 and $15 per pill. The retail price varies between $8 dollars in Atlanta to as much as $40 in Savannah. Ecstasy is extremely popular in the hip-hop scene and is readily available in Atlanta's nightclubs, as well as underground *rave* parties and concerts which target the younger population. An emerging trend among young adults is *candy flipping* which is a method of mixing MDMA and LSD."

The lights shifted as the projector switched to a picture of a marijuana field hidden on a farm in south Georgia. Agent Cooper took a sip of water and cleared her throat.

"Now marijuana...," Cooper started again, "...marijuana is the most commonly abused drug in Georgia, and is readily available throughout the state. Mexico and the southwest border states are the usual sources for marijuana imported and distributed in Georgia. The primary wholesale suppliers of marijuana are Mexican nationals. Local outdoor cannabis cultivation sites are increasing due to the normally ideal growing conditions in Georgia. But we've found that because of the DEA's recent eradication program and the recent drought, some dealers have resorted to the *hydroponic* cultivation of marijuana."

* * *

Mike night-dreamed he was on a beach. The heavy crash of waves soothed his aching head. There was soft beige sand for miles along the coastline. She was there. Her back was to him as she walked toward the edge of the water, dipping her feet into the incoming tide. He called out to her, but no sound escaped from his lips. She kept walking, the water steadily rising above her waist, until she disappeared beneath a giant crashing wave.

The door clicked and Mike snapped from his sleepy fantasy, wiping the slimy drool from his bottom lip.

"Rise and shine, convict. Time to earn your keep," Agent Cooper greeted him.

"That was a rousing speech. You're pretty hip for a Republican. And did I actually hear you say *hip-hop?*" Mike joked, mimicking her verbal delivery.

Agent Cooper smirked, "Why yes, I believe you did." Normally, she would not have taken such insolence from any Agent beneath her rank, but their relationship was one of both admiration and respect. She had personally raised him.

"Michael Antonio Drakeire, you look like hell-run-over," Cooper sneered as she sat down. "My God, son! You smell even worse."

"So I've been told," Michael murmured. It felt good to hear her use his real name. It reminded him of the man he used to be.

Agent Cooper laid a plastic bag on the table. It was labeled *Atlanta Police Evidence.* "Thought you might want these back."

"Hey, ladies." Mike took his guns from the bag, kissed them both, and tucked them back in his waistline where they belonged. *Irene* and Marlene were safe again.

Agent Cooper tossed a file folder on the table, its contents spilling out. "Recognize your new buddy?"

Mike opened the folder and his face turned cold.
A glossy, black-and white surveillance photo of Officer David Alexander glared back at him. Alexander was smiling with a wicked, shit-eating-grin. *The kind of grin that only a killer with a badge and a gun could produce.*

"He's the one that planted the coke on me." But of course Cooper already knew that.

"He also tried to bury you with a rusty .45 with no serial numbers. Ballistics don't lie. That gun killed one of Jorge's nephews. Did Alexander put that lump on your head too?"

He pointed, "Nah, *this* lump I got from a goon over on Rice Street." Mike touched another spot on his sore head. "*This* lump is the fine work of some robbin' crew running around town dressed in Fulton County Sheriff's gear. They like to turn dope boys inside out for profit," Mike replied as he repositioned the melting ice pack on his head.

"The Diablos?" Cooper asked with an air of omnipotence. Only God had access to more information than she did.

"Probably. They were definitely locals. Atlanta country."

"As opposed to New Orleans country?" Cooper offered. Since the destruction of Hurricane Katrina, homeless New Orleans crews had also come to Atlanta on robbing sprees.
It had already hit the local news with Atlanta crews vowing on TV to *"kill any out-of-towners looking for an easy lick."*

"Some of Atlanta's finest."

"How can you be so sure?" Agent Cooper asked just for the hell of it. If Drake said it then it was usually as good as gold.

"They knew me by name." Mike didn't realize how proud he sounded.

Agent Cooper slowly reeled back in her chair, her face cropped in both amusement and shallow concern. Her killer toy soldier had grown up before her eyes, and here he was—a dangerous man, seething with pride, falling into the abyss.

"Tell me, Mike. How are you holding up?" she asked softly.

Mike shook his head at the probing question. He wasn't in the mood for a psychiatric evaluation, especially from a career woman who had the emotional depth of a cold bullet.

"This isn't the part where you get worried that I'm losing my focus, is it?" Mike huffed. "I don't need the therapy."

Agent Cooper leaned toward him with an inquisitive smirk. "As long as you're still in control."

"Let me be the first to fill you in," he assured. "I am not. You come to my job for a few days, see how you feel about gettin' up in the morning."

"I understand how being this deep can rub off on you. There's a lot of temptation. Old loyalties can fade as your pleasures and priorities change."

"You don't give a damn how deep I fall into the pit," Mike replied with a respectful grin. "All that matters is that you get to stamp your name on a few high-profile arrests and catch a few press conferences on your way to a White House party." Mike winked at her.

"One of these days, Michael. You and I are going to have long talk about what this job really means to me," Agent Cooper winked back and rose from her chair. "Is there anything going on with Vargas that I need to know about?"

"Since his nephews died, Jorge's been slowly losing it. He's more dangerous than I've ever seen him. He has Manuel and Hector bringing in half a ton of pure tar heroine. Maniac wants to let it loose on the city like the *Plague of Babylon* as he called it."

"Mass extermination. He's a ruthless bastard, isn't he?" Cooper shrugged it off.

"What's takin' so long to unseal the indictments against Vargas?" he asked. "It's getting harder and harder for me to stay alive out there."

"It's your newfound relationship with Todd Graham."

"Fat Todd is who you want now?"

"Todd Graham is already gone. The DEA office in South Carolina has had him under surveillance for two years. With the supply he's been getting from you, he's sealing the last nails in his coffin as we speak."

Then it hit him. "You want his wife."

"Namath has his crosshairs on Mayor Franco," Cooper informed him. "To pull the trigger, he needs to prove that Kylie Graham is somehow involved with her husband's business."

Mike rubbed his sore knuckles, keeping his silence. Kylie Graham had once delivered him a plastic shopping bag stuffed with one-hundred-and-fifty thousand dollars in cold cash. Todd had missed the last flight from South Carolina that evening and couldn't make the overdue payment himself.

"You haven't dealt with her at all, have you?" Cooper asked.

Mike shook his head. "It's usually just Todd and sometimes his two partners. I've never even see her around."

"You wouldn't lie to me, would you?"

"Of course I would."

"Stay on point, Drake. Try to get me times, dates, transport points for Vargas's shipment of heroine, anything we can work with. I'll talk to Namath about shutting it down. Now go home and bathe."

"First, I'm going to get my car."

"Don't get too attached. We own that car," she reminded him. Mike climbed to his feet and limped toward the door.

"What happened to you?" she noticed.

"Alexander tried to have me killed on the seventh floor," Mike grunted in pain. Cooper rested her hand on Mike's shoulder and opened the door for him as she whistled a somber blues tune.

"And by the way..." Mike almost forgot. Agent Cooper froze with her hand still grasping the door handle. "...I was listening to your speech on club drugs," Mike continued. "It was impressive, but you're wrong about the ecstasy." Mike enjoyed knowing more than the almighty FBI section chief.

"How so?" Cooper's attention was baited.

"Atlanta's no longer the ecstasy drop-off zone for the West Coast. There's a major manufacturer right under our noses," he revealed.

Agent Cooper smiled radiantly and let go of the door handle. Her star recruit had done it again.

51

RANSACKED

Mike sat parked in his condo garage--his life a sitcom, surreal and dangerous, his rampant thoughts disorganized. Next thing he knew he was stepping off the elevator, treading down the hallway, jingling his key ring. He abruptly stopped at his door. It was pried open, the deadbolt lock crumpled. Mike drew his guns and crept inside.

The condo was destroyed--chairs overturned, cushions slashed open. His king-sized mattress was torn to shreds. The jewelry boxes were empty. Dirty Cop Alexander and the Diablos had wiped him out while he was stuck in jail. Mike now knew what it was like to be invaded--your privacy and the serenity of home sweet home violated. He laughed.
It really was rape.

Michael swept the house. Satisfied that he was alone, he went to the kitchen and slid the refrigerator away from its nesting spot. Behind it, a dummy fuse box was mounted in the back wall. Mike popped open the gray metal door and the front wall of switches slid out, leaving a steel black box.

He unlocked the steel case and pulled a sealed, cloth bundle from inside. Unwrapping the cords, he laid banded stacks of cash out on the table. *Stupid jackasses.* They had walked right past nine-hundred thousand dollars in cash. *Dumb fucks missed their payday.*

Forty-five minutes later the locksmith had replaced the dead bolt and a door knob. Miss Layla, his cleaning lady from Trinidad, finished with her chores, and pulled a sweater onto her narrow shoulders.

"Is there anythin' else ya need me to do, Mister Drake?"

"Two years you've been working here, Miss Layla. Two years, and you still won't call me by my first name."

"That's right, Mister Drake. Since it not bein' a proper *t'ing* for our relationship. This be *business*. Now is there anythin' else I can do for ya while I'm here?"

"This is goodbye for me and you. Things are dangerous right now," he said, shaking his head in worry. "I wouldn't wanna get you caught up in none o' my crazy business."

"I ain't scared of these criminals!" she threatened in her Caribbean accent. "They oughta have their heads busted open! Breakin' into a man's home."

Michael handed her twenty-thousand dollars in small bills.

"I don't deserve all this!" she gasped.

"'Have you done anything *not* to deserve it?" he calmly asked.

She paused, tracing her memories. "Well, no. Not that anythin' comes to me mind. No."

"Then take it. You don't want it, then give it to somebody who needs it."

"Everything's alright, isn't it, Mister Drake?" Layla asked as she reached for the door.

"I'll be retiring soon, Layla. It's just always better to go out on top," Michael said.

"Then good luck to you, Mister Drake. I wish you God's grace in all that you do."

"Thank you, Layla." *I'm gonna need it.*

* * *

A speedy thirty minute ride took Mike deep down I-85 South to an exit at Collinsworth Road in Palmetto, Georgia. He entered the small country city and finally pulled off the black asphalt, disappearing into a nondescript opening in a batch of trees.

The Lamborghini's headlights trailed along a dense wall of forestry that surrounded the narrow, winding dirt road.

Mike drove until he came to a clearing where a white, wooden ranch-style home stood beneath a single giant Pine tree. Nearby, a pristine lake sat under the bright stars. As Mike parked and exited the car, a soft breeze wind traced across the lake, rippling the moonlight reflecting from the water's surface.

Mike unlocked the hidden compartment in his trunk, grabbed the duffel bag of cash, and went inside the house. He flicked on the lights and the *real* Michael Drakiere was home.

His real furniture was plain and simple. In the living room a small television sat on the floor, always playing, with a single chair in front of it. A single glass table was covered with fading pictures of young Momma Drake holding a naked baby son of the '70s, snapshots of li'l Mike and his father, photos of Aunties Irene and Marlene and li'l man Mike all Sunday-suited up in front of the Mount Zion Baptist Church.

The master bedroom had one king-sized bed. The bare kitchen simply held a refrigerator, and old sports trophies-- football, baseball, and track. *No million dollar circus out here in the woods.*

The hallway walls were an artist's gallery that told his life story in framed chapters—a Benjamin Mays High School Diploma mounted next to a U. Penn Ivy League degree, both facing an opposite wall that held several pictures of his Airborne Ranger Division stationed in Afghanistan, Kuwait, and Somalia--the soldier of fortune story, preceding a framed picture of his graduating class from the FBI Academy in Quantico, Virginia.

The art show ended with a wooden plaque that bolstered a bronze engraving that outlined the FBI's guiding principles....

Rigorous obedience to the United States Constitution...Respect for the dignity of all those we protect...Fairness...Compassion...Personal and institutional integrity.

52

THE EXECUTIVE GAME

"Plant Man, what'd I tell ya?" Mike greeted their gracious host in the penthouse living room.

"San Antonio just got lucky, ya bum. That's all it was!" The Plant Man laughed back. He was a short, stocky dark skinned man. A diamond pendant hung from a long platinum necklace that stopped just over the top of his bulging stomach.

"Let me hold something? That was a six-hundred-thousand dollar pickup."

"Six minus your transaction fees," Mike complained.

"Just cause I don't mess with that cocaine like you big time cats," the Plant Man defended, "that mean I can't eat too?"

The Plant Man's specialty was the *hydroponic...*the *'dro, him,* that *grown man, bubba kush,* that *presidential*-to smoke anything less was uncivilized. *You watch the ESPN sports channel? Then you already know about him.*

The Plant Man was in contact with ninety percent of the athletes who had failed a random league drug test by way of the good weed in the last five years. *Million dollar NBA and NFL stars with million dollar contracts, they only smoke the good shit.* At last count, the Plant Man was the cause of a measly two-million dollars in team and league fines. But what the Plant Man was really known for was the *Executive Game.*

"And the major league home run record finally fell yesterday. Bonds hit number 756 within a week of the tie," the Plant Man remembered. "You owe me three-grand on that bet too."

"Steroid homers don't count," Mike joked. "Barry Bonds is juiced the fuck up."

"I could give everybody in this room a shot in the ass of the finest monkey ball steroids you got, and none of y'all could hit a ninety-five mile an hour fastball even if ya life depended on it. Now can I get that?" the Plant Man asked as he held out his hand, wiggling greedy fingers. "Trust me, I know baseball."

Mike dug into his pocket, peeled off three stacks, and slapped the money into the Plant Man's palm.

"Just like I don't see why my man Justice was on TV throwing out the first pitch at Turner Field," the Plant Man rambled aimlessly as he shuffled the dollar bills into order. "It's the curse of the Atlanta Braves. They should've never traded David Justice after he hit that home run to win the World Series. They'll never win another one."

"First he lost his job, then he lost Halle Berry," Mike remembered.

"Bastards did the same thing to Dale Murphy," the Plant Man nodded. "Greatest center fielder we ever had and they send the poor man to Philly."

"When you get a chance I need to sit down with ya," Mike said.

"Business is business and gambling is gambling," the Plant Man replied as he walked off, thumbing through crisp hundred-dollar bills. "Grab a drink, lose some money. Make me rich. We'll talk later."

Here was the *Underground Atlanta* that special agents and federal prosecutors wanted to get inside of the most. This penthouse gaming night was an exclusive soiree for rich visitors and some of the city's most powerful insiders. The real black power structure came to lounge and play here. They were part of the establishment that put Cheryl Franco into office. And some were still seeking to protect her legacy.

"Mike Drake! You bring any party treats?" Terry Dreyer greeted with an outstretched hand. Mike rudely brushed past the offended businessman, never acknowledging him.

I don't deal with pedophiles. Dreyer was a wealthy real estate developer who had a lust for fourteen year old girls or younger if he remembered to bring lollipops. But his lofty and seemingly untraceable City Hall payoffs and visionary land deals kept his sick fetishes completely ignored. He'd met Mike once through Tatianna Olazaban, Jorge's real estate partner.

Gorgeous women in short dresses and high-heels worked the room--all of them available for your personal pleasure. Todd Graham sat at the Texas Hold 'Em poker table, waiting on the dealer to flip his river card. A sexy young temptress hung on Todd's shoulder whispering in his ear. Todd's partners Scott Duval and Ray Hackett stood with mixed drinks in hand, conversing with Tony Starks.

Now ain't that somethin."

Tony Starks was the DEA mole planted inside the Atlanta hub of the Black Family Mafia. He'd single-handedly infiltrated the top ranks of the BMF crew and had been a respected soldier for three years now. Starks had once told Mike about some of the unspeakable things he'd been forced to do in order to maintain his cover. *Hang in there brother.*

Mike spotted another familiar face. Tracy Vick, Atlanta's hundred-million-dollar quarterback sat at the blackjack table with an impressive pile of casino chips.

"A hundred stacks say I'm right all night!" Mike proclaimed as he dropped thick bands of hundred-dollar bills on the crap table.

"We have a new shooter!" the casino host shouted. And stiff drinks flowed like water as the dice rolled heavy, and the night went on.

I took Mike another hour to grow his bankroll to a respectable two-hundred-twenty-thousand dollars--and all of two seconds to crap-out on a heartbreak nine and lose it all.

"Heyyy! You smile when you win! You smile when you lose!" Mike cried out in drunken laughter at the end of the high stakes saga.

"How's the craps treatin' ya?" The Plant Man appeared again in the late night.

"Damn dice just slaughtered my wallet. I lost it all," Mike joked.

"Ohhh! I'm really glad to hear that. You'da bucked that

heartbreak nine and I'd be in the hole four-hundred-thousand deep," the Plant Man said, realizing he'd just dodged a bullet.

* * *

Mike and the Plant Man walked out to the balcony and leaned over the railing. The panoramic view from the Buckhead penthouse was a spectacular portrait that stretched for miles, highlighted by a glowing crystal city that shimmered against a black sky canvas.

"I hear you're having problems with the Diablos," the Plant Man started out of nowhere.

"There are too many small time robbin' crews runnin' around Bankhead using the Diablo name, claiming to be them," Mike said. "I need to know who the real Diablos are--the four in the sheriffs' uniforms. So don't act like you don't know."

"Of course I know who they are," the Plant Man smiled as he began to roll a blunt of *bubba kush*. "But if I tell you and you go kill them all, or they'll probably kill you first," he quickly corrected, "then I'll be responsible in some way no matter what happens and that ain't what I do. So don't act like you don't know."

"Then just let 'em know that I have powerful political friends who want to see them off the street," Mike offered. "Tell 'em all, the Diablos, crooked cop Alexander, the whole strip."

The Plant Man nodded and that was that.

Mike smirked at the chess move he'd just made. *The Diablos would soon know that he could reach out and touch them whenever he wanted them to die.*

That was the Plant Man's third claim to fame. He was a concrete ambassador. His calm deliberations had avoided a few murders, returned stolen property to hard core rap stars who didn't have the balls to get it back themselves, gotten the sons and daughters of politicians out of legal binds, and saved a few Bankhead neighborhood homes from foreclosure. *A hustler's job is never done.*

"You ever run into any of the fellas over at our ol' bar on Cascade?" Mike asked, reminiscing about better days.

"Not anymore," the Plant Man answered regretfully. "There's hardly anybody left on the streets. Big Cokie got twenty years. And poor Tim Noid--Feds up in Virginia drove down here, took him back, and gave him ten years for making a phone call about the dope. Fat Kelvin's gone; he got ten years. Big Fran got life. Richard Shelton and ol' Rodney Sinkfield got jammed up in Douglasville—crackers gave 'em both life sentences. Just about everybody we grew up with is *down the road*."

Tracy Vick stumbled out to the balcony with two cackling women in his clutches.

"I see you got Mister QB spending his Nike money now," Mike noticed.

"He spends a dime or two every now and then," the Plant Man admitted with a devious smile, "but he pays me better when he's on the field."

"Tell me something." Mike lowered his voice. 'When we bet against the Falcons in that Eagles playoff game, how come you were so sure?"

"I can't give away all my secrets for free."

"Didn't I shoot ya somethin' extra for the tip?" Mike argued. "Fifty-thousand *somethings* to be exact."

"You really wanna know? Gimme a hundred dollars." Mike reached into his pocket and pulled out a crisp C-note. The Plant Man took the bill and flipped open a gold cigarette lighter.

"Vick bought a quarter-pound of my best smoke less than two days before the game. Now there's no way in hell you're gonna blow my dope, then fly north to subzero temperatures, and beat them Eagles with the defense they had," the Plant Man expertly explained. "On-the-road in Philadelphia? Just wasn't gonna happen."

The Plant Man stuffed the finished blunt in his mouth, set the hundred-dollar bill on fire, and leaned his cigar into the smoldering flames.

53

CASTING THE NET

United States Attorney's Office
Northern District of Georgia

Today, we announce that "Operation Meth Defense" has resulted in forty-one indictments of sixty individuals and twenty corporations associated with convenience stores in North Georgia.

The named defendants are charged with selling ephedrine and pseudoephedrine and other products and materials, knowing that the buyer's purpose for the product was to manufacture methamphetamine. Law enforcement officers executed 35 federal search warrants at stores and residences associated with these crimes. The task force focused on convenience stores in nine Georgia counties (Fulton, Dekalb, Gwinnett, Catoosa, Floyd, Whitfield, Chattooga, Dade, and Walker) based on numerous complaints received from the outraged public.

Law enforcement sent cooperating witnesses into each store to purchase ingredients used to manufacture, methamphetamine, but only after telling the clerk or owner that the items--such as pseudoephedrine, ephedrine, Coleman fuel, antifreeze, and matchbooks--were being purchased to make meth.

Note that the ephedrine-reduction method of manufacturing methamphetamine requires ephedrine and pseudoephedrine, along with red phosphorous, iodine crystals and other chemicals and solvents. Ephedrine and pseudoephedrine are commonly found in over-the-counter cold and sinus products, such as *Sudafed, Tylenol Cold and Sinus*, and many other brand name and generic cold and sinus products. *Max Brand Pseudo 60's, Ephedrine Plus* and similar products are sold as over-the-counter products for the treatment of asthma in convenience stores, truck stops, and gas stations.

Ephedrine and pseudoephedrine is extracted from these products by using a household solvent, such as "Heet", which contains methanol. "Heet" is legitimately used as a gas line antifreeze product for gasoline engines. Red phosphorous is extracted from the striker plates affixed to matchbooks by removing the striker plates and then soaking them in alcohol to soften the red phosphorous for removal and collection.

Businesses involved in the distribution of common chemicals and other ingredients utilized in the manufacture of methamphetamine inflate the price of those products, and stock and sell large quantities of these products, thereby generating enormous profits.

Beginning when the stores opened for business, over 200 law enforcement agents executed arrest and search warrants at each of the targeted stores. The United States is seeking forfeiture of all funds traceable to the alleged crimes, the defendants' interests in corporations and businesses involved in the offenses, and real estate where several of the stores are located.

At the news conference announcing the indictments and arrests, United States Attorney David Namath said, "Methamphetamine is an extremely addictive and dangerous drug that is poisoning our communities. Its manufacture poses a serious threat to people in the area of the laboratory, especially children. Its production creates dangerous and expensive environmental hazards. And it is utterly sad to see that some businesses seek profits in knowingly selling items to produce meth. These owners will face harsh federal prosecution, long prison sentences, and complete forfeiture of their business assets."

* * *

Hector turned the television down and pointed, laughing at the Pakistani man being arrested on the screen.

"The Indians can't make the *ice* like we do back in Mexico," Jorge said. "My crystal meth is premium."

"You gotta hand it to them Feds," Mike interjected, noticing the majority of the arrested store owners were foreigners. "They're an equal opportunity prosecutor."

"Punjab the thug is going to jail. Hope he's got a good lawyer," Hector chided in his best Hindu voice. Everyone laughed out.

"*Thug*...the word, it comes from the Indian term *thugi*," Jorge smugly noted. "They were a cunning band of thieves that befriended travelers, then murdered their victims by strangulation, then buried their bodies in shallow graves."

"Where in hell do you get these tid-bits of useless ass information?" Michael wondered.

"I watch the History Channel. I learn," Jorge answered. "Cable TV was sent by God to educate the simple man."

Manuel entered the room drawing, Jorge's attention.

"Well, where is she?" Jorge asked.

"I still can't find her," Manuel answered.

"I call...she doesn't answer," Jorge frowned. "She hasn't been dancing in those bars, I know this. Mike, you seen her?"

"Seen her who?" Mike toyed with him.

"Adrianna!" Jorge was pissed.

"Not in a week or two. I've been too busy countin' the money and drillin' new pussy to worry about keepin' up with your mistresses," Mike complained boldly.

54

WAR IS COMING

Manuel and Hector drove down Morosgo Drive and turned into the Northmoor Apartment complex. Their plush Mercedes drew wanting stares from the packs of young onlookers posted on the corners. And nosey heads poked from open windows.

Muchachos were posted up on the sidewalk, their exposed arms covered in *SUR-13* tattoos-- *Members of La Grand familia.* Garcia Abrego, a young SUR-13 lieutenant in jeans and a khaki shirt walked up to the driver's window and gripped Hector's large hand.

"*Ola*," Garcia greeted. "You're a long way from uptown."

"We always take the time to come see our people," Hector said.

"I hear our friend is having troubles with the locals. It's sad what they did to Alejandro and Cesar," Garcia said.

"Our friend is counting on you to help make this right. We all have to stand together if we want to keep the city under control," Manuel said from the passenger seat.

"*La Raza, esse*," Garcia said reverently. "All you gotta do is show me where to place the blame, and I'll put these black fuckas' whole block outta order."

"That's always what we like to hear," Hector smiled. "Your loyalty to us will not be forgotten. And it will of course be rewarded. Name your price."

"I'll take four...five kilos for my trouble and expenses. But let Jorge know that I'd do this for him for free if I had to."

"Then, why don't you?" Manuel smirked.

"Shit, *esse*...'cause Vargas got more loot than he needs."

55

WEST END

"*O*pen Up! This is the FBI! We have a warrant to search the premises!" They were pounding at the front door when Kylie Graham dropped the phone, and raced through her sprawling home. She rushed to a file cabinet in her husband's private office next to the master bedroom, and snatched a pile of money orders, frantically stuffing the evidence into a grinding paper shredder.

* * *

"Has he come in yet? U.S. Attorney Namath excitedly asked as he threw on his coat and straightened his tie.

Agent Cooper ended her cell phone call. "He just arrived."

Downstairs, Todd Graham walked into the Richard B Russell Federal Courthouse.

* * *

Traffic jams along I-20 forced Mike to drive the scenic hood route up Martin Luther King, past Washington High School into the *Atlanta University Center*. Along the way, he passed by the now deserted Morris Brown campus, and turned right on Northside Drive. The Morris Brown administration had stolen and mismanaged millions of dollars in school endowments and rigged financial aid records. *What kinda shit is that? You let Harvard go under...some heads are gonna roll.*

It was the start of a new school year and droves of young college co-eds had been dropped off in the belly of the beast. A billboard on Northside Drive prominently displayed an advertisement for the *Pleasers* strip club on Cleveland Avenue. The sign said they were *"...always hiring the young and the beautiful."*

Now that's inspirational for any enterprising young college woman. Bet there ain't none of these kind of billboards around Yale or Duke recruiting white college girls. Only in Atlanta. Mike wondered if their parents had any idea of the kind of city they were sending their college age kids too. *Stay the hell away from the locals, youngbleeds.*

The Lamborghini rumbled past the West End Mall and turned south on Ralph David Abernathy.

West End Park. Mike stopped at a red light. Across a grassy field he could see children laughing and running across the playground inside the small neighborhood park. He slowly remembered a time when it wasn't always this way.

Jamil Abdullah Al-Amin was his name--also known to you '60s and '70s soul brothers and sisters as H. Rap Brown, and author of the classic 1969 book *Die Nigger Die!* Al-Amin had cleaned up this once drug infested neighborhood and given a safe and vibrant park back to the community. Quiet as kept, he murdered a few persistent dope pushin' brothers in the process. *But 'round here ain't nobody talking.*

Then one night, Fulton County Sheriffs came to arrest Al-Amin on a warrant out of Cobb County for failing to appear in court on a traffic citation for speeding and impersonating a police officer. Apparently, Al-Amin had shown the arresting officer the honorary badge that was given to him by the city for cleaning up the West End. *Cracker cops from Cobb County didn't have the balls to come get him.* Al-Amin murdered both black sheriffs and took off on a run for freedom that led to an interstate man hunt. *Die Nigger Die!*

Mike drove through the streetlight and raised the volume as the news broke on the radio, *"Todd Graham, the son-in-law of Atlanta Mayor Cheryl Franco appeared in Federal court today after turning himself in this morning on cocaine trafficking charges out of South Carolina. The bond for Graham has been set at five-hundred-thousand dollars. Graham made arrangements with the DEA and the U.S. Attorney's office to turn himself in at the U.S. Marshal's office at the Richard B. Russell Federal Building here in Atlanta. Graham is one of fifteen suspects charged in a drug trafficking operation that pushed drugs through South Carolina and Georgia. Graham will remain in the custody of U.S. Marshals until a Friday hearing in Greenville, South Carolina."*

56

BOULEVARD BURNING

Garcia Abrego sliced the gas line behind the rusty, battered old stove, and set the digital timer on his handcrafted flash fuse. The slow, quiet leakage started to fill the roach infested kitchen with the pungent aroma of natural gas.

Garcia lifted his tool box and calmly walked out of the apartment, passing an arguing lesbian couple in the dingy hallway. Outside, he crossed the complex and exited, ignoring the white T-shirted black boys standing guard at the corner, smoking reefer, and laughing their lives away.

At the curb, Garcia calmly climbed into a waiting Chevy Denali.

"When is Thanksgiving, Garcia?" the driver asked and cranked the truck.

"Tomorrow...we eat good," Garcia answered.

* * *

The Wednesday morning air was crisp and the skies too clear. It was a beautiful day before *Thanksgiving.*

The bow-legged, grey-haired man banged on wooden doors with all the fury his arthritis cramped fists could muster.

"Get outta here y'all!" he spat, and coughed mucus. "This here whole place's on fire!"

Frantic mommas scooped up half-dressed babies and plastic bottles, clean diapers, and what little else they could carry. Shaking grannies clinched family heirlooms, fading pictures, and outdated jewelry. The panicked tenants scurried for any available exit from the smoldering Bedford Pines apartments, escaping into the 400 block of Boulevard Drive, just on the edge of downtown.

The horseshoe-shaped complex had been built in 1930, survived the turbulent civil rights movement of the 1960s, endured the crack infested '80s and '90s, and was now about to meet its demise in a raging wave of fire and black smoke.

The massive, four-alarm fire drew sirens, police support, and medical crews from the nearby Medical Center. Beleaguered firefighters swiftly closed off Boulevard Drive while they fought to extinguish the rampant blaze.

"Shut down the whole grid!" a lieutenant ordered to a fireman waiting on his walkie-talkie, and with the official decree, electrical power to four-thousand residents was immediately cut. For five hours the fire aged on, seeming to fade, only to erupt again several times as the November winds ebbed and flowed, feeding its frenzy. Several more times the flames fanned outward, threatening to grab and destroy neighboring buildings. In the end, some fifty-six families were burned out of their homes.

"Me, my wife and kids, we got outta there. If you ain't dead, then you got plenty to be thankful about," a brother said in his debut television news interview.

Amen, brother. Amen.

57

"What'd you do, ya sick psycho-maniac?" Michael blasted into the phone! He was barefoot, feverishly pacing back-and-forth across his balcony. In the distance, a menacing black plume of smoke billowed over downtown, blotching the otherwise tranquil blue sky.

"Didn't I tell you they made a mistake when they crossed paths with Jorge Moreno-Vargas?" His angry voice hummed back on the other end of the line! "I make them pay for what they do to me! I burn them out! They don't eat! They don't sleep!"

"This shit ain't goin' down like this, Jorge! Not in my city!"

"No, it's not going down. It's *burning* down!" Jorge laughed.

"Burn, baby...BURN!" Manuel and Hector cheered in the background.

"I ain't pissin' around with ya, Jorge! You went too far, and I ain't gonna back you on this when Boulevard comes back at ya ass."

"I don't need you to watch over me! I make you. I give you the product. I give you the big time!" Jorge's voice strained.

"And I got you movin' on the street!" Mike fired back. "You keep this shit up, and I'm gonna turn my back on you. Then we'll see how long you last without my protection!"

"Protect me? You think you protect me? I got the balls! I got the guns!..."

"But you ain't got the fuckin' brains!"

"*Condenado!*" Jorge exploded, *Damn you!* "You don't talk to me like I'm stupid! *No me quiebres el culo!*" *Bustin' my ass.*

"And you don't keep fuckin' with my business!" Mike screamed at the top of his lungs. "I gotta live and eat around here! Do you see me burnin' down Mexico with a sombrero on my head, tap dancin' and pissin' all over your fuckin' fiesta?" Then silence struck.

"What time you say you come for dinner? I want to try this new place in the Virginia Highlands," Jorge calmly asked like they'd never been arguing. "I hear Jane Fonda, she really likes to go there. If I see her I want her autograph."

"I'll meet you at nine," Mike replied peacefully, "and this ain't over, Jorge. You just killed yourself."

"Hey, amigo...no man wants to live forever," Jorge said and hung up the phone.

* * *

Todd Graham was *under* federal indictment, *out* on a half-a-million dollar bond, *under* house arrest, watched *over* by the electronic tracking monitor strapped to his ankle, and he still went back *in* to work. He was nervous, too jittery when he climbed into Mike's car. *Under pressure.*

"I gotta keep workin'," Todd said. *I still gotta eat.*

"I can't fuck with you," Mike laughed. "You're hotter than a firecracker on the Fourth of July. Shit, you so hot right now you're radioactive."

"Don't you think I feel crazy comin' to you? Especially after this already hit the news. The lawyers are draining me. I still got the mortgage on my house. And man, my mother-in-law is about to shit on herself right now."

"What do you want me to do?" Mike shrugged. "Hell, what would you do in my situation?"

Todd Graham shook his head in despair. *'Cause pressure will bust steel pipes.*

"Alright, I'll help you when I can," Mike offered in consolation. "You just call me when you need some work. Don't say nothing else, no numbers, no code words, no nothing. And...

...I'll call you back with a safe spot to meet, and we'll hustle from there."

"I appreciate this, Drake," Todd whiffed as his shoulders sagged in defeat. "Things went from sugar to shit overnight."

58

FALLEN ANGELS

"This is late breaking Channel Two live news coverage... Pittsburgh Steeler's all-pro running back, and former Atlanta high school star, Ahmad Lewis has been arrested on charges of conspiracy to distribute narcotics."

"There goes the Super Bowl," Michael grunted as he shuffled through the hallway, half-awake, his bare feet pressing on the cold hardwood floor. He leaned in the door frame, watching the news report--the NFL running back rose from the back seat of an FBI car, his broad shoulders filling an expensive tailored suit, his hands cuffed behind his back.

"A meeting with an FBI informant...at a local restaurant on Ponce DeLeon...Co-defendant DeAngelo Woods...." Mike backed away, absorbing all the dates, times, and that one location, then it him.

That night in the rain...I waited for her outside...I'll just be damned! He rushed to his computer, tapping away at the keyboard.

"Come on, hurry the hell up!" He pounded the computer monitor, as if violence would convince the modem to download faster. Michael sat motionless in front of the computer screen, reading:

U.S. Attorney's Office Northern District of Georgia

David Namath, Acting U.S. Attorney for the Northern District of Georgia, Peter Fallwell, Special Agent-in-Charge, Federal Bureau of investigation, Ronald Simeon, High Intensity Drug Trafficking Area Task Force (HIDTA), and Victor Koenig,

Director, Georgia Bureau of Investigation, announce that Ahman Lewis, 26, of Atlanta, Georgia, today pleaded guilty to using a telephone to facilitate a drug-trafficking crime.

Lewis was indicted by a federal grand jury along with DeAngelo "Angel" Woods, 29, of Atlanta, Georgia, with conspiring to possess with the intent to distribute cocaine and using a telephone to facilitate a drug trafficking crime. The United States also filed a superseding indictment. Lewis pleaded guilty to count two of that superseding indictment before United States District Judge Annette Ethridge, admitting that he was guilty of using a cellular telephone to facilitate Woods' attempt to possess cocaine with the intent to distribute it.

Pursuant to a written plea agreement, Lewis admitted that he used his telephone to arrange a meeting between a confidential informant working for the Drug Enforcement Agency and DeAngelo Woods. At the time, Lewis didn't know that the confidential informant was cooperating with the DEA and the FBI but rather believed that the confidential informant was in contact with high-level cocaine traffickers who could supply the product he required.

Lewis openly and candidly admitted that he made the phone call to facilitate Woods' attempt to purchase cocaine from the confidential informant. Later that evening, Lewis introduced Woods to the confidential informant at a Krispy Kreme restaurant on Ponce De Leon Avenue in Atlanta. According to the evidence, Lewis made this introduction because he knew that Woods was interested in purchasing cocaine.

Lewis has agreed to cooperate with the United States, including testifying in the upcoming trial of Woods. The United States and Lewis have agreed to recommend that the court sentence Lewis to six months of incarceration, four months to be served in prison followed by two months in a halfway house. Lewis will also perform 500 hours of community service following his release from prison.

The investigation of Lewis and Woods arose during a broader investigation into drug trafficking in the Bowen Homes and Bankhead Highway area of Atlanta. That investigation has lead to the conviction of more than 40 defendants and the dismantling of a significant cocaine distribution network.

Acting United States Attorney David Namth said of today's plea, "We're satisfied that we have reached a fair resolution concerning Mr. Lewis' role in this offense. His guilty plea reflects that participating in a drug transaction in any manner is serious and can end in prison time. We hope that the time Mr. Lewis spends in community service speaking to young people about the dangers of getting involved with drugs will help better their lives and prevent them from making similar life-altering mistakes."

FBI Special Agent-in-Charge Angela Cooper said of the case, "The Atlanta Division of the FBI will continue to investigate and prosecute any and all people who choose to participate in drug-related activities, regardless of their fame, social status, and prominence in our community."

Mike leaned back in his chair, relieved but far from satisfied. Adrianna's name wasn't mentioned.

Was she the informant? Either way for Ahmad Lewis it was a bullshit arrest, followed by a mere slap on the wrist--a small stroke of justice, if that, but useless in the overall enormity of the big picture. *He could've gotten ten years.*

Michael had followed Ahmad Lewis' career from AAAA Georgia State football, through his record breaking seasons at Auburn University. The detail starved newspaper stories and the federal indictments wouldn't tell how Ahmad Lewis had spent forty-thousand dollars from his NFL signing bonus to pay for a cancer operation for an old elementary school friend.

I guess saving another man's life is inadmissible in court. Nigga can't even buy a break.

Mike's cell phone chirped and he dug into a pile of clothes, locating it. "Adrianna, where the hell have you been? Jorge's about to go nuts lookin' for you."

"I'm back at home now...bored outta my mind," her nervous voice squawked back. "You busy?"

"I'm keeping any eye on the news. Feds just scooped up Ahmad Lewis this morning."

Patience. She's callin' to feel me out.

"Who? Who's that?" she asked innocently.

"You don't know?" he asked, testing her, giving her room to squirm.

"Why would I know him?"

"He's a local cat. Thought maybe you'd tricked some o' that NFL cash out of him."

"You need to get a life. Turn that stupid TV off and come get me. I'm dying for a gourmet lunch and some stimulating company," she sighed.

"After I shit, shower, and shave, I've gotta go see Jorge for a minute. If I got nothin' or nobody better to do after that, I *might* come spend some money on ya."

"Don't make me break your heart, playboy. Believe me. If you don't see about me, somebody else will," she sweetly threatened and hung up the phone.

This damn woman is gonna get us both killed. And I still can't let her alone.

As Michael showered beneath a stream of boiling hot water, he outlined the brewing scenario. Adrianna had called to check his mood and lied to him about knowing Ahmad Lewis.

Why? It's simple. *If Jorge knew she was making any kind of side-play he'd be furious. But if he found out that same side-play was a job for the DEA...he'd kill her.*

Michael stepped from the shower, dried himself off, and wiped the fog from the mirror over the sink. Confused, he stood staring at his reflection, debating the facts....

If Adrianna thinks that I know about her being part of a bad deal, then she's worried about me going to Jorge. If Jorge finds out that I knew about this, and didn't tell him first, he'd kill me quicker than he'd kill her. Then there's Officer Alexander; he was there that night too. But who was he watchin'?

* * *

Richard B. Russell Federal Courthouse

"The U.S. Attorney's office is aggressively investigating whether Kylie Graham helped her former husband launder tens of thousands of dollars of drug money," David Namath confidently spoke into the microphone. "Miss Graham's lawyers contend that she was completely unaware that he was a drug dealer because he never revealed it to her. The lawyers claim that he simply explained away his piles of cash — sums as much as $60,000 or $70,000 at any given moment — as lucky gambling winnings. Now, I have to ask you in the interest of justice, and prudent judgement, how could she not know?"

"You're getting a little too comfortable in the spotlight," Agent Cooper teased as the flock of news anchors and journalists dispersed.

"Are you kidding me? I was born to do this," Namath bragged. "Did you find any kind of money trail between Graham and her father's airport concession business?"

"Not so far," Cooper answered firmly and untruthfully. "She was just an employee and daddy's little girl. There doesn't seem to be a direct correlation between any of their bank transactions, but we're still digging. Sooner or later we'll strike oil."

With her small deception, Agent Cooper had drawn her line in the sand. She would protect Mayor Franco's legacy only as far she could under the letter of the law, while the Mayor's daughter and son-in-law would have to get their devil's due in court. The couple had already stepped too far over the line, and Agent Cooper saw no reason why that fact should taint the Mayor's honorable track record anymore than it already had. But it was going to be a difficult struggle to navigate treacherous legal waters with a shark like David Namath swimming in your pool.

59

DEA Dismantles Black Tar Heroin Trafficking Group

Atlanta, GA – Today the Drug Enforcement Agency (DEA) announces the successful completion of Operation Black Rush. The multi-jurisdictional investigation breached a major black tar heroine trafficking enterprise. The architects of this international smuggling syndicate were headquartered in Sonoloa, Mexico, and were involved in money laundering and drug trafficking operations that spanned from central Mexico to communities throughout the United States. Operation Black Rush involved investigations by DEA offices in 26 U.S. cities, and has resulted in the arrest of 143 suspects and the seizure of over 1,000 pounds of heroin. More than half of those arrests occurred within the DEA's Atlanta Field Division.

Operation Black Rush began with a seizure of five-pounds of heroine in Corpus Christ, Texas, but intelligence leads soon unraveled a multi-million dollar black tar heroin trafficking enterprise. The cartel leaders employed 'human smugglers' to illegally sneak Mexican nationals across the border, from Mexico to the U.S., to work solely as drug couriers in various cities. These immigrant couriers would be used as runners in a "take out or delivery" system of heroine distribution, where a customer could literally receive his drugs while standing at his own front door. The illegal proceeds were then laundered by the cartel's financial managers, accountants, and lawyers, using a complex web of bank wire transfers, real estate investments, and bulk currency shipping.

* * *

10:00 PM. *Buford Highway Plaza.* The expansive parking lot of the giant strip mall swayed with a sea of bodies. There were two large Ferris wheels with fluorescent lights illuminating its circumference. Dozens of carousels, mechanical rides, and small zoo animals littered the landscape. Droves of children bounced inside giant inflatable playhouses. And Mariachi bands blazed live instruments in colorful songs, drawing applause, cheers, and sing-a-long chants, as Spanish families reveled in the festive community atmosphere.

The bad news had reached Jorge less than an hour after the conclusion of the DEA's *Operation Black Gold* raid on his Memphis hub. The poisonous heroine shipment he had been waiting for was not coming.

"Now it was funny to ya when all the Indians in the 7-Eleven's were getting jammed up for selling crack pipes and meth supplies," Mike mocked as he walked alongside Jorge, through the crowded carnival.

"I had plans for that shipment," Jorge scowled.

"They were evil plans--better left unfinished," Mike argued. Adoring benefactors greeted Jorge, some shaking his hand, others seeking a hug, while an old woman patted his face and prayed for him. Jorge was a celebrated man who provided construction jobs, medical and dental care, immigration lawyers, scholarships, and whatever else he could offer his countrymen.

Near the concession stand, Garcia Abrego met with Manuel and Hector.

"Is this her?" Garcia asked as he took the photo from Manuel. "Damn, she's hot! Can I bang her before I choke the shit outta her?"

Manuel shrugged, "Vargas has turned his back on her. Do whatever you like."

* * *

"There are other pressing concerns on my mind," Jorge said as they walked on.

"Anything I can take care of?"

"Manuel tells me about the girls he tortured...the things they said." Jorge watched for Mike's reaction. "They say they met my nephews through Adrianna.'

Mike held his emotions, allowing no trace of them to contaminate his facial expression. His next words were crucial.

"People will say whatever you want 'em to say when there's pain involved. And even if Adrianna introduced them, you know in your heart, that she'd never do nothin' to hurt you or your family. Those dirty bitches were probably using Adrianna the whole time, trying to get to me and you," Mike finished, and prayed that it was enough to keep Adrianna alive.

"It was too easy for Adrianna to bring them to us. She already knew them," Jorge regretfully concluded. Popping balloons echoed in the background. Mike desperately thought of what to say next. Children ran past them in whirling bands, playing and laughing. Cheers rang from the crowd, while singing and melodic voices coiled in a chaotic orchestra.

"Every year, I throw this carnival for the people," Jorge said. "I do it to bring joy. That's all. I ask nothing in return, not even their gratitude. But there's been no joy for me this year. Not when everything I cherish must die."

Mike's heart dropped. *Adrianna's fate was sealed.*

Manuel and Hector escaped from the massive crowd with two lovely female escorts at their side.

"You don't look too happen there, Mike," Manuel smirked. He reveled knowing that Jorge had already delivered Adrianna's death sentence.

"Sorry to hear about your crew in Memphis." Mike speared back at Manuel. "You can rebuild after everybody gets out in twenty years."

"I've lost my heroine, but I have other plans to compensate for the setback," Jorge interjected. "Mike, you'll get more than you need for the next couple of months. We'll triple the coca supply, and the money. Let the world pay us for our troubles."

Jorge climbed aboard the stopped Ferris wheel with a stunning blonde mamacita in a white mini-skirt, and stiletto heels.

"You ever been fucked on a Ferris wheel?" he asked her as the carnival ride lunged to life.

60

RUNAWAY BRIDE

Mike pushed the Lamborghini south, running red lights, swerving between cars, as he held his dialing cell phone. He had rang her twice already and nearly had two accidents. *God don't let me be too late. The phone clicked....*

"Adrianna!" he burst out. "Adrianna!"

"Hello?" she finally answered.

"Adrianna listen to me. I ain't pissin' around. Get your ass up right now. Pack a suit case, grab whatever cash you got 'cause there ain't no coming back. Jorge knows about you and his nephews, everything."

Adrianna was stunned into silence.

"I'm on my way to get you. Turn off all the lights, lock the doors. Don't answer the phone." He slammed into second gear and the motor roared.

* * *

Adrianna frantically packed her favorite designer clothes into two Louis Vuitton suitcases as she rummaged through her closet, yanking dresses from hangars, picking shoes from dozens of pairs.

"I can't leave all my shoes behind!" she complained as she dumped a hat box full of cash into her suitcase.

Suddenly, the cell phone rang again, startling her out of her packing dilemma. Her heart sunk as she read the screen: *Jorge V.*

She paused--too scared to face her fate, too scared to let

it all go. *This is it. I have to know for myself.* Adrianna poked the call-button.

"Jorge," she timidly said.

"*Mija*, do you remember that night?" Jorge grumbled softly. "You were sleeping so peacefully. I wanted to kiss your lips and take you with me. You didn't deserve what you saw the next morning. But business is business. I look back now and think that if I had killed you too, then my nephews would still be alive. Fate is strange."

*The shadow in my bedroom doorway that night...*She keeled over as flooding anxiety mixed with disbelief, fury, and sadness, balling into a gut wrenching pain deep in her stomach...*He's the ghost that writes my nightmares.*

Adrianna gasped when she heard the front door *slam*, and she dropped the open phone on the carpeted floor....

She backed away as heavy, deliberate footsteps neared the bedroom door. She knelt down behind the bed in the dark. The cell phone still glowed as it sat on the floor. The bedroom lights flicked on.

"You need to knock before you come into my crib," she complained in relief. He had a gun in one hand dangling by his side.

"Knock these nuts," he joked, squeezing his crotch. "Why I would I have to knock? I gotta key," Mike said nonchalantly as he thumbed through a row of books stuffed on the shelf. Still stunned from Jorge's heartless revelation, Adrianna paced nervously, staring at Mike's gun.

"Ah, here we go." Mike pulled her high school yearbook, and cracked open its aging pages. Thumbing through the senior section, he soon discovered a young, bright-eyed picture of Adrianna Guevara.

"Owww! You were kinda hot your senior year. What happened to you now?" he laughed.

"I started screwin' around with degenerates like you," she said as she sat down, crossing her legs nervously. "Come to think of it, I've never seen any of your old pictures. I'm beginning to think you aren't who you say you are. I might need to get a background check on you."

"I can save you the trouble," he hinted. "I've never been who you think I am." Michael flipped the yearbook pages back to the sophomores, and there he found a picture of future Pittsburgh Steeler running back, Ahmad Lewis. He looked like a little kid.

Mike sat the book down in front of her, tapping the picture of Lewis. Adrianna tensed up, unfolding her legs, interlocking her fingers.

"When did they flip you?" Mike calmly asked.

"What?" she trembled.

"That night we stopped on Ponce De Leon. I waited while you went inside to set Angel and Ahmad up," Mike said as he slowly approached her with the gun in his hand. Adrianna stood from the bed, wringing her fingers.

"You're getting too paranoid," she returned, trying to maintain her composure.

"Don't lie to me," Mike said calmly. "Your life depends on it."

His words sunk into her, sending her heart fluttering in sheer panic! She spun, diving over the bed, reaching for the dresser drawer, as Mike grasped for her.

"Adrianna...come here!" He caught her arm, but she jerked free, reached into the drawer, and.... *Click*—the hammer of the .38 Special locked into firing position. Mid-breath, his lungs froze. Less than six inches away, Adrianna pointed the chrome, pearl-handled pistol at his chest. Her small hands shook and her weight bobbed anxiously on the balls of her bare feet.

"You have to let me leave, Mike. That's all you have to do."

"Or you'll do what?" he asked, taking a short, controlled step toward her. She measured the hate in his voice, finding none.

"This doesn't have to end like...like this, Mike," she

begged. "You and me are too close."

"You're right. It don't have to go do down like this," he assured her as he took a second step. "But I ain't the one standing here pointing a loaded gun. It's loaded, ain't it?"

"Can't laugh and joke through this one," she whimpered as her voice cracked and tears streamed from her eyes.

"After all I've done to protect you, you'd shoot me?"

"I need to know whose side you're on," she hardened, taking aim at his head. Mike gulped a ball of air into his lungs. "You and Jorge have too much to loose, Mike!"

Be, easy woman.

"You think Jorge...or anybody else could order me to kill what I love most? You know I got bigger nuts than that."

Her arms grew heavier with the pull of love and gravity weighing down on tired hands.

"Jorge killed them!" she broke down. "Every night that same stinkin' nightmare, and he did it. I can't believe I let him touch me!" She teetered on the edge of madness; the gun was too heavy, slowly falling to earth. "Bastard killed them, now he wants you to murder me," she fumed, sucked up the pain, and raised the gun.

Be, real easy woman! Mike tossed his gun on the bed.

"There's three of us standing here," Mike said. "You kill me and you won't get a dime of child support. I kill you, and I kill my child. Is that the kinda man you think I am?" He took the last step--no more time and distance between them—and the cold gun barrel nudged into his chest. She could feel his steady heartbeat echo through the gun and reverberate into her hands. Mike slowly took the gun away from her and tossed it on the bed next to his. *That coulda been ugly.*

"I got caught driving down to Orlando with two bricks in the car," she explained. "I never gave you up, Mike. I didn't tell 'em shit about you or Jorge. But they needed something major and I wasn't going to prison for ten years. I'd rather die first."

Adrianna collapsed, weeping into his warm chest. Mike threaded his fingers through her hair and clinched the locks in his fist.

"I need to be able to trust you," she said. "You're all I got now."

"Your next lie is your last," Mike grasped her throat, squeezing. She winced, enjoying the pain. He pulled her near, leaving them eye-to-eye, his pupils burning through hers.

"Are you with me?" he asked angrily and released her.

"Till death do us part," she purred.

Down on the floor, the cell phone finally clicked off.

* * *

Moments later, they rushed out of her condo, scurrying to his car with the heavy luggage. That's when Mike saw the headlights of the Chevy SS Impala barreling down on them with Garcia Abrego climbing from the widow. A bright flash sparked the flurry of shots--the blasts centered on Adrianna. Mike covered her, wrapping his arms around her, as bullets tattered his back, spinning them both like a top. They crashed to the sidewalk. Adrianna shrieked in terror!

The Chevy Impala mashed off, hot tires smoking.
Adrianna screamed, crawling on her knees, reaching for Mike as he cringed in sheer pain.

"Mike! Mike!" she repeated, lost in her own fear.

"Sonnuvbitch!" he gasped, rolled over on his back, and sprung to his feet. Mike drew his *tools*, and ran out into the middle of the street, straddling the yellow divider line as cars whipped past him in both directions. He aimed his gun, lining up the site, waited, and squeezed off a shot!

With deadly accuracy, the blast ripped through the Chevy Impala's back window and the driver's head disintegrated in red spray all over the front windshield. The car swerved across the center line and Garcia quickly grabbed the wheel, punching the brakes. The car skidded to a stop. Garcia leaned over, opened the driver' side door, and kicked the headless corpse out of the car. Garcia slid behind the bloody steering wheel and screeched off in a cloud of rubbery smoke.

"Ah, carnal!" Garcia moaned as he sped away. "You got brains all over my dashboard."

* * *

"You alright," Adrianna caringly asked while checking his body for new holes and slow leaks.

"Machine gun bullets don't kill they just sting like shit!" Mike painfully joked as he ripped his shirt off--a tattered Kevlar vest lay underneath. *Twice this damn thing's saved my ass.*

"Woman, you're more trouble than your worth," he grimaced in excruciating pain.

* * *

Michael drove into the night, knowing that he was about to make one of the deadliest mistakes of his life. But the city wasn't safe anymore for either one of them, and he had to hide her from Jorge.

"There's no turning back, ya feel me?" Mike cusped her face in his right hand as the car raced down the highway. She closed her eyes, melting in the warmth of his fingers.

"I need to know that I can trust you with my life, Adrianna."

Her eyes opened and she leaned into his ear and whispered, *"Tienes mi Corazon en tus manos."*

You have my heart in your hands.

* * *

That night they drove to his Palmetto hideout where she learned for the first time that she never knew Mike Drake at all.

61

UNCLE SAM'S WAY

U.S. Attorney's Office Northern District of Georgia
RUDOLPH SENTENCED IN ATLANTA FOR THREE
BOMBINGS

Atlanta, GA.   ERIC ROBERT RUDOLPH, 38, of Murphy, North Carolina, was sentenced today by United States District Judge Charles Barnett for three bombings in the Atlanta area, including the bombing at Centennial Olympic Park during the 1996 Olympic Games. Rudolph was sentenced to five life sentences, two 50 year sentences, and two 30 year sentences. Rudolph plead guilty to charges in Atlanta and in Birmingham, Alabama. Rudolph was indicted in the Northern District of Georgia for the fatal bombing at Centennial Olympic Park on July 27, 1996, which killed Olympic spectator Alice Hawthorne and seriously injured dozens more.

Rudolph was also convicted of the bombing of a Sandy Springs, Georgia, family planning clinic, which injured more than 50 people; and the bombing of a Midtown Atlanta nightclub, the Otherside Lounge, which injured five people. As well, Rudolph has been sentenced in the Northern District of Alabama for the fatal bombing of a Birmingham family planning clinic which killed Birmingham Police Officer Robert Sanderson and critically injured nurse Emily Lyons.

Eric Rudolph executed plea agreements with the United States Attorney's Offices for the Northern Districts of Georgia and Alabama. Rudolph agreed to plead guilty to the three Atlanta bombing attacks, and the Birmingham bombing attack. The Plea Agreements provide for multiple life sentences for Rudolph without the possibility of parole, and all subsequent appeals have been waived.

Rudolph disclosed the existence of more than 500 pounds of dynamite buried in several locations in the Western North Carolina area. Rudolph provided the locations of the explosives, and other potentially hazardous materials, and provided information to the government allowing them to find and safely remove the dangerous items.

The FBI and ATF, with assistance from state and local law enforcement, successfully located the dynamite without further incident. RUDOLPH was sentenced to two life sentences in the Birmingham cases. At today's sentencing hearing in Atlanta, the court heard testimony from victims of all three Atlanta bombings, and entered into the record written statements from other victims.

"Eric Rudolph's terrorist attacks in Atlanta and Birmingham destroyed the lives of two innocent people and injured hundreds more," stated Attorney General Roberto Gonzales. "Our thoughts and prayers continue to be with the victims of theses vicious crimes. They will witness justice being served as he spends the remainder of his life behind bars. I am grateful to the dedicated officers, agents and prosecutors who relentlessly pursued this case, and I'd like to thank them for the persistence and hard work that brought it to a successful ending."

After the sentencing hearing, United States Attorney David Namath commented, "We hope that people will quickly forget Eric Rudolph as he sits alone in his prison cell for decades. Swift justice came through the excellent work of law

*enforcement officers and our judicial system. We'd like
everyone to remember the image of Centennial Olympic Park
when it reopened. Strong and proud Americans refused to stay
home in fear as Eric Rudolph had hoped. Instead, thousands of
people--Georgians, Americans from across the country, and
visitors from around the world--they all returned to the Park,
to show that they could not be intimidated and would continue
to live their lives freely. This is a vital lesson as we confront
terrorism on a wider scale. Eric Rudolph has learned what all
of our terrorist enemies ultimately will--that their violence may
cause pain and suffering to innocent people, but it will not
defeat the citizens of this great country."*

***

Agent Angela Cooper unfastened her last coat button
and tossed the suit jacket into the back seat of her car. She was
parked on the top floor of a three-story parking deck and the
mid-day sun was bearing down at full beam. Cooper walked to
the edge of the parking deck and peered through a pair of
binoculars. In the near distance, she could see the caravan of
black Chevy Suburbans parked behind the Richard B. Russell
Federal Courthouse. Armed federal agents were escorting the
infamous Eric Rudolph to his date with a prison cell.

Agent Cooper smiled proudly. Another chapter in
bureau justice had been summarily closed and the legend of the
Olympic Bomber would soon fade into obscurity. *Rot slow and
die, Rudolph.*

Soon, the rumble of the steel gray Lamborghini broke
Cooper's vengeful thought. Behind her the polished car climbed
the parking ramp and stopped. The car's butterfly door swung
up and Michael Drake escaped.

"They're hauling Eric Rudolph away." Agent Cooper
offered the use of her binoculars. Mike refused.

"Nobody delivers the fist of God like we do," she noted.

"You're beginning to remind me more and more of
Condoleeza Rice everyday."

"If I could only be so blessed," Agent Cooper fondly imagined. "If I were sitting next to the President...downtown Baghdad would be a giant parking lot right now."

"You should've told me Adrianna had been turned," he said.

"Adrianna owed the DEA a favor for some problems she had in Orlando. It was none of our business."

"Officer Alexander knows about her too. He's blackmailing her over it," Mike worried.

Agent Cooper rested her palm against his throbbing chest. "Feel your heart pounding? That's not the adrenaline or the gut instinct you'll need to finish this. This is a cold emotion that you think you can turn into love. In another life, you wouldn't have given her a second look."

Michael dropped his head, hoping that she was wrong.

"All you would've seen was another burned-out stripper with no future, and a very bad ecstasy habit," Cooper finished. Mike's head whipped around in surprise.

Agent Cooper laughed. "Only God knows more than I do, son. Years ago, I told you to never forget that. I know about all the gambling and the nest eggs you've been stashing away. London, Las Vegas, Paris, Bahrain. Stop me when I go astray."

Mike scratched his head in bewilderment. She had kept a tighter leash on him than he realized.

"Right now that sexy little thing is prancing around your Palmetto hideaway," Cooper said. "You show her your prom pictures?"

"I know it was a risky move to make but..."

"It was the wrong move!" Cooper interrupted. "Whatever she means to you, don't let it cost you your job and your life. She's expendable. Let her go." Agent Cooper chirped her car alarm as she turned and left him standing alone in the sun.

"Ain't gonna be that easy, *Boss*," he jabbed.

Cooper sneered, "Only thing that really matters is which side of the sledgehammer she's on when it falls." That was his first and last warning.

"She walks outta this with me!" Mike yelled.

I got three-million ways to make it happen. That was her first and last warning.

"Don't get killed on my watch," Agent Cooper replied. "She's not worth it."

Hell if she ain't. Now, stay alive.

* * *

Late one balmy Wednesday night, Jorge Vargas received the tragic word from Mexico City. Drowning in despair, reeling from the assassination of her two sons, his sister, the beautiful Renee Vargas Castillo, had fatally shot herself in the head.

With nothing to lose and no heart to feel, Jorge Vargas ordered his faithful SUR- 13 soldiers into action....

Vicious Latin soldiers preyed on black gangsters, stalking them in drive-by shootings that ruptured into full-fledged street corner shootouts on Boulevard 4th Ward, Campbellton Road, Old National, and Martin Luther King Drive....

Everyday the news story told the saga--even if all the pieces of the wicked puzzle didn't connect in a single Action News Hour.

Murderous Black crews from Thomasville, M. L. K., Bankhead, East Point, Ben Hill, The Bluff, Mechanicsville, and Jonesboro South blindly headed north to Gwinnett, Tucker, Lawrenceville, and deep into Douglasville and Cobb County, south to Clayton County, hunting for any Mexican that was holding too many rubberbands of that mean green deniro, too many pounds of dirty Tex-Mex mote, or a whole lotta bricks of that sweet, coca candy.

This was concrete war.

62

7:00 PM. Hartsfield Jackson International Airport.
Delta International Departures. The vacationing couple swiped their passports under the ticket kiosk terminals and checked the luggage.

"Is there any particular reason why you've been trying to keep me up all night and all o' today?" Adrianna whined like a sleepy toddler.

"I keep telling you it makes the flight easier," Mike argued. "You pass out on the plane, and next thing you know we're there."

"I'm going to pass out right here," she stomped.

* * *

"*All passengers this is the final call for Flight 89 to London-Gatwick. Now boarding all passengers. This is your final call.*"

On board the plane, they shimmied through the narrow aisles, stored their carry-on bags, and settled into their first-class seats. Adrianna propped her head against the pillow and buried herself beneath a blanket. Mike sat staring at the open plane door; a stewardess stood near it taking on the last few passengers.

"Go on sleepy head. Rest your soul. I'm going to take a leak before when we hit the friendly skies." Mike stood and scurried down the aisle.

Adrianna rolled over and close her eyes. Minutes later, the plane lunged as it backed away from the gate. Turbine engines roared to life and the plane slowly crept toward the runway for takeoff. Adrianna's eyes opened. She was facing out of the window. Dusk was slowly dying.

"I'm going to miss this place," she said. "How about you?" The plane lumbered out to the runway and throttled into a slow roll before rushing to full takeoff speed.

"Don't you hear me talkin' to you?" She rolled over....
Mike wasn't there.

The plane defied gravity, tilted, and climbed into the night. Her Blackberry PDA *chimed.* It was a new text message.

* * *

Mike Drake boarded the train back to the main airport terminal and parking decks. As the underground transit rolled along inside dark tunnels, he stood looking at his phone.

Time to go back to work.

* * *

The airplane pitched hard and rose steadily as the moan of the rising landing gear filled the cabin. Quietly, Adrianna sat reading her text message:

Look in carry-on bag. Read instructions.
2 many things left 4 me 2 finish.
I will C U both again soon.

M.D. 404city

* * *

As the plane leveled off at thirty-two thousand feet above her new life, the seatbelt signs extinguished, and Adrianna quickly grabbed her bag from the overhead storage bin. Inside she found a white envelope stuffed with ten-thousand British Pounds—at current exchange rates just under twenty-grand U.S.

There was a credit card from a bank she'd never heard of and a pin-number taped to the back. A short, hand-written letter outlined her itinerary and intermediate destinations. *Don't look back.*

She closed her eyes--saddened that he had left her, but feeling safe and free, and exhilarated by an intercontinental run that would be her biggest adventure yet. She rubbed her growing stomach and prayed that they would both be safe.

Their journey was just beginning.

63

WHITE CHRISTMAS

Mike Drake calculated the hefty weight and added the loftier numbers. He had fronted Fat Todd Graham another thirty kilos at cost—*four-hundred-eighty-thousand dirty dollars* was tonight's payoff. Feeling more suspicious than ever, Mike showered a naked dancer with money, finished his drink, and left the *Onyx Club.* Todd was an hour late and he wasn't answering his cell phone.

Mike tipped the eager valet and slid behind the wheel of his car. Boredom set in as he the punched the radio presets, hearing voices and new channels shuffling, *"...In a botched late night drug raid, three Atlanta Police officers accidentally shot and killed ninety-two year old Kathryn Johnston in her southwest Atlanta home. Undercover narcotics officers were initiating a 'no-knock' search warrant when they stumbled upon...."*

Mike sat there for another hour, waiting for his money, redialing Todd every fifteen minutes or so. *No answer.*
Todd Graham never showed up.

I hope you get to stay free long enough to spend that money. Mike cranked the car and smiled like a hungry fox.

'Cause the rabbit's on the run.

* * *

United States Marshals Service

U.S. Marshals Add Todd Graham and Scott Duval to South Carolina's Most Wanted

Todd Graham and cohort Scott Duval have been placed on the U.S. Marshal Service list of the ten most wanted South Carolina fugitives. Graham, 33, and Duval, 36 are both defendants in a federal indictment alleging their involvement in a conspiracy to possess, manufacture, and distribute cocaine and 'crack' cocaine in the Greenville, South Carolina area.

"Our search for these fugitives has unearthed some very useful leads, and we're close to apprehending our suspects. I guarantee that we will find them," U.S. Marshal Jason Durham promised.

Graham and Duval are avid gamblers and golfers who enjoy playing at some the finest resorts in the U.S. Both suspects are known to frequent Las Vegas casinos and have been seen gambling at the high-limit tables. Suspects have access to large amounts of money and have shown a propensity for expensive foreign automobiles. Anyone with information relating to Graham and Duval, please contact the U.S. Marshals Service.

64

BYE-BYE

* * *

United States Drug Enforcement Agency

DEA Deals Motor City Mafia a Knock-out Punch
Detroit Drug Legends Facing Twenty Years to Life

Washington, D.C.- The Drug Enforcement Administration has arrested 41 members of the self-named Black Mafia Family, also known on the street as BMF, and has seized more than $3 million in money, assets, 90 kilograms of cocaine, and a cache of illegal assault weapons.

The DEA labeled BMF a large-scale cocaine and money laundering enterprise that operated in Detroit, Michigan, Columbus and Atlanta, Georgia, Los Angeles, California, Miami, Fort Lauderdale and Orlando Florida, St. Louis, Missouri, Greenville South Carolina, and Louisville, Kentucky.

The DEA said prior to today's arrests, they had already arrested 27 members and seized over 750 kilograms of cocaine, $5.3 million in money, and $8 million in assets.

The DEA further claims brothers Terry "Southwest T" Flenory and Demetrius "Big Meech" Flenory were the founders and ringleaders of BMF. They began selling crack during their high school years in the mid-1980's, and their efforts expanded across the country during the 1990's, evolving into a multi-million dollar criminal cartel.

"The BMF was a sophisticated and ruthless drug smuggling and money laundering organization, led by brothers that operated in some twenty U.S. states. The Flenory brothers had direct links and full access to major Mexico-based drug trafficking organizations," said DEA Task force commander Stuart Weismore.

The DEA also alleges that BMF distributed thousands of kilograms of cocaine and laundered millions of dollars in drug proceeds. BMF members and associates were responsible for trafficking at least 2,500 kilos a month out of their Atlanta hub. BMF used hidden compartments in stretched limousines to conceal and transport drugs and money. And many of their vehicles were equipped with special devices to mechanically dispel drug-tainted-air that would alert drug-sniffing dogs. The proceeds from the sale of illegal narcotics were funneled through Atlanta's untaxed, underground economy. BMF Entertainment was even backing a local artist named Bleu DaVinci, who released an album titled, "The World Is BMF", which was nominated for a Source Award in 2004.

"For far too long, these drug dealers have poisoned our streets and cast dangerous shadows of death, fear and intimidation across our cities and small towns. Today's arrests have nearly dismantled this entire drug mob and will significantly impact drug-related crime in the communities where the BMF operated," Weismore added.

* * *

The Bad Boys from Motor City had suppressed cocaine prices with shameless abandon, ran through the city like they owned it, murdered like assassins, and it finally cost them the ranch. Now, with a gaping void in supply to fill, the price of a kilo of cocaine would re-adjust--for inflation, and the cost of living and dying--to a firm twenty thousand. But there was still a better bargain in town—an offer you couldn't refuse from the one man who had outlasted them all. The Atlanta underground would have to call on him if they wanted to eat at a decent price. *There was one general on top now...Mike Drake.*

65

CAPTURED

United States Marshals Service

U.S. Marshals Capture Todd Graham in California
A nationwide manhunt ended today with the help of law
enforcement officers from the United States Marshal Service
(USMS) District of South Carolina, the USMS Southeast
Regional Fugitive Task Force (SERFTF), and the DEA.

A federal judge in the District of South Carolina issued
a warrant for Graham's arrest when Graham violated his bond
on a drug conspiracy case. Both Todd Graham and co-
defendant Scott Duval have been on the run since last year. A
third co-defendant Ray Hackett and his girlfriend, Missy
Carter, were murdered in their Atlanta condominium.

Three days ago, Tony Rivera was arrested in Los
Angeles, CA while in possession of twenty-five kilos of cocaine.
During the police interrogation, Rivera revealed that he was an
associate of wanted fugitive Todd Graham, and that Graham
himself was hiding out in Los Angeles. This afternoon, during
surveillance in Van Nuys, CA, Task Force investigators
positively identified Graham as he exited a red, 2006 Cadillac,
and entered a Starbuck's Coffee shop in Van Nuys.

Minutes later, Todd Graham left the shop and
approached his vehicle. He was immediately blocked in, and
U.S. Marshals and regional Task Force personnel swooped in to
subdue the suspect. At the time of his capture, Graham was in
possession of a valid California driver's license under the name
of Alfred Jenkins. Todd Graham will be held in federal custody
until he is extradited back to South Carolina to stand trial for
extensive drug charges.

PART III

Humpty dumpty sat on the wall.
Hope he don't ball 'til he fall.

El hombre sabe que hacer con la vida desde que sabe
que hacer con su propia mierda.

Man learns how to deal with life once he knows how to cope
with his own shit.

66

Department of Justice
Greenville, South Carolina

Federal Judge William Cartwright sentenced Todd Graham to life in prison for his role in a drug ring that smuggled at least 2,200 pounds of cocaine from Atlanta to South Carolina, Alabama, and Maryland. The drugs had a street value between $25 million and $35 million. Graham, 33, pleaded after prosecutors alleged he ordered the killing of a co-defendant and his girlfriend. Before moving to Atlanta in 1992, Todd Graham worked as a courier for a South Carolina drug dealer while attending Clemson University. When he met Kylie Franco a few years later, he had already become an established cocaine dealer and was a leader in a drug ring called the Sin City Mafia.

Graham's car dealership, 404 Eurosports, on Cheshire Bridge Road in Atlanta, was a money-losing front used to evoke an aura of legitimacy. The 404 Eurosports website showed an array of luxury cars including BMWs, Bentleys, and Ferraris. The dealership had numerous celebrity clients such as Atlanta rappers Ludacris and Young Jeezy, and Sean P. Diddy Combs. There were sport star clients such as Hines Ward, Takeo Spikes, and Jamal Anderson. They even sold a car to the pastor of New Birth Missionary Baptist Church and televison evangelist Bishop Eddie Long.

Graham's drug ring had accumulated about $10 million in profits at the time of his marriage to Kylie Franco. This money fueled a number of high-dollar acquisitions for the newlyweds. They immediately purchased a $650,000 house in Fulton County, expensive jewelry, and a Porsche Cayenne sport utility vehicle. Todd Graham traveled regularly to Maryland and South Carolina to oversee drug shipments from Atlanta, according to court testimony. He was in Los Angeles in April when his wife called him with bad news. Federal agents with a warrant were searching their home. A federal grand jury in South Carolina had indicted Graham in a case that ultimately would net a dozen guilty pleas. Graham returned to Atlanta and turned himself in.

A judge released him on a $500,000 bond, secured by an Atlanta bail bond company, Free At Last. When Todd Graham went on the run the bonding company was forced to pay a top Miami bounty hunter fifty-thousand dollars to find the fugitive. Even while Graham was under house arrest, he continued to oversee the distribution of drugs from Atlanta. Graham then became worried because Ray Hackett, a drug courier who also worked for 404 Eurosports, had been arrested while making a delivery and could give authorities damaging information.

Prosecutors allege Graham acquired a gun from a fellow drug dealer and hired another co-conspirator to murder Hackett and his girlfriend, Missy Carter. Atlanta police never made any arrests in the case, and federal authorities have recently taken over the investigation. Weeks after Hackett died on Labor Day weekend, just before his trial was scheduled to begin in South Carolina, Graham snipped his electronic ankle bracelet and fled. He took most of his wife's jewelry and left behind a $5,000-a-month mortgage and his $500,000 bail bond.

While Graham was a fugitive in Los Angeles, he even purchased a brand new Ferrari. Graham and his former wife remained in regular contact, according to evidence presented during his sentencing hearing. Graham's co-defendants testified that while he was a fugitive, he sent drug money to Kylie Graham in cash bundles of $50,000, another with $70,000.

In California, Graham bought a pre-paid cellular telephone to call only his wife, believing that it would be impossible to trace. In his testimony Scott Duval referred to the device as "the Kylie phone." Kylie Graham regularly sent bills to the house where her husband was hiding in suburban Los Angeles. Duval said Graham told him "that Kylie was still his wife, and it was his responsibility to take care of her." Graham used postal money orders to pay Franklin's bills, an Internal Revenue Service agent said. They apparently took elaborate measures to make the transactions difficult to track.

U.S. Marshals captured Tremayne near his California hideout, where they also discovered more than 650 pounds of cocaine, $2.9 million in cash and eight weapons, including an AR-15 assault rifle. This time, Graham was held without bond. In March, he agreed to plead guilty to charges that could send him to prison for several decades. But prosecutors promised to seek a lighter sentence of 35 years, if he cooperated with their continuing investigation.

During a lie detector test, Graham said, "...his wife was unaware that she had handled drug money." The examiner told Graham the machine showed he was lying. Graham, the examiner later reported, simply laughed and shrugged his shoulders. In court Graham told the judge in his case, "I'm sorry if my tragic life story wasn't grand enough for the FBI's sick tastes. But the terms of my plea agreement and the truth don't require that it be that way. Now give me what you gotta give me."

Consequently, prosecutors revoked their deal, and the judge handed down the maximum sentence: life, with no chance for parole. Graham's lawyers have said that they plan to appeal. But, for the moment, he is serving his time at the maximum-security U.S. Penitentiary in Atlanta.

67

THE DEVIL'S DUE

The Diablos were brothers in blood, in murder, and in life. They signed their deal with the devil a long time before this day came. They promised to bring the pain, and in return, whore Atlanta was there for the taking. They didn't have to ask. Whatever you had was already theirs. But like I said, Atlanta has its way of dealing with legends, in its own way, in its own sweet time.

* * *

Special Agent Stanton stood in the corner, his legs crossed, arms folded, staring at the dangerous man now squirming in the hot seat.

Danny Diablo sucked on the gold teeth lining his dry mouth as he sat twisting his hands in the shiny handcuffs. His heart was heavy. *We lived like kings.*

The door opened behind him.

"Uncuff him." Her voice was powerful and bitter. Agent Stanton unlocked the restraints and left the brightly lit interrogation room.

Agent Cooper faced Danny Diablo.

"Good evening, Mister Diablo." she welcomed him. "You don't look much like the devil to me."

* * *

Zone 1 Police Precinct. Roll call ended with a vulgar pussy joke from the Watch Captain and the laughing troop of blue-suited officers disembarked on another day of *Tragic City* patrol.

Officer Alexander laughed with a few fellow officers, grabbed a bag from his locker, and stepped out of the precinct into the morning sun. *What the hell is this?* He stopped in his tracks, and squinted, taking in the commotion in the parking lot.

Shiny black car doors flung open, spitting FBI Agents in dark shades, who rushed in with their guns drawn.

"David Alexander. FBI!" An eager agent huffed. "You're under arrest. We need you to come with us."

Alexander smiled, calmly dawned his aviator shades, and raised his hands.

"If you don't mind, I'll remove your sidearm," a second agent said as he flanked and reached for Alexander's gun, dislodging it from the utility belt. Agents swiftly patted Alexander down, finding a second gun in his leg holster. The handcuffs *clicked* and led him to a car.

Behind the frantic scene, a platoon of stunned Atlanta Police Officers watched as one of their own took a federal fall. *Good cops shouldn't have to see this kinda shit.*

68

U.S. Attorney's Office Northern District of Georgia

SUPERCEDING RICO INDICTMENT CHARGES OFFICER AS PART OF GANG

United States Attorney David Namath announces that a federal grand jury has returned an indictment against David Alexander, 37, as part of a superseding indictment against sixteen individuals, with charges of Racketeer Influenced and Corrupt Organization Act (RICO).

The indictment charges the defendants, Daniel Jones, 28, a/k/a "Danny Diablo," William Rainer, 30 a/k/a "Reo," Eddie Sims, 29, a/k/a "250," and Demarcus Jackson, a/k/a "Debo, with RICO violations, including acts of murder, attempted murder, robbery, violence, drug sales, and distribution, threats and kidnapping, as part of a pattern of racketeering activity. The superseding indictment adds the name of defendant David Alexander who was employed as a police officer with the City of Atlanta during the period of the conspiracy, and charges that Alexander played a pivotal role in the management of this criminal organization.

The defendants, acting as an organized group called the "Diablos," a gang operating in Northwest Atlanta, used threats of violence and intimidation in a continuous effort to obtain money and drugs for the organization. The indictment details a history of violent attacks, drug transactions, and other actions designed to maintain and expand the geographic area controlled by the Diablos which was located in Zone One of the Atlanta Police Department. Defendant David Alexander, at the time a police officer working in Zone 1, is charged with working closely with the identified leader of the gang, Daniel Jones, a/k/a "Danny Diablo." The allegations against Alexander include bribery, aggravated assault, and attempting to recruit persons into the Diablos organization; transferring cocaine from a suspect he had captured to Daniel Jones, warning Jones of a planned execution of an APD search warrant involving the Diablos, and threatening to kill and injure persons.

* * *

"With your cooperation, you may do less, but ten years is what you're facing," Agent Cooper promised.

No way in hell I can do ten years. Too much time.

"What if tell you about a cop way worse than me," Alexander offered. He was sweating under the interrogation room lights. "You're already looking for him, but you just don't know it yet."

"Go on," Agent Cooper said as she stood from the table. "I'll let you know if it carries any weight."

Alexander perked up. "I know about a cop, a buddy of mine, who has a strange hobby you might be interested in."

"What kind of hobby?" she asked.

"During his lunch break...he likes to rob banks," Alexander squealed like a pig.

Agent Cooper smiled and sat back down.

69

U.S. Attorney's Office Northern District of Georgia

ATLANTA POLICE OFFICER DAVID ALEXANDER
SENTENCED TO PRISON IN "DIABLOS" GANG CASE

David Alexander, 37, of Atlanta, Georgia was sentenced today by United States District Court Judge Walter Suttles, Jr., on charges of depriving of his civil rights by misusing official authority. According to U.S. Attorney David Namath and the evidence presented in court:

Alexander was sentenced to 8 years, 10 months in federal prison. There is no parole in the federal system. Alexander is also ordered to serve ten years of supervised release. Alexander pleaded guilty to a federal civil rights violation in connection with his association with the "Diablos," an Atlanta-based street gang. Alexander had been an Atlanta police officer for approximately 15 years prior to his indictment and arrest.

Alexander admitted that he associated with the Diablos and that he committed civil rights violations with the aid of at least one Diablo gang member. Alexander admitted that he misused his authority by summoning an individual under threat of arrest. Once the victim appeared, Alexander and several men abducted the victim and took him to a Diablo-controlled area where the victim was severely beaten. The victim sustained injuries including broken ribs and a shattered cheekbone which required reconstructive surgery.

David Namath said of the case, "This police officer, sworn to uphold the law, instead used his authority to assist a violent gang. He will now serve a long hard sentence along with the criminals he joined."

70

SUICIDE RUN

Wild Bill popped a handful of pills into his mouth, slammed a glass of port wine, gulped the ecstasy cocktail down, and waited for the pain to numb. It was all over--the pill labs, the sex, the cash--and *Ecstasy World* was officially out of business. *Good night boys and girls.*

The television was blinking an old black-and-white John Wayne movie--guns blazing, American outlaw. "This is the last ride, partner!" Wild Bill laughed maniacally, his senses fading from reality. "We had it all, Marco! We fuckin' had it..." Wild Bill collapsed to a chair, burying his aching head in his hands.

We'll take the money we got saved up, and get the best lawyers in the city. I can beat the case. If we lose, then what? 24hours...365days...Five, ten, twenty years? This is my fuckin' life! Cold steel bars and lonely nights in a dark cell--the stark images crackled like fireworks, echoing inside his skull. *Help me.* There were unbearable mental screams and more charged visions of demonic judges, unholy correction officers, and cell block rape and torture. *I can't do this.* "I can't make it!" *God, I can't do this!*

He lifted his eyes and trained them on his destiny. Dazed, he stood and nervously walked across the room, his sights focused on something in the distance. Labored steps carried him along his path until he reached for a rope that hung on the antlers of a mounted skull from a Texas-bred longhorn steer. *There's no other way, this can end.*

Wild Bill plodded up the carpeted steps at stopped at the top of the stairwell, trying to calm his shaking hands, Wild Bill lassoed the rope over the stair railing, dropped the trailing end, and slowly tied a hangman's noose. He tossed the loop around his neck, and raised his head, sucking in a hearty last breath. *God forgive me.*

"Now...take it like a man." Wild Bill jumped over the railing, snapping his neck in the clutches of the tightening rope. Slowly, his dangling body rocked back-and-forth, a human pendulum, until his spastic, jerking final motions ceased. *Good night boys and girls.*

* * *

U.S. Attorney's Office Northern District of Georgia

DEFENDANTS SENTENCED IN GEORGIA'S LARGEST
ECSTASY MANUFACTURING CASE

Today we announce that three defendants were sentenced today for up to twenty years in prison for organizing the largest ecstasy manufacturing operation ever brought to trial in Georgia. The defendants in the manufacturing conspiracy constructed and maintained at least nine ecstasy laboratories in the Atlanta area. According to U.S. Attorney David Namath and the documents and information presented in court:

The ringleaders of the operation were Marco Nobles, 29, of Decatur, Georgia, and William "Wild Bill" Ogden, 27, of Atlanta, Georgia. Ogden committed suicide after his arrest. Nobles cut off an electronic monitoring bracelet after posting bond before his trial was to begin and still remains a wanted fugitive.

Nobles and Ogden began manufacturing ecstasy in small laboratories inside residential homes in Atlanta and in communities outside the city such as Jonesboro and Rex, Georgia..

Afterward, Nobles and Ogden determined that it was more lucrative to train others to run ecstasy laboratories for their pipeline and distribute the final product. Through all the labs, Nobles and Ogden's organization manufactured an estimated 44 kilograms of ecstasy packed into gelatin capsules or pressed into tablets and distributed in Atlanta and elsewhere. At the close of the investigation, agents seized four laboratories established by Nobles and Ogden operating inside residences in Alpharetta and Duluth, Georgia.

According to the evidence, the discovery of the Duluth lab was vital to the prosecution of the case. Drug investigators working for Gwinnett County, Georgia, Sheriffs' Department and the Georgia Bureau of Investigations responded to a complaint from a neighbor about putrid odors coming from a house in Duluth, Georgia. The agents searched the residence and discovered a fully operational ecstasy laboratory, described by the DEA as the largest in Georgia history. Agents arrested Jonathan Morgan, 24, of Atlanta, Georgia, in connection with that laboratory, and the subsequent investigation immediately tied the laboratory to Nobles and Ogden.

Four months later agents raided another lab tied to the organization at 789 Monserato Drive, which is an upscale residential neighborhood in Buckhead just off Roswell Road. The combined laboratories manufactured enough ecstasy to produce 850,000 ecstasy tablets, with an estimated street value of $10 million. The Nobles and Ogden partnership benefited from a surge in the popularity of ecstasy amongst young adults involved in the club scenes during the late 1990's.

William "Wild Bill" Ogden first initiated the plan to manufacture ecstasy while he was in college where he met fellow student Marco Nobles, who earned a chemistry degree from Georgia Tech.

"This is the first prosecution of this kind in Georgia, and one of the few instances in the entire Southeastern United States where drug dealers have manufactured their own ecstasy," said David Namath. It's an intricate chemical process that requires an advanced level of sophistication and scientific acumen to complete. This is an unusual drug prosecution because it involves some extremely well-educated men who used their advanced university degrees to unleash a dangerous and utterly addictive drug on the community. Like vultures,

they heartlessly preyed on innocent and vulnerable young people, and college students and who don't understand how deadly club drugs like ecstasy really are."

Ogden and Nobles were manufacturing ecstasy in the basement of a residence in Alpharetta when a container of chemicals exploded in Ogden's face. Investigators obtained hospital records that showed Ogden received treatment for serious burns and lacerations on his face and arms.

Ogden and Nobles were the victims of a home invasion robbery by members of the "Diablos" gang, which targeted high-level drug dealers for robberies while wearing Fulton County Sheriffs' uniforms. During the robbery, members of the Diablos gang handcuffed and beat Ogden, locked him inside a closet, and stole $100,000 in cash and five kilograms of ecstasy powder. The members of the Diablos gang were later arrested and indicted by the Atlanta U.S. Attorney's Office.

U.S. Attorney Namath urged citizens who have any information regarding the whereabouts of Marco Nobles to contact the United States Marshals Service immediately.

71

TRAGIC CITY

Department of Justice

THREE ATLANTA POLICE OFFICERS CHARGED IN FATAL SHOOTING OF ELDERLY ATLANTA WOMAN

Two Officers Plead Guilty to State and Federal Charges

ATLANTA—Two Atlanta Police Department Officers plead guilty today to both state and federal charges in conjunction with the fatal shooting of Kathryn Johnston, a 92-year-old woman, in her southwest Atlanta home. Ms. Johnston was killed during the execution of an illegal search warrant.

As well, a third officer was indicted by a Fulton County Grand Jury on additional charges related to the death of Miss Johnston.

Officer Gary Junier, of Buford, GA, and Officer Jerry Smith of Woodstock, GA, plead guilty in Georgia State Court to violation of oath by a public officer, criminal solicitation and false statements, and voluntary manslaughter. Smith also entered a guilty plea for one count of perjury. The two defendants also plead guilty in federal court to a civil rights conspiracy violation.

The third officer, Barry Tessler, of Jonesboro, GA, was indicted on state charges of providing false statements, violation of oath of office by an officer, and false imprisonment.

"Every single act of police impropriety, especially a case as heinous as this one, threatens to undermine public trust in

our law enforcement," said Attorney General Roberto Gonzales. "The majority of law enforcement officials are men and women of exceptional honor and integrity who risk their lives everyday to protect ours. Day in and day out, they perform their duties with dignity, honor and uncompromised professionalism. As a community, we will not allow misconduct of this level to destroy the lawful efforts of so many other dedicated civil servants.

"The execution of Miss Kathryn Johnston by sworn Atlanta police officers was a horrific and unforgivable tragedy," said David Namath. "These outlaw officers violated their sworn oath, the Constitution, and the civil rights of the very citizens they were sworn to protect. They will be held accountable for their reckless actions. Miss Johnston's family has been remarkably strong and they are an inspiration to us all. They have said to me repeatedly that they want to see something good come out of her death. My staff and I have made a commitment to find out just how deep the cancer of misconduct that led to this death has spread within the Atlanta Police Department. I promise you, we will bring any other officers who have violated the law to swift justice."

Fulton County District Attorney, Steven Howard called the murder of Miss Johnston, "...one of the most horrific tragedies to ever happen in our Atlanta community. More shocking was that our investigation revealed that many of the lawless practices that led to her death were common practice in this Narcotics unit of the Atlanta Police Department."

"The unlawful conduct of these police officers is unnerving. As law enforcement officers, we take a solemn oath to preserve law and order, and to protect innocent people," FBI Special Agent in Charge Angela Cooper added. "These rouge officers selfishly chose to trample everything we stand for and consequently, they stole the life of an innocent elderly woman. We've discovered through this investigation that other Atlanta Police Officers have engaged in similar misconduct, and we will be seeking additional indictments."

Agent Cooper also commended Atlanta Police Chief Dale

Harrington for "having the foresight to refer this controversial case outside of his department, and for taking stark measures to revamp police training procedures in light of this recent investigation."

* * *

Like the Chief had a choice. Three outlaw cops had viciously riddled an elderly woman with dozens of hot bullets, shredding her to pieces, then handcuffed her as she still lay bleeding, waiting to die. In a devious plot to conceal their sins, the *goons* bribed a confidential informant to lie about the investigation by saying that *"he'd been to that house earlier in the day and made a drug buy."* Under the strain of the investigation that same confidential informant revealed the entire plot.

Dirty cops and robbers went lookin' for the money and the dope, and ended up at the wrong house.

American justice in all her glory.

72

MI CASA ES SU CASA

"Release the Dogs!" Jorge screamed and reached for his M-16 assault rifle, jamming in a clip. "The barbarians are at my gate!" Enraged, he peered at the bank of video monitors on his bedroom wall; their color digital images tracked the disrespectful trespassers trampling his yard....

* * *

With steel battering mounts protruding from their front bumpers like ram horns, four armored FBI trucks pummeled the front gate, turning it into an abstract wire sculpture. The convoy also included five bulletproof Chevy Suburbans trailing at high speeds.

In the kennel, the Mexican guards released twenty snarling pits bulls from their cages, then trained deadly AR-15 rifles on the invading caravan.

Shielded in full black tactical gear, fifty Agents sprung from their SUV's and armored support carriers, and clamored into firing positions shielded by their vehicles. Overhead, two roaring FBI choppers whirled across the skyline.

The Mexican guards triggered in a thumping shower of gunfire as the barking dogs raced in on the entrenched FBI forces.

"Knock 'em down!" an order fired from the FBI ranks, and the return gunfire erupted in a blistering fury. With a craving for human flesh, the furious pit bulls charged into a blistering hail of metal slugs that ripped into their streamlined bodies, tumbling them to the ground in bloody heaps.

Jorge leaned against the glass patio doorway, peered down his gun site, and took aim at an FBI helicopter.

"Back the choppers off!" Jorge ordered, and triggered the assault rifle as he raced across the courtyard. Laying down suppression fire, Jorge's fearless bodyguards trained their guns on the two black metal ravens storming above. Their heavy line of gunfire traced off the tail rotor of the lead bird and the crippled metal propeller grinded on its shaft, sending the vulture into a slow tailspin.

"Set it down! We took a hit to the tail!" The black bird twirled downward two-hundred feet, gravity rapidly increasing its tilted velocity, and crashed into the green lawn. Spinning rotor blades dug into the earth, vomiting rock, red clay dirt, and razor-sharp, metal shrapnel. Agents on the ground ducked behind their vehicles, as debris shot past them in massive hunks and smaller disintegrated puzzle pieces.

The intermission ended. Agents sprung back to their firing positions and returned a volley of gunfire, tattering the bodies of Mexican gunman--their dead fingers locked on depressed triggers.

On the helipad, Jorge climbed into his personal helicopter as the propellers peaked at full throttle.

"Make it fly!" Jorge pointed his gun at the rushing pilot and the helicopter quickly ascended, racing into the sky.

"Vargas is in the air!" the pilot's headset squawked while the surviving FBI helicopter banked hard left, and roared away in the chase. The rotor blades thumped, echoing for miles as the helicopters screamed over a green sea of trees.

On the horizon, a thick, smoggy haze covered the downtown skyline. Down below the helicopters, Highway 400 coiled along, surrounded by a dense foliage of trees.

Jorge aimed his rifle through a sliding glass window and fired at the trailing helicopter, sending it veering out of harm's way

"Haa! Haa!" Jorge cheered at his precision.

"Punch his pressure lines! Just below the top rotor!" the agent ordered to a gunner poised in the cargo door, his sniper rifle aimed at Jorge's chopper. And fire vaulted from the FBI rifle in measured bursts that pierced the hull of Jorge's helicopter. Inside the bird, Jorge squirmed, ducking from a ricocheting bullet that snapped through the glass near his head.

"Hold your fire!" the agent told his sniper. "We can't afford to have him crash over the city."

The steel hawks streaked along the I-85 corridor, headed due south into downtown. Suddenly, a plume of hydraulic fuel sprayed from Jorge's helicopter. *Beeping* cockpit gauges registered the dangerous wound. The pilot tightened his grip on the control stick, and shuffled his feet, stomping on the rotor pedals, as the helicopter tilted wildly. Jorge tumbled over in his seat.

"Do I need to fly this thing? Jorge raged. "Fly straight or I'll shoot you!"

"I have to land, we're losing hydraulic pressure!" the pilot yelled. The injured helicopter veered over downtown Atlanta, slowly losing altitude, the pilot fighting to maintain control. Finally, in a last ditch effort, the bird landed atop the Grady Memorial Hospital Life Pad. The landing skids scraped against the roof and Jorge sprung from the door, his gun aimed at the approaching FBI chopper. He clicked the trigger. *Empty.*

Jorge dropped his gun and walked to the edge of the roof, and climbed to the top of the railing. Sixty-yards out, the FBI helicopter hovered like a menacing, metal bumblebee--a sniper poised from its cargo door with his hand aiming the killer stinger. "Should I take the shot?" the FBI sniper hoped.

Jorge wobbled dangerously on the edge, almost losing his footing. He laughed at the fact that his free fall would end a dizzying twenty stories below, on gray concrete, in a land far from his Mexican home.

There are still seven ways to die in Atlanta...so Jorge Moreno-Vargas closed his eyes, spread his wings, and stepped off the edge....

* * *

His legs went weak and his pounding heart tore at his chest.
I better sit down before I fall down.

The raid had gone down one day before he was to make
his final cash drop to Jorge Vargas. *And nobody knows this but
me.* Mike drooled on himself and wiped his bottom lip. Stacked
in front of him, neatly piled in two-foot columns, was a money
cube totaling out at four-point-three million dollars. *Karma's a
sonnuvabitch.*

73

OPERATION ENIGMA

*I don't want the cheese, I just want to
get out of the trap.*
                    --Spanish Proverb

* * *

U.S. Attorney's Office Northern District of Georgia

**"OPERATION ENIGMA" DEFENDANTS SENTENCED FOR
DISTRIBUTING OVER $90 MILLION IN DRUGS IN LESS
THAN 1 YEAR**

*JORGE MORENO-VARGAS, 36, of Mexico was sentenced by
United States Chief District Judge Mallory Evans to life
without the possibility of parole in federal prison on charges of
conspiracy to possess and distribute cocaine, marijuana,
methamphetamine, and possession of a firearm in furtherance
of a drug trafficking crime; conspiracy to commit murder, and
money laundering.*

*According to the evidence, Moreno-Vargas led and
directed over 50 co-conspirators in a nationwide drug
distribution enterprise. Moreno-Vargas, while based in Corpus
Christi, Texas, directed the shipment and distribution of
thousands of kilograms of cocaine and thousands of pounds of
marijuana and methamphetamine, much of it through the
Atlanta area for sale nationwide.*

*Additional members of the organization, sentenced
on related possession and drug distribution charges include:
Hector Avila, 33, of Mexico; 60 years in federal prison,
Manuel Avila, 33, of Mexico; 60 years in federal prison,*

Adrianna Guevara, 29 of Peru; 25 years in federal prison.
Marco Vargas, 25, of Mexico; 40 years in federal prison.

The arrest and conviction of Moreno-Vargas, and the others resulted from a several month long investigation by FBI, DEA, and ICE agents in Atlanta, and Corpus Christi, Texas.

The Atlanta portion of the investigation culminated in the execution of more than 25 search warrants and the arrest of 34 people. Pursuant to these searches, agents seized sizable quantities of marijuana, cocaine, methamphetamine, numerous firearms, and more than eight million dollars in American currency. During the course of the investigation, agents seized approximately eleven million dollars from the organization that was destined for Mexico. The money had been concealed in cars which were then loaded on a car hauler for transportation to Mexico.

The evidence showed that the seizures of money and drugs however, represented only a fraction of the amount of drugs this cartel was responsible for distributing. Evidence produced at trial showed that in eleven months, this organization distributed more than $60 million worth of drugs in the Atlanta area alone. The investigation further revealed that the drugs were smuggled from Mexico, across the southwest border into Texas, where they would then be transported to Atlanta, and other destinations via tractor-trailer.

Upon arrival in Atlanta, the drugs were re-packaged, and distributed to the Atlanta-based distributors and customers. In the case of methamphetamine, it was often processed into its more potent form "ice", before being distributed. This cartel was also responsible for the distribution of drugs to other locations in the Southeast and along the East Coast. These destinations included South Carolina, Tennessee, Ohio, and New York. Evidence presented at the trial proved that this cartel often used violence, or the threat of violence, to collect drug debts and to protect substantial inventories of drugs and money.

Moreno-Vargas was the head of this Mexican-based drug trafficking organization. Manuel Avila directed distribution operations in Atlanta, while his brother Hector Avila was in charge of transporting drug shipments to the Atlanta area.

Other members of the cartel performed various duties for the organization including transporting drugs and money between Atlanta and Texas; processing and distributing drugs in Atlanta; and providing security for the cartel's various stash houses, where drugs and money were stored.

Adrianna Guevara was sentenced for her role as liaison between Vargas and individuals prominent in the local Atlanta drug community. Guevara was responsible for introducing high-level dealers to the cartel supply chain. After additional investigative leads were obtained, Guevara was implicated in the murder of two Atlanta women found in an abandoned car in the Chattahoochee River. Adrianna Guevara was sentenced in absentia and, while still on the run, she remains on the FBI's most wanted fugitive list.

At an earlier sentencing, Tatianna Olazaran, 41, was sentenced for her role in fraudulently securing various commercial and residential properties for members of the organization to sell, lease, reside in, and to utilize as store-houses for drugs and money. Olazaran, a real estate professional, was sentenced to eight years in prison, and will be deported to Mexico after the completion of her sentence.

United States Attorney David Namath said, "This series of prosecutions has wiped out the ability of this organization to distribute drugs, particularly here in Atlanta. The tireless work of both federal and local agencies in this case have set the benchmark for future investigations into the dangerous trafficking cartels that seek to destroy our communities with poisonous drugs."

If you have any information regarding the whereabouts of federal fugitive Adrianna Guevara please contact your nearest FBI Office.

74

SPANISH REFUGEES

The dead bolt locks ripped from wooden frames as splintered doors tore from metal hinges! Dozens of FBI and DEA Task force agents swarmed the apartment complex. Barefoot Spanish mommies held crying babies, as they shuffled into the street at Morosgo Drive. Helicopters hovered above the chaos, beaming bright spot-lamps over the urban terrain below.

"Check for tattoos!" the Agent barked. "Anything branded Sur-13 is going to jail." Gang affiliates, construction workers, cooks, landscapers, janitors, Mexican fugitives, and tattooed comrades were slammed to the ground. They cursed and spat at the Agents. Heavy gun butts knocked the most belligerent suspects to the floor.

"Hey, captain! We got us another loser!" an agent roared as he found a Sur-13 insignia inked on a Mexican soldier's stomach. "Roll over dickhead," the agent said and reached for his cuffs.

The raids continued deep into Gwinnett and Dekalb counties. Warrants, confessions, and familia betrayals fed investigations that spiraled into new leads, netting busts that cut directly into the last of Jorge Vargas's pipeline. In one raid alone, Gwinnett County Police seized one-point-five-million in cash, and four of Jorge's best delivery drivers. The family had completely unraveled, and all the federal dominoes were falling fast.

* * *

U.S. Attorney's Office Northern District of Georgia

FEDERAL INDICTMENT UNSEALED AGAINST EIGHTEEN MEMBERS OF SUR-13 STREET GANG

David Namath, United States Attorney, announces the unsealing of a federal grand jury indictment against 22 members of a violent street gang known as "SureZos-13," also known as "SUR-13." The indictment charges 15 defendants with being part of a racketeering conspiracy and three additional defendants with violent crimes related to racketeering.

Regarding the racketeering charges, the indictments alleges predicate crimes including murder, attempted murder, carjacking, armed, robbery, and drug dealing. The indictment also charges nine defendants with conspiring to possess and possessing with the intent to distribute methamphetamine and marijuana; four defendants with armed carjacking; and twelve defendants with firearms charges including possessing, carrying, using, and discharging a firearm during and in relation to violent crimes and drug trafficking.

Seventeen named defendants have been arrested on the sealed indictment. The operation included the arrest and federal prosecution of seven other SUR-13 gang members, the deportation of forty members, and the seizure of twenty firearms, and $600,000 in cash over the course of the investigation. Also arrested this weekend were approximately eleven SUR-13 members and associates who were residing illegally in the U.S. and who will now face administrative deportation.

* * *

At the news conference, Namath made his way to the bank of microphones. Nearby, Agent Cooper sat on her cell phone, conversing with Mike Drake. Camera shutters clicked. Lights flashed.

"As alleged in the indictment," Namath breathed into the microphone, "members of SUR-13 were responsible for a significant amount of drug and violent crime occurring within Fulton, Dekalb, Gwinnett, and Cobb Counties over the past several years. This indictment is an important step in combating the problems that violent street gangs pose throughout the state. We will be able to use federal racketeering and drug conspiracy statutes to attack the gang's entire leadership. Members of the public are reminded that the indictment contains only allegations. A defendant is presumed innocent of the charges and it will be the government's burden to prove a defendant's guilt beyond a reasonable doubt at trial."

* * *

Bullshit! Federal allegations were worth their weight in gold and were going to stick no matter what the Mexican consulate had to say about the raid on Spanish communities. Mike pondered the lavish and meaty words.

Presumed innocent...Reasonable doubt...Government's burden...just intricate ways to say you're fucked.

The capture of the deadly twins Manuel and Hector Avila brought down a storm on the gang members of SUR-13. To avoid a life sentence, Manuel had given up the names of his gang contacts, and implicated them in the Boulevard arson case and four murders in Fulton and Dekalb Counties.

From there, full-time triggerman and part-time arson Garcia Abrego confessed to more than a dozen robberies and murders over the past two years.

American justice in all its glory.

75

BOOTLEG BLUES

Candler-Smith Lofts. West End. Battering rams pummeled the steel doors as armed ATF Agents swarmed in well formed teams. The exits were blocked off. Fleeing African workers were rounded up, dropped to their knees, and restrained with tie-straps.

Mubarek screamed, "It's all coming down!" He was quickly handcuffed and shoved outside into the boiling sun.

Resisting every step of the way, Mubarek shouted defiantly, "You thieves! You rob me! I no criminal! You the criminals!"

Federal agents packed a large U-haul truck with CD's, DVD's, watches, handbags, clothes, laptop computers, and every other item Mubarek had cloned, bootlegged, or forged.

It was a massive show of force for an organization dedicated to protecting the manufacturing and distribution of copyrighted music and films. *Intellectual property.*

The Recording Industry Association of America (RIAA) had spoken in no uncertain terms and delivered a fatal blow to Atlanta's million dollar underground bootlegging trade.

Down here, we don't just make hot, new music. Hell, we'll steal your shit, copy it, and distribute it too.

Michael Drake watched from his car as Mubarek was loaded into a waiting van. *Mubarek set up the raid on Wild Bill's house and almost got me killed...dead as a doorknob.*

Payback's somethin' else, ain't it?

* * *

U.S. Attorney's Office Northern District of Georgia

$10 MILLION CD COUNTERFEIT OPERATION
SHUT DOWN

Today we announce the federal indictment of Khalid Mubarek, 34, of Atlanta, Georgia and the raid of a major CD counterfeiting operation by the Atlanta Police Department and the FBI in connection with the case.

A federal grand jury had already returned a 15-count indictment, charging Khalid Mubarek, a/k/a "DJ Afrika" and Abdulla Muhammed, a/k/a "Taliban Joe" with conspiracy and pirating of copyrighted material, with a gross retail market value to the recording industry in excess of eighty-million dollars U.S. ($80,000,000).

The indictment specifically charges that Mubarek and Muhammed manufactured and distributed counterfeit and pirate CD's, counterfeit audio cassette tapes, counterfeit labels and trademarks in various locations through the Atlanta metropolitan area, and in Columbus and Macon, Georgia.

Mubarek and Muhammed manufactured counterfeit compact discs and counterfeit audio cassette tapes through the unauthorized recording of popular music protected by copyright and the unauthorized duplication of artwork, graphics, and photographs which were protected by copyrights contained on labels of popular music, often manufacturing "compilation" recordings and individual recordings by artists such as: Usher, Trick Daddy, Cee Lo, Run DMC, Beastie Boyz, R. Kelly, LL Cool J, No Doubt, Pink, Britney Spears, Mandy Moore, Christina Aguilera, Nelly Furtado, Lenny Kravitz, Alien Ant Farm, B2K, N Sync, Whodini, Eazy E, Master P, Snoop Dogg, Ludacris, Ashanti, Nappy Roots, and the Commodores.

Mubarek registered "Mandingo Media Corporation" to conduct business in the State of Georgia, for the purpose of purchasing bulk orders of blank CD-R's and jewel cases.

Mubarek opened a counterfeit CD label plant at 679 Oakdale Plains, Suite 3-J, Atlanta, Georgia, and produced CD labels. Around the same time, Mubarek purchased $25,000 to $30,000 worth of CD copying equipment from the defendant Abdullah Mohammed in New York City. Mubarek leased office space at 179 Peachtree Street, Atlanta Georgia, using the business name of "Afrika Enterprises."

Mubarek also began acquiring vans and other vehicles pertaining to the business, including a Chevrolet C15 and received a prestige tag reading "AFRIKA."

The business quickly spread to other locations: Mubarek established a CD copying plant at 754 Clifton Place, Macon Georgia; a counterfeit CD and CD label plant at 1911 Cleveland, Avenue, Atlanta, Georgia. Mubarek and Muhammed hired workers from Columbus, Ohio and relocated them to Atlanta, Georgia, to work in the plant at 528 Mundy's Mill Road in Jonesboro, Georgia. Mubarek operated a storefront in the Bankhead Highway flea market, 2716 Bankhead Highway, Atlanta, Georgia, selling and shipping counterfeit and pirate CDs, counterfeit labels, and counterfeit trademarks.

With the Bankhead address as another main location, Mubarek and his "bodyguard" went to the residence of a competitor who manufactured counterfeit CD's, followed him and confronted him. The next day, Mubarek sent his "bodyguards" to the Stewart Avenue flea market to intimidate his competitor by attacking him.

As part of the investigation, in a raid last Thursday at 1149 Lee Street, Atlanta, the Atlanta Police Department and the FBI seized over 350,000 illegal CD's.

At a news conference announcing the case, David Namath said, "Mr. Mubarek was indicted for creating an illegal market for the sale of counterfeit CD's. The scope of his illegal activity was enormous and his indictment shows our commitment to investigate and prosecute those who commit intellectual property crimes."

FBI Special-Agent-In-Charge Angela Cooper added, "The FBI will continue to work hand-in-hand with local, state, and federal agencies, and along with industry representatives to aggressively investigate any violations of federal law."

Khalid Mubarek appeared before United States District Judge Beatrice Marlowe on Monday, and was held without bond to await his trial. No trial date has been set.

* * *

"What did they do to my son?" the frail African mother asked her anxious sister in their Yoruba tongue. "I want to talk to him." She shuffled out of her favorite leather recliner chair, reaching for the telephone. Her small apartment was neat and well furnished. *Gifts from a loving son.* The same prodigal son who had left them sixteen years ago, but sent back CD's and DVD's, electronics, books, and cash, *so much cash,* to bribe doctors, lawyers, and politicians just to get them to feed people, free people from jail, and care for sick children in the same slums that had birthed and almost killed him.

Hungry African brothers and sisters had eaten from the labor of DJ Afrika in a place they called Atlanta.

Word of Mubarek Akujyoe's arrest reached Lagos, Nigeria on a cool winter's dawn. And a legend was born.

76

GETAWAY

If you have built castles in the air, your hard work
need not be lost; that is where they should be.
Now put foundations under them.

--Henry David Thoreau

The Lamborghini roared down M. L. King Boulevard, crossing Fulton Industrial in a silver blur. The guard at the gate waved him through as he entered the Charlie Brown Regional Airport. Michael parked the car and lifted a large Louis Vuitton duffle bag from the trunk.

A young aviation mechanic wiped grease from his hands and stared at Michael and his exotic ride.

"That's a hot set of wheels, man! Lamborghini Gallardo right?" the mechanic beamed excitedly.

"Mercialago."

"I'm almost an expert on foreign cars. That's my specialty!" the mechanic grinned.

You really like this car?" Mike asked.

"Hell yeah, I do. Don't you? I know it's gotta keep the ladies lined up for ya."

"I never liked this car one bit," Michael admitted as he tossed the car keys to the stunned mechanic.

"Here ya go, boss. She's all yours," Mike granted with a sigh of relief.

"What?! Ya bullshittin'!" the mechanic drawled.

"I was always a Chevy man anyway," the *real* Mike confessed.

"God Bless you!" the mechanic danced in circles, then dove inside the Lamborghini.

"Watch out for third gear...she's hell." Michael warned as he tossed the duffle bag over his shoulder and strolled off to Vargas's Gulfstream jet waiting at the edge of the tarmac.

77

Department of Justice
Richmond, Virginia

Richmond, VA--Atlanta Falcons quarterback Tracy Vick was indicted early this morning by a Federal Grand Jury in Richmond, Virginia, with violating federal laws against competitive dogfighting, procuring and training pit bulls for fighting, and conducting the enterprise across state lines. Vick will now have to turn himself into authorities under federal law. The unsealed indictment alleges that Vick and three co-defendants began sponsoring dogfighting in early 2002, the former Virginia Tech star's rookie year with the Falcons.

It accuses Vick and three additional defendants: Ronald Pearson, Quanis Bolton and Thomas Taylor of "knowingly sponsoring and exhibiting an animal fighting venture," of conducting a racketeering enterprise involving gambling, as well as buying, transporting and receiving dogs for the brutal and illegal purposes of an animal fighting venture. Vick became the focus of a federal dog fighting probe after an April 25 drug raid on his Surry County, Va., home. At that time, authorities seized seventy dogs, including sixty pit bulls, and equipment used in the training, and disposal of animals in a dogfighting operation. Papers, filed earlier this month by federal authorities in U.S. District Court in Richmond, noted that dog fights have been sponsored by "Bad Boyz Kennels" at the property since at least 2001. Fifty-four animals were rescued from the property during warrant searches, along with a "rape stand," used to hold dogs in position for mating, and rolls of carpeting stained with animal blood. Investigators also uncovered the graves of nine pit bulls that were slaughtered by members of "Bad Boyz Kennels" following scrimmage matches to test whether dogs would be good fighters, the documents revealed.

Vick claims he rarely visits the Surry County home and was unaware of any criminal enterprise.

* * *

Six months later, Tracey Vick agreed to a plea deal, and was sentenced to fourteen months in federal prison. *This shit is chess not checkers.*

* * *

Twelve hours later, the outdated charter plane touched down in a wave of sunlight. The warm sky was crystal blue and a strong wind blew over the plains. Mike emerged from the plane door, inhaled the fresh air, and descended the stairs. There wasn't a cloud in sight for miles.

From the Airport, the private car traveled for another hour through rugged terrain to a small train depot. He bought his ticket and clamored onto an old coal powered train where a collection of natives chattered in their tongue-rolling dialect. For miles the iron horse road the railway tracks, chugging through the lush green countryside, climbing into the cavernous mountains. After a much needed nap, he awoke and exited the train at a tiny, rustic building in the middle of nowhere.

Mike dialed his cell phone...

* * *

Agent Angela Cooper sat at her desk surrounded by four inept analysts who were trying to update her on the escalading narco-political violence in Bogota, Colombia. Suddenly, the phone rang, and she excused herself as she answered, "Agent Cooper." Her face tensed. Agent Cooper dismissed her personnel with a wave of her hand, and they quickly left her alone in the office.

"Do you know what happens when black sheep stray too far from the farm?" Cooper set the receiver down and clicked on the speakerphone. "They get slaughtered."

"I think I might've grown on you over the years. It would take a lot for you to push the button on me now," Mike's voice buzzed over the speaker.

"Don't fool yourself, Drakiere. If it was either a matter of personal business or a question of national security, you wouldn't live to see the morning."

"Good thing for me America's safe and you really don't give a damn what I do."

"Where is Vargas's plane?" she remembered to ask. "That's a forty-million dollar trade-in."

"I left it at small airport outside London. It'll be washed and all gassed up when the repo'-man gets there."

"Call me later, and give me a clue to your final whereabouts. I'll send your last paycheck," she transparently offered.

"I brought my paycheck with me," he said. "If you ever need to find me, just...call...," Mike spun, taking in the beautiful scenery, "...*Paradise*." A vast, wind swept mountain range filled the horizon, stretching beneath a tapestry of white clouds that shifted across a fiery orange-hued sky.

"1-800-Paradise. I'll put you in my book."

"Forget about me. This is my last go round. I ain't too sure about my loyalties no more," he finally admitted.

"You go ahead and take that vacation, Mister Drakeire. Clear your mind. Watch the big blue waves roll in. Oh, and if you get a chance, you must swim with the pilot whales. It's a spiritual experience like no other," she slowly teased.

She already knows where I am. "I've done all I can do for you. Almost died twice in the process." The conversation stalled in silence.

"Everybody still wants the girl, Mike. Vargas. The Avila twins. And especially us. She's a fugitive and as long as you protect her, so are you. Bring her back or I will."

As Mike walked, a frown weighed heavily on his face. Cooper had just threatened to dangle Adrianna's life like a piece of raw meat over a cage full of starved lions. *Crazy bitch is serious as a heart attack.*

"I wouldn't want anyone other than us to get a whiff of her trail," she added for good measure, but Mike had already gotten her drift.

Jorge, he'd love to bury her. And the twins, Hector and Manuel they'd kill both us for fun.

"Lucky for us, you're here to watch over me," Mike offered. *I could run a million miles from this job and still couldn't get a good night's sleep.*

"Enjoy the coast, son. It's a little chilly this time of the year, but the sunsets are amazing."

"How long do I have?" Mike asked, hoping she would give him another head start.

"The hounds are already on the way. And Namath sends his thanks. Anything you want me to tell him?" Cooper asked, her stern demeanor pierced by a trace of softness.

"You tell 'em I said to look out for my favorite lady shepherd, or I'll be back to see 'bout 'em."

"That a veiled threat against a sworn U.S. Attorney?" she hardened again.

"I've never threatened a man in my life."

"I'm going to go now. I'm busy mapping out a plan to hunt your girlfriend down. Take care of yourself and that sweet little baby boy. If he's anything like you, he has a future with us."

Stunned, Mike stopped in his tracks. "Is there anything you don't know, you psychotic bitch?" he asked.

"Nope," she confessed. "Rest up, Mike. We have a lot of

work to do when you get back. I'll be in touch, Mister Drakeire." And she hung up.

Mike walked up the winding dirt road, the sun beaming down across his sweltering forehead. With less than half a mile to go, his pace hastened into a slow run. Within the sound of his pounding feet, he figured his position in the chess game and calculated his next move. And with the very next step he knew for certain. *She'll never let me out.*

78

DEATH ROW

The emotional trial had been a sensational blend of heart felt testimonies, courtroom jousting, blinding media coverage, and a dogfight to avoid the death penalty. Millions of tax payer dollars had been spent defending a man whose fate had already been sealed the day he escaped from jail.

After just two hours of deliberation, a unanimous jury convicted Fulton County Courthouse shooter Ryan Nichols on forty-nine of the fifty-four felony counts against him.

During the death penalty phase, Nichol's attorneys pulled out all the pro-life arguments they could muster--cruel and unusual punishment, unacceptable disparities in the dispensation of the death penalty according to geography and race, malice murder versus felony murder, express versus implied malice, and a nagging statistic that ominously revealed that among all homicides with identified suspects, those convicted of killing white victims are nearly five times as likely to get the death penalty as those who killed black people.

Mister Nichols killed two white folks. You do the math.

Nichols was sentenced to die by lethal injection and sent to wait for his pending date with destiny on death row. His appeals to the Georgia Supreme Court and the governor finally exhausted, and his weary soul prepared for the next journey. He had outlived most of the witnesses, prosecutors, and friends and families of his victims.

Exactly twenty-two years, eight months, and seventy-six days from the second Ryan Ray Nichols mercilessly killed a state judge and two courthouse employees, he was executed at 11:53 PM on a stormy, wind swept night in Georgia. 2028 A.D.

79

Department of Justice
Northern District of Georgia

Atlanta, GA – Today we announce that a federal grand jury has indicted Kylie Franco, 35, of Atlanta, on charges of money laundering, perjury, and tax evasion. She is the former wife of convicted drug trafficker Todd Graham. Scott Duval, who was Todd Graham's partner in the drug business, introduced Graham to his future wife in an Atlanta strip club.

The superseding indictment alleges that she knowingly utilized funds received from her husband's illegal drug enterprise. The couple purchased a large mansion in a gated suburb of Atlanta, and Kylie Graham amassed a personal collection of jewelry estimated at a value of more than $350,000. When her mother became Atlanta's first female mayor, the couple celebrated at the side of Cheryl Franco during her inauguration dinner.

Details of Kylie and Todd Graham's opulent lifestyle are outlined in countless interviews, court testimony, and additional public records. Scott Duval testified that Todd Graham invested $220,000 of their drug funds in David Franco's Atlanta-based company, Franco and Colbert Airport Concessions Inc. The firm was owned and operated by Kylie Graham's father.

Scott Duval was ultimately sentenced to 28 years in prison, and testified that he expected to receive monthly paychecks from Franco and Colbert to disguise his illegal profits as legitimate income. Instead, the company only sent a check each month to Kylie Graham. Prosecutors could not establish in court when the alleged payments were made or how much of the investment funds Kylie Graham actually received. The Mayor and David Franco have been divorced since 1988.

David Franco told federal investigators that the investment "Was a complete fabrication." Franco's company operates six retail outlets at the city-owned Hartsfield-Jackson International Airport. The firm's contracts are approved by the City Council, but Mayor Franco has denied any role in the bidding or selction procces.

Kylie Graham made no mention of payments from her father's company when she filed for bankruptcy in June 2006. In court papers, she claimed income of close $2,500 a month in unspecified family donations. She also showed itemized debts of more than $450,000, not counting the mortgage on a rental property in Alpharetta, GA. She reported $2,250 in the bank, and jewelry valued at approximately $8,000. However, witnesses at her former husband's sentencing contradicted her claims, painting a deeper picture of her involvement. Duval testified that Kylie Graham routinely mailed bills to her husband while he was a fugitive. Todd Graham would then pay them with postal money orders. IRS Agent Reginald Wright testified that federal agents seized the dated receipts for more than seventy-five such money orders covering credit card, utility, car payments, and mortgage bills for both Kylie and Todd Graham.

There were numerous money orders purchased at multiple post offices in Atlanta on the same day. And each money order was issued for less than $3,000 to avoid federal reporting requirements set to detect illegal transactions. The indictment further alleges that Kylie Graham used money from her husband to make payments on three Porsche sports utility trucks while he was a fugitive. Eventually, the luxury vehicles ended up in the possession of a Detroit-based drug gang, the Black Mafia Family. The gang had laundered large sums of money through a luxury car dealership, 404 Eurosports, that Todd Graham owned and operated.

80

DEAD END

The shackles that clasped his hands and feet jangled like a fortuneteller's chime, singing of the doom to come. A platoon of armed U.S. Marshals and ATF agents flanked the monster as he stepped from the transport van parked in the center of a long line of government vehicles. The escort was massive for one man. But this wasn't just any ordinary *bandito*.

United States Penitentiary Administrative Maximum Facility (ADX). Florence, Colorado, USA.

Supermax. It was an impressive compound--unofficially known as ADX Florence, Florence ADMAX, or the *Alcatraz of the Rockies.* It was operated by the federal government and housed the scurge of America--some of the most dangerous men in the world. *Outlaws.* For the rest of this life and the first forty years of the next one, Jorge Moreno-Vargas would be under constant surveillance by closed-circuit television cameras. The new Vargas Estate would be sparsely decorated, but built to last--poured concrete walls and floors, and cold metal furniture. Soundproofed cell walls and plumbing would prevent him from communicating, plotting, and scheming with other inmates.

Uncle Sam would choose who moved into the neighborhood next. His unseen neighbors were a cadre of convicted terrorists, gang leaders, and the notorious prisoners of bomber row: Eric Rudolph, Atlanta Olympic Bomber; the September 11th terrorist Zacarias Moussaoui, also serving life; Theodore Kaczynski, otherwise known as the *'Unabomber'* who attacked via mail bombs; and Richard Reid, an Islamic fundamentalist serving life for attempting to board an aircraft and detonate explosive materials in his tennis shoes. *BOOM!*

Jorge's closest neighbor would be Mutulu Shakur, stepfather of slain rap legend Tupac Shakur. Soul brother Mutulu was serving sixty years for masterminding a plan against the oppressor, against *The Man* that just so happened to involve an armored car robbery that left two New York Policemen and a Brinks Security guard dead.

At night, you could hear the ghosts of John Gotti, Mafioso *Boss of all Bosses*, and the infamous Tim McVeigh, the man who bombed the Federal Building in Ohlahoma City. McVeigh was the first federal prisoner to be executed since 1963.

23 Hour Lockdown. Vargas would live slow and die slower in solitary confinement, no wine, but fine dining on drab meals catered through food slots, *bean holes,* in the steel door of his cell. He would be allowed out of his concrete condo for only an hour a day. Twice a week, he could shower. There would be no work detail, no access to leisure activities, and definitely no television. To keep him strong for the long mile he'd be allowed to workout in a small, enclosed area where he would exercise alone once a week. *If he's a good boy.*

J orge Moreno Vargas had it all--big guns and bigger dreams, a beautiful daughter born from a gorgeous wife he loved to hate, slutty local mistresses, fleets of exotic cars, yachts, private jets, mansions and more mistresses all over the world, and millions of dollars to burn.

Then...*Poof!* Like harsh dreams melt in the heat of reality, it was all gone. Now you have to ask yourself...

Was it worth it?

81

Ensancho de mi Corazon

The Comfort of My Heart.

The rustic nine room chateau overlooked a mountainous range deep in the heart of La Palma, Spain. $1.2 million dollars U.S. had made this real estate purchase through an intricate series of wire transfers from Atlanta. *Now she's all mine.* As Mike climbed the gravel driveway, he could see her looking down at him.

Adrianna stood at the patio wall, beaming a radiant smile. Her hands rested on a plump stomach bulging through a white, linen dress. Mike rushed through the house, sliding across the Italian marble floors.

Out on the patio, they crashed together in a wrenching hug, kissing deeply.

"We made it," he sighed in relief.

"I missed you," she said, tracing her hands across his cheeks, remembering what he felt like. Then she punched him in the stomach! "How're you gonna just leave me on a plane by myself, and send me half-way around the world?"

He blocked her next punch, and tied her limbs up in a tight hug. "I saved your life. Now show me some love."

"Are we safe?" Adrianna fearfully asked.

"Yeah, for the first time... we're free," he lied.

Now...Stay Alive.

NOWHERE NEAR THE END...

The 404 Saga Continues...

A.T.L. CHRONICLES
www.myspace.com/fultoncounty404

EPILOGUE

A Hard Head Makes A Soft Ass Every Time

"Our destiny is largely in our own hands. If we find, we shall have to seek. If we succeed in the race for life it must be by our own energies, and our own exertions. Others may clear the road, but we must go forward or be left behind in the race for life. If we remain poor and dependent, the wealth of others will not avail us. If we are ignorant, the intelligence of others will do but little for us. If we are foolish, the wisdom of others will not guide us. If we are wasteful of our time and money, the economy of others will only make our destitution the more disgraceful."

--Frederick Douglass

ACKNOWLEDGEMENTS

All praises due to the King of Kingz.
Love, admiration, and thanks to Granny Catherine, Kim and
the boys---Bubba, Tank, & Jersey Joe, Dwayne, Sabrina,
Junior, Warren, P. Y. Cooper, Johnnie Lin', Sonda, Adrian,
Demetrius, Tim Diesel, Shawny Boy, Chris B., Gina G.,
Robin P., Ed-X, James, Chipper, Dennis the Menace,
Hardhead Nard, T.C. Rainer & George, Twin, Marcus C.
and the BodyMan.

Peyton Affiliates:
Miss Liz, Eddie B., Lando, Tat and Basil,
EJ, Gary J, Them Carter boys, Bruzah Cody,
G. Wynn, Ragsdale, Marty Ray, and Chip Favors.

Philadelphia affiliates: Donald and Miss Bell.
Los Angeles affiliates: Ledon B., Calio Devin
Free them Diablos.

Rest in Peace,
Big Otha, Sheila, Calvin, Uncle Mike, Dot & John Henderson.
And a whole lotta other sons and daughters of this tragic city.

We'll see y'all again...when our journey is done.

REVELATION7 ©2007